Where's my daughter!

She was thirty yards away, talking to a man. He was tall, dressed in tight jeans and boots, his face shadowed by a cap. Before I could yell in warning, they started walking.

I cut the distance to a few scant yards, then hurled my body through space. His muscles braced against me, but the dive took him down.

"Nice tackle," he said.

I realized I was spread-eagled on top of him. And that his eyes were the translucent, amber-warmed gray of winter twilight.

"If anybody sees us like this, my reputation'll be shot to hell," he continued. "Think you could let me up?"

Seeing the lazy sensuality in his grin, I scrambled to my feet. "Who are you?" I finally managed. "And where are you taking my little girl?"

ABOUT THE AUTHOR

Elizabeth Morris has lived most of her life as a resident of Washington, D.C. A wife and mother of three grown sons, she is a heavy reader of mystery, suspense and horror. Of her writing, she says, "Since my youth, I'd spin out these plots, and more often than not they'd have some element of suspense in them. I feel comfortable with the form and find it a real challenge." Besides writing for Harlequin, Elizabeth has penned several young-adult titles.

Books by Elizabeth Morris

HARLEQUIN INTRIGUE
125—A TEASPOON OF MURDER

HARLEQUIN AMERICAN ROMANCE
178—THIS DAY FORWARD
221—A TOUCH OF MOONSHINE

The First Horseman

Elizabeth Morris

Harlequin Books

TORONTO • NEW YORK • LONDON
AMSTERDAM • PARIS • SYDNEY • HAMBURG
STOCKHOLM • ATHENS • TOKYO • MILAN
MADRID • WARSAW • BUDAPEST • AUCKLAND

To
Marc, Patrick and Eric,
with the crazy lady's love
and for Eddie,
the wind beneath her wings

Harlequin Intrigue edition published December 1992

ISBN 0-373-22208-4

THE FIRST HORSEMAN

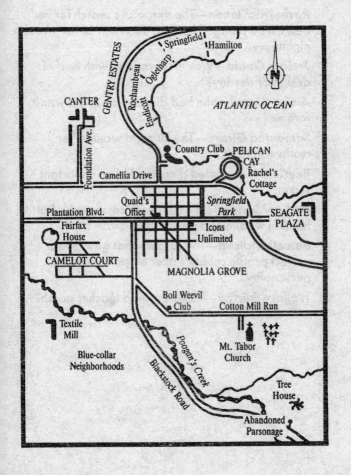

CAST OF CHARACTERS

Rachel McKinnon—The desperate search for her best friend plunged her into the terror of her worse nightmares.

Jericho Quaid—Was his encounter with Rachel design or destiny?

Alison Girard—She had disappeared, but was it forever?

Samantha Girard—The little girl wanted her mother.

BeeCee—The stuffed dinosaur hid an important secret.

Michael Springfield—His death came early, but familial wealth and power lived on.

Barrett Endicott—The surgery that gave him a perfect profile couldn't alter his poisonous personality.

Wallace Fairfax—Did the retired teacher gamble with the devil?

Chapter One

The instant the heavy door creaked closed behind me, I knew I was in terrible trouble. The air was so thick with the smell of roses that it was hard to breathe, and as I stared at the grotesque pattern in the stained-glass window high above me, my mouth went cottony with dread: this was not the enchanted fairy castle I'd thought it to be—it was a truly evil place.

Leave now, little girl—run as fast as you can. If the ghosts find you here, you will be punished.

The warning came from everywhere—echoing from the high-vaulted ceiling, whispering from the cobwebbed corners, shouting inside my own head. I tried to obey, but my feet dragged me to the gleaming golden chair at the front of the room.

Too late. They're coming now.

I could hear a chorus of wordless moans coming from outside, counterpointed by guttural laughter that changed into a shriek as it climbed the scale. With no protection except the "Now I lay me" prayer that I dredged from my frozen soul, I shrank back into a shadowed alcove beside the throne just as a crimson form melted through the door.

Its face was blank except for terrible eyes, and its tight fist was clutched around a coiled whip. The purple-and-green specters who followed dragged a struggling man between them. They would surely have seen me if they hadn't been busy beating their prisoner. The chamber echoed with his screams, the crack of the lash against his back, and rising

*above the brutality of the assault was the measured sound
of a church bell. The funereal tolling quickened to an un-
relenting alarm.*

*The crimson specter turned to stare toward my meager
shelter, saying, "You belong to us, Rachel, and one day we
will come to claim you..."*

"No!" THE WAIL THAT TORE from my throat came out a
whimper, and I hunkered down among the pillows, shaking
and damp with a gelid perspiration. The rainbow hobgoblins had haunted my sleep for as long as I could remember,
and although the recurring nightmare was now only a once-
or twice-yearly event, over time it hadn't lost one iota of its
punch. Disoriented by my latest tête-à-tête with the spooks,
it took awhile for me to realize that the ringing in my ears
wasn't the echo of the dreaded church bell. When it finally
hit me, I switched on the lamp beside my bed and, fumbling for the telephone, mumbled a less than gracious,
"Rachel McKinnon here. What do you want?" into the receiver.

"After you finish calling me every nasty name you can
think of for waking you up at this hour of the morning, I
surely would appreciate a long distance hug if you have one
to spare," came the answer.

A fierce joy jerked me to complete wakefulness. Although it had been over two years since I'd heard my best
friend's voice, there was no mistaking its soft blend of
honeyed sunshine and magnolia-touched gentility. "Alison, is it really you?" I breathed in a hoarse whisper.

"Last time I checked." Her words reached for lightness
but fell a shade short. "Lord, but it's good to hear you
again, Cricket. You have no idea how much I've missed
you."

The use of my childhood nickname raised a lump in my
throat. For a second I straddled the fence between joy and
anger, finally tipping toward the latter. "Don't you 'Cricket'
me, Alison Girard. I've been worried sick about you and
Samantha. Why did you pull a disappearing act on me? And
where in the hell have you been?"

"For the past six months Sam and I have been living in Maine, but we're in Boston at the moment. We have tickets for the noon bus, and we'll arrive in D.C. tonight. Would it be too much trouble for you to meet us at the Greyhound terminal?"

"Say the word, and I'll drive all the way to Massachusetts and pick you up," was my heartfelt offer. "I can hardly wait to see you and Sam. After all this time, I hope the little munchkin hasn't forgotten me."

"You're the first person she God-blesses every night, and nothing on earth could part her from BeeCee."

The assurance triggered a mental videotape of my godchild unwrapping the silly stuffed dinosaur I had scoured Georgetown to find for her fourth birthday. Again, I caught the sweetness of her little-girl scent, the warmth of chubby arms clasped around my neck. And with the poignant images came the remembrance of darker emotions: the confusion and bereavement I felt when a scant week after the party, Alison and her daughter vanished from my life. The cryptic note Alison had left instructed me not to try to find her. It ended, "For right now, it's better if you don't know where Samantha and I are." In the two years since, the ache of what I considered a betrayal had never left me.

But this was hardly the time for airing the grudge, I cautioned myself, repressing another spate of accusing questions. The most important thing was that they were coming back to Washington. "Don't plan on getting much rest for a while. We've got a ton of things to catch up on," I told her.

There was silence at the other end, then the thin whisper of a suppressed sigh. "I'm afraid we'll only have a few hours together. I have to leave for Magnolia Grove first thing tomorrow."

"You're going back to South Carolina?" I tightened my grip on the receiver, and, swallowing the sourness that pruned my lips, forced a humorless chuckle. "What's in our dearly beloved hometown beside killer mosquitoes and terminal boredom?"

"Freedom—I hope," was the enigmatic response. I was about to probe its meaning when Alison hastened to add, "A few loose ends there have to be tied."

The undercurrent of fear I thought I detected beneath the words filled me with an inexplicable uneasiness. "Are you in some sort of trouble?"

"I'm just going down to finish some old family business, nothing earthshaking. I'll explain it all when I see you," she promised. Her tone was bright, almost careless.

Family business? At four in the morning, I'm always a bit slow on the uptake, but that one speeded my reflexes. Alison had no relatives in South Carolina. Burdett and Viola Compton, the middle-aged couple who'd adopted her when she was five, were long gone. Even before they'd died, she'd been estranged from them. In one final slap from beyond the grave, they'd left all their property to a televangelist.

"I'm afraid the trip might be a bit much for Sam. Can I leave her with you for a few days?" Alison added in a rush.

I sat bolt upright, as much with astonishment as pleasure. It was completely out of character for her to want to leave her child with someone else—even me. I'd never known them to be separated for more than a few hours. "I can't think of anything that would make me happier." I rummaged through the clutter atop the nightstand for a pad and pencil. "What time will your bus get in?"

"Nine-forty tonight." Another infant silence, an intake of breath that sounded suspiciously like a sob. "Thank you for being there for us, Rachel," Alison said. "Watch for the moon."

I hadn't the foggiest notion what she meant by that, and before I could ask, she broke the connection. As I cradled the receiver, a shiver traversed the length of my spine. Neither Alison nor I were fond of Magnolia Grove, South Carolina, but her aversion was much more deeply entrenched than mine. No reason I could think of was compelling enough to induce her return.

Retreating under the covers, I still felt chilled by the eerie juxtaposition of the call and my recurring childhood nightmare. Fragments of a gathering apprehension, unbidden and certainly unwelcome, flapped at the edges of my mind like the wings of rapacious crows. To hold the scavengers at bay, I forced my thoughts back to the dozens of things that required my immediate attention.

For starters, the spare bedroom was currently a combination studio and storage space for boxes of photographs that I hadn't had the willpower to discard. The room needed new curtains, a matching spread and all the amenities that might make my tiny guest feel at home. Although the deadline for submissions to the ad campaign I was hoping to freelance was only a month away, completing the photographic shoot and putting together a portfolio would have to wait. Until Alison returned from South Carolina, my top priority would be Samantha.

In the midst of planning a whirlwind tour of Washington, it suddenly dawned on me that entertaining the child might be the least of my worries. Bottom line, I knew less than squat about the care and feeding of little people. Going back to sleep was no longer a viable option, so I pulled on a sweat suit and marched off to do battle with the dust bunnies multiplying in the corners of my Georgetown row house.

If cleanliness was next to godliness, the next few hours assured my reservation at the Pearly Gates. Remembering Samantha's curiosity and penchant for mischief, I was down on my knees ferreting potential health hazards from under the kitchen sink when the knob on the back door rattled.

"Come on in, Maggie," I called out.

Not that Margaret Peace, my elderly neighbor, confidante and self-appointed supervisor, needed a formal invitation. She frequently used the spare key I'd given her—not always, I might add, at the most convenient moments.

"This is a miracle," Maggie breathed as she circumnavigated the bucket I'd left near the entrance. Her dark-eyed gaze was amused and more than a little curious as she surveyed the scrubbed expanse of the tile floor. She set a thermos on the table, and on her way to retrieve two mugs from the rack on the counter offered the dry observation, "You've made six trips to the Dumpster since dawn, so I figured you might be ready for a cocoa break. Is it that time of the month or have you landed yourself a new beau?"

"Neither. I'm about to become a mother," I shot back, grinning.

"It's just as well. Your biological clock is on the shady side of thirty-one and running down fast." Appropriating a chair beside the table, she raised a quizzical eyebrow and awaited further explanation.

After detailing the bare bones of Alison's phone call, I stripped off my rubber gloves and wandered over to slump into the seat across from the old woman. "I don't mind admitting I'm nervous about baby-sitting. What do I do if Samantha gets sick?"

"Call me, of course. Having a son and five grandbabies qualifies me as an expert."

I should have been reassured, but I wasn't. "I've forgotten every fairy tale I ever knew, and I was always terrible at kiddy games. Suppose she gets bored?"

"Why do you think God invented television cartoons?" Maggie uncapped the thermos, filled the cups with creamy, steaming cocoa and slid one across the table toward me. "Isn't Alison Girard that friend of yours who took off a couple of years back?"

I nodded absently, a host of concerns still lurking in my subconscious. Now restless, I rose to wander over to the window, glancing across the backyard at the luxurious full-blossomed geraniums clustered around Maggie's flagstone patio. The innocent brilliance of the July noon made my premonition of disaster seem groundless. Worse than that, they seemed outright paranoid.

"Do you suppose her business in South Carolina is connected to her disappearance two years ago?" my neighbor mused aloud.

The expression that drifted across her café-au-lait face, the anticipation of a bloodhound hot on the trail, made me instantly wary. At the slightest nudge, Margaret Peace, the widow of a D.C. policeman and a confirmed detective novel addict, was apt to go off on a mystery binge.

"I doubt it." To forestall one of her far-out scenarios, I retrieved a yellow pad from the counter and began scribbling a grocery list. Two items down, I abandoned the task. "It'll be late when we get back from the terminal, and Alison and Sam will probably be too tired to eat much. Maybe I'll just pick up a chef salad at the deli so I won't have to cook."

"That'll be a blessing for all concerned." The corners of Maggie's mouth lifted in amusement. "When you go to the supermarket, just buy things for breakfast. I'll take care of the rest of the meals while Samantha's here. I always fix way more than I can eat by myself."

The firm set of her shoulders told me there was no point in objecting, not that I was of a mind to put up much resistance. My own culinary expertise was limited to stuff that could be nuked in the microwave.

"You've got a deal, Maggie, but only if you promise to hang out with us. We're going to hit every shopping mall within a twenty-mile radius."

"Sounds good to me." Striding briskly across the kitchen, she turned to smile from the doorway. "My considerable grandmother skills have been going to waste since Junior moved his brood to Seattle. It'll be so good to have a little girl to fuss over again! And I'm just tickled to death that you've finally found your friend."

"So am I, Maggie." I blinked back a sudden mist that blurred my vision. "So am I."

FIFTEEN MINUTES AFTER the last stragglers departing the 9:40 bus from Boston had claimed their luggage, there was still no sign of Alison Girard and her daughter. My spirits yo-yoed between depression and concern. I was hurrying back to station myself at the terminal's main entrance when an amplified voice caught me mid-stride.

"Rachel McKinnon, please report to the information desk."

I must have set a new record for the cross-concourse dash. A few feet from my destination, a uniformed woman with arms like Arnold Schwarzenegger stepped from her position beside the counter to intercept me.

"Rachel McKinnon?"

"Yes. Is there a message for me?"

"May I see some identification?"

I usually didn't have much patience with people who answered questions with questions, but I wasn't about to tangle with Ms. Biceps. After a brief search through my purse, I handed her my driver's license. As she scanned the laminated card, her facial muscles relaxed.

"Sorry for the mug check, but I had to be sure you were the right party." She extended her hand, adding, "I'm Wilma Clanahan."

Her grip made me wince. "How do you do. Is there a message for me?" I said a touch testily.

"No, but I've got the boy."

I favored her with a blank stare. "Pardon?"

"Sammy Girard," she explained, an almost-smile tugging at her thin lips. "He sure is a cute little fellow, smart as a whip, too. It's hard to believe he's only in the first grade."

If my jaw had dropped any lower, it would have hit the floor.

"I drove the 9:40 run from Boston. When Sammy's mother put him on the bus, she asked me to look after him until you picked him up," Ms. Clanahan informed me.

"Where is Mrs. Girard now?" I stammered, struggling against a monumental confusion.

"Still in Massachusets, as far as I know. She said to tell you there had been a change in her plans and that she would contact you as soon as possible."

How could Alison have entrusted her daughter to the care of a complete stranger? And why would she have passed off Samantha as a boy? The panic that clutched at my stomach must have been telegraphed to the bus driver; her gaze narrowed to wariness.

"If there's a problem, maybe we'd better contact the transit authorities," she said, folding her arms across her ample bosom.

I swallowed hard, forcing a confident smile. "Everything's fine. I'm just anxious to get Saman—er, Sammy home. Where is he?"

"Follow me." As Ms. Clanahan ushered me through a hall off the concourse, she confided, "Poor little thing conked out just past Baltimore. When we arrived, I stashed him in the drivers' lounge so he could finish his nap."

Left to my own devices, I would never have recognized the child sleeping on the couch in the lounge. The angel's glory of golden, waist-length ringlets was gone, cropped to a gamine halo and colored a deep chestnut brown that was approximately the same shade as my hair. Samantha's face was thin, the cherubic cheeks I remembered were still delicate, like rose-tinted porcelain. Her features were so like Alison's that my breath caught in my throat.

"Sam," I murmured, kneeling beside the couch and touching her shoulder with careful fingers.

Her lashes fluttered and slowly lifted. Her eyes were the color of Indian turquoise. The recognition in her unfocused gaze sharpened to resentment. She scrambled to a sitting position, and retrieving the bedraggled stuffed animal that had served as her pillow, she clutched it to her chest. "Ms. Clanahan?" she quavered, looking past me.

"Right here, tiger," the bus driver interjected from behind. "I found your Aunt Rachel for you."

A strained expression pinched Samantha's face. I wanted to scoop her up in a hug, but when I made a move to sit beside her, she shrank away. The rejection twisted a knot in my heart. Don't rush it, I cautioned myself, struggling to view the world from her perspective. She was separated from the person she loved above all others, exhausted from a ten-hour bus ride, and confronted by someone she'd been away from for a third of her life. Under the same circumstances, I probably would have screamed bloody murder.

Operating on pure instinct, I turned my attention to the stuffed animal clutched in her arms. "I know you're tired from your trip, BeeCee, but after you take a nap, you'll have to tell me the latest gossip from dinosaur land. I'm dying to know how Mrs. Brontosaurus's face-lift turned out."

This bit of nonsense was rewarded by a small snort, possibly the beginnings of a giggle. I tweaked the animal's padded tail. It was connected to the threadbare once-plush torso by a ragged line of stitches. "That bad, huh? She should've gone to Dr. Neanderthal's clinic. I hear he does marvelous work on wrinkled snouts, too."

"You're silly," Samantha said. A fledgling grin revealed the absence of two front teeth.

"Nope. I'm Willy-Nilly. Silly's my twin sister." I held out my hand, willing it not to tremble. "Ready to go home, Sam?"

After a split second's hesitation, she nodded. "First, I've got to say goodbye to Clanahan."

Though I would have given large dollars to be the recipient of the hug she gave the bus driver, I contented myself with the belief that if I didn't force the issue, I had a better-than-even shot at reclaiming Samantha's trust.

On the way to the car, my first tactical error was asking about Alison. At the mention of her mother, Sam's body stiffened and she disengaged her fingers from my grasp. Although I purposely kept the conversation innocuous during the drive to Georgetown, her answers to my inquiries about school and life in Maine were limited to unenlightening monosyllables.

When we walked into the silent house, I immediately checked my answering machine for messages: there were none. Fighting disappointment and a mushrooming attack of worry, I ushered my guest into the newly decorated spare bedroom. "When I bought these curtains, I remembered that your favorite color is pink," I said, knowing I sounded overly enthusiastic.

"I like purple better now."

"Strike two," I muttered under my breath. I set her suitcase on the bed, turning with a determined smile. "Would you like for me to help you unpack?"

"I'm not a baby. I can do it myself." Her tone stopped just short of disdain.

"Right." I took in a deep breath and moved along to the next topic. "The bathroom's just across the hall if you'd like to freshen up. While you're getting settled, I'll go fix us something to eat."

"I'm not hungry."

Neither was I, but in the face of such resistance, there was nothing to do but beat a strategic retreat to the kitchen. I still had one ace in the hole: the little girl I knew had a sweet tooth that almost equalled mine, and the double-fudge layer cake Maggie had baked that afternoon was sure to send her into chocoholic raptures. Bribing Samantha with dessert may have been dirty pool, but I desperately needed information.

The sound of water running in the bathtub detoured my worries onto yet another path. When I'd told the child to freshen up, I meant face-washing and tooth-brushing, not total immersion. What if she slipped on a bar of soap and drowned? The possibility had me halfway through the door when I caught myself. She was six years old, after all, and insulting her independence would only serve to alienate her further. After fifteen minutes—probably the longest of my entire life—I added cocoa with marshmallows to the cake tray and marched back to confront the tight-lipped first-grader.

A reluctant "Come in" answered my tap on her door.

Sam was perched cross-legged on the bed, the unisex Levi's and striped T-shirt she'd worn replaced by a lavender nightgown, the look on her oval face so lost and lonely it nearly broke my heart.

"I know how hungry dinosaurs get, so I brought BeeCee a snack," I chirped, my voice sounding brittle even to my own ears.

"He can't eat. He's just a toy."

So much for the therapeutic powers of chocolate. Setting the tray on the nightstand, I sauntered to the bookcase to retrieve a shoe box of photographs I'd run across during my cleaning binge. "These are some pictures I took when you and your mommy used to live in Washington. Would you like to look at them?"

"I'm too tired." She hunkered down among the pillows, pulled the spread up under her chin and squeezed her eyelids shut.

I couldn't recall ever feeling so frustrated. I sat down beside her to make one last plea, my fingers clenched so tightly that the nails bit deep into my palms. "All the while you were away, I never stopped thinking about you and loving you for a single minute. You must miss your mother very much right now, and so do I. As long as I live, she'll be the dearest friend I'll ever have...." I slumped, the rest of the words I'd planned frozen in my throat, my muscles numbed to immobility by the heaviness that suddenly came crashing down on me—the helplessness of not knowing where Alison was, the fear that something was terribly wrong, the weight of my responsibility for her child.

I didn't even realize I was crying until Samantha began to wipe away my tears with her dinosaur's tail. The comfort she offered was the sweetest I'd ever known. Her small fingers cradled my chin, smoothing back the hair from my brow. After a moment, she climbed down from my lap and padded to the bathroom, returning with a length of toilet tissue and the firm instruction, "Blow."

Who's the adult here? I wondered, meekly complying with the order.

"That's much better." Fetching a plate, she appropriated a big bite of cake for herself then guided a forkful into my mouth. "Don't worry, Cricket. Me and BeeCee are gonna take very good care of you till Mommy comes Saturday morning."

I swallowed convulsively, almost choking in my haste to follow up the lead. "Is that when she's supposed to come back?"

"Uh-huh." I had to wait until the lion's share of the dessert disappeared before she continued. "It's my birthday, and she said she'd bring me a two-wheeled bicycle. I get to spend the whole day learning to ride it."

That Alison would appear on schedule was a blue-chip certainty as far as I was concerned. She would never let business—no matter how urgent—interfere with a promise to her daughter. The breath I'd been holding came out in a relieved whoosh. "That's terrific, honey. We'll put together a huge party—grape soda, purple balloons, funny hats—the whole nine yards," I proposed, ruffling her still-damp curls. The gesture gave me the opportunity to segue into the next topic. "Your hair looks cute this way. When did your mommy cut it?"

"Yesterday at the motel in Boston. She did hers the same way so we would match. I didn't much like it at first, but she said it would grow back again pretty soon."

Alison Girard's honey-colored mane was her pride and joy; it was hard for me to imagine any circumstance that would cause her to tamper with her hair, or Sam's, either, for that matter.

"Did she say why she wanted to change the color?"

"Just because," Sam said, with what was either annoyance or apprehension.

I interpreted the wariness that crept back into her eyes as a not-so subtle hint to back off, so I made the tone of my next question casual. "Do you know where she went after she put you on the bus with Ms. Clanahan?"

"The tree place."

"Magnolia Grove?" I pressed.

"Uh-huh. That's where she lived when she was a little girl." Samantha downed half her cocoa, then licked the froth from her upper lip. "Can we look at the pictures now?"

I kept up a running commentary as we sorted through the photographs, more to keep my mind from going off on a dark tangent than to provide the little girl with information.

Exhaustion was obviously taking its toll, but fighting to keep her eyes open, she plucked a snapshot from the array on the bed and held it up. "Who's this man?"

"Kevin is—was—my husband," I explained, regretting that I hadn't previewed the display more carefully beforehand.

The gaze that swept my face was solemn, sympathetic. "Did he go to heaven like my daddy did?"

"Nope—to California."

"Why didn't he take you with him?"

"Because we're not married anymore."

"How come?"

I squirmed under the weight of her probing glance. "We decided we'd both be happier if we didn't live together." That pretty much summed up a long-closed chapter in the life and times of Rachel Bodine McKinnon. I banished my ex back to the shoe box.

"My friend Jennifer's parents did that, too. She told me that people who get a divorce always have 'wreck-consiled distances,'" Sam persisted with a yawn, adding a drowsy "Does that hurt as bad as when you get your tonsils out?"

I worked hard to hide a smile. "It's certainly not something I plan to go through again."

As I started to pack the rest of the photographs and take them into my room, she selected a three-by-five close-up of Alison.

"Can I keep this one?" she asked, clutching it as she nestled down beside her stuffed toy.

I nodded, making a mental note to hunt for the negative the very next day: a framed enlargement would be my contribution to the birthday festivities. "If you get lonesome tonight, you can come sleep with me," I offered as I leaned down to kiss her forehead.

"I'm okay by myself," she murmured groggily. I was about to switch off the lamp on the nightstand when she objected. "BeeCee likes the light on so he can see if any monsters come out of the closet."

Although a shower alleviated some of my stress-produced fatigue, sleep that night was hard to come by. Alert to any sounds that might come from the room across the hall, I sat on the edge of my bed an hour later absently going through the cache of pictures.

Near the bottom of the stack was a color Polaroid of two children, one of them the preschool version of my best friend. The resemblance between her then and her daughter now was more than startling: the two could easily have been identical twins. The dark-haired boy standing behind Alison, hands resting protectively on her shoulders, was in the all-ears-and-feet stage of post-pubescent growth. He was painfully thin—the arms extending from his T-shirt showed no prospect of muscles to come—and the freckled face he turned to the camera was screwed into a goofy, adolescent grimace.

Who was he? The answer came in a rush that transported me to an August Sunday in my ninth year.

Magnolia Grove was in the grip of a record heat wave that summer, the drought and South Carolina sun an unforgiving combination that withered the corn in the fields and seriously shortened adult tempers. In deference to the lack of air-conditioning in Mount Tabor Presbyterian, my father—normally good for a half hour in the pulpit—had chopped his "Thou shalt nots" to five minutes flat, dismissing his grateful and perspiring congregation. Alison and I were first through the church door, not wanting to miss a second of the afternoon her adoptive parents had reluctantly agreed to let her spend with me.

Burdett and Viola Compton, advocates of the 'never spare the rod' school of child rearing, were humorless and stern. In their presence, Alison's spirit and imagination wilted into hopeless resignation. Which is why my mother and I conspired to rescue her at every opportunity.

"Mama made lemonade and caramel cupcakes. I took them up to the hideaway before Sunday school," I had confided, giggling with anticipation as we dodged through the crowd. Our target was a playhouse the church sexton had built for us among the branches of a huge oak in the grove in back of the parsonage.

When we reached the beginning of our shortcut through the cemetery, Alison's footsteps lagged, her cheeks blanching with a sudden pallor. "I'm scared."

The words were so soft that I nearly missed them.

"It's broad daylight, and everybody knows ghosts can't come out on Sunday," I had scoffed. "Besides, we've been through this graveyard a zillion times, and nothing's ever bothered us yet."

"I'm not afraid of what might happen now. It's about later."

In spite of the temperature, a shiver of cold zipped up the nape of my neck. Alison's wide eyes were fixed and empty, as though the main part of her were no longer there. I'd seen the same look on her face when she told Beanpole Sykes his pet raccoon was going to die. Two days later, it had been squished to a pulp under the wheels of a semi.

"Quit fooling around," I had commanded, shaking her arm.

At my touch, the color flooded back into her cheeks and she grinned at me like nothing had happened.

I was inordinately relieved. "Race you to the treehouse."

"Okay, but first I have to give you something." She had fumbled through the patent leather purse that matched her Mary Janes and produced a photograph. "She doesn't know

I still have it, and if she sees it, she'll make me throw it away."

The 'she' in question was old Viola. Whenever possible, Alison avoided calling Mrs. Compton the required "Mother Dear."

"I'll keep it for you." I had taken the picture, frowning as I scanned the two subjects. "Who's the goofball standing behind you?"

"My brother Daniel."

My mouth dropped open in a startled O. We'd been best friends for a whole year, and this was the first I'd ever heard of a sibling.

"He's not really a goofball. In fact, he's kind of cute," I had amended lamely.

"No, he isn't, but he will be when he grows up."

There was no doubt in my mind that she adored her big brother. Her face glowed with love and a longing that far surpassed anything in my meager experience.

"Where is he now?"

"Don't know. When they adopted me, they wouldn't take Daniel, and they say it's better if I forget about him."

Speechless, my nine-year-old brain filled with an outrage it had never known, I could only imagine the magnitude of Alison's loss.

"It's okay," she soothed, patting my arm. "One day, Daniel's coming back to find me. And guess what?"

I could barely squeeze the obligatory "What?" between my clenched teeth.

"You're gonna marry him, and we'll all live happily ever after."

It was a prediction she never made again, and, in fact, that was the last time we spoke of her brother. As I shook my head to loosen the grip of the memory, I wondered if she even remembered giving me the photograph.

"Cricket?"

The forlorn figure in the doorway was so achingly familiar that the breath caught in my throat. "Having trouble sleeping, short stuff?" I queried, extending my arms.

Sam was on my lap in nothing flat. "No, but BeeCee is. Want us to keep you company?"

"I thought you'd never ask." I gave her an extra hug before I tucked her under the covers, for the first time regretting that Kevin and I had skipped parenthood. Given the skittishness with which I currently viewed the male half of the population, I probably wouldn't get another shot at maternity.

Although Samantha fell asleep as soon as she was settled beside me, I lay staring into the darkness. It occurred to me that Daniel might be the "family business" that had pulled Alison back to Magnolia Grove, but the theory didn't hold water. If she had found her beloved brother, she'd surely have taken Samantha to the reunion.

There was bound to be some logical explanation for it all, but if there was, I couldn't think of it. It was almost dawn before I drifted off, one arm cradling my godchild, the other stretched toward a phone that refused to ring.

Chapter Two

After one hectic sortie to the National Zoo, my plans for doing D.C. were canceled; it seemed much more urgent to wait at home for Alison's call than to explore the Smithsonian. As four days inched past us with no word, Margaret Peace became the balance in our equation, her optimism a palliative for my fears, her ingenuity providing a wellspring of activities to keep Samantha happy and occupied, not an easy task considering the child's increasing anxiety level. Quite a few of the little girl's waking hours were spent on the window seat in the living room, where she fitfully scanned the flow of traffic along Dumbarton Street.

"What are you doing?" I was finally moved to ask.

"Practicing a game Mommy made up. The first one who sees the blue car gets a double-dip chocolate cone," she explained.

"Sounds like fun. Can I play with you?"

She scooted over to make room for me, never shifting her attention from the scene outside. In less than a minute, one of my neighbors turned the corner and pulled his navy Toyota into his driveway, but Samantha completely ignored it.

"I win," I gloated, pointing at the vehicle.

Sam shook her head in firm dismissal. "That's not it."

"But you said blue. You're not supposed to change colors in the middle of the game."

"That one's not the right kind of blue."

The impatience evident in her fledgling scowl sent me into strategic retreat. "Oops—it's nearly two," I said, checking my watch with feigned surprise. "You and Maggie have a date to make brownies this afternoon."

"Gingerbread people," she corrected me, brightening. "We're gonna use M&M's for their eyes." Sunny disposition now restored, she wiggled down from her sentry post and skipped off to her appointment. She was barely through the kitchen door when my neighbor came to meet her.

Watching the two of them walk hand in hand across the backyard, I breathed a heartfelt "Thank the Lord for Margaret Peace," then headed for the telephone.

The number provided by the long distance information operator was busy, but after five minutes of punching the redial button, I finally got through to Magnolia Grove's chamber of commerce.

"Miz Bloomer speakin'. How may I serve you?" drifted through the line in a gush of honeysuckle.

My request for a listing of all the motels in town met slight resistance until I hinted that I was on the staff of *Southern Style*. It wasn't exactly a lie. An occasional date of mine was one of the editors of the prestigious travel magazine; over lobster at Phillips, we'd casually discussed the possibility of my doing an article for him. I also knew a senior editor there.

"Is that all?" I queried after Miz Bloomer had given me three locations.

"All that we would recommend," she advised. "Magnolia Grove doesn't cater to the usual type of tourist. Most of our *visatahs* lease private cottages."

"As you probably know, our readers are very discriminating. They're also interested in reviewing the full range of accommodations," I insisted, adding the merest touch of steel to my tone. "I'd like the numbers of all the boarding houses, bed-and-breakfast establishments, and realty companies."

The inventory she finally provided was still brief, but I was satisfied that it was complete. "Your assistance has been invaluable, Ms. Bloomer. Rest assured you'll receive proper recognition in my article," I promised, disconnecting her before she continued with her packaged patter on the historical glories of the town.

For the next half hour, I waded through my list: skirmishes with recalcitrant desk clerks and sullen innkeepers established the fact that my friend wasn't registered at any of the public accommodations. I also determined that most cottages were rented by the month and that the rates started at astronomical. It was a cinch Alison hadn't gone that route.

At the end of the last call, I sat staring into space, back to square one with nowhere else to go. I'd only been fourteen when my father had died and mother and I had moved to her family home in Arizona. At best, my ties to Magnolia Grove were tenuous. Without a phone directory to jog my memory, the names and addresses of people I'd once known were hard to come by.

"I hope you've got some eggs. Sam just dropped my last dozen." Maggie reported as she bustled into the kitchen. At my listless wave toward the refrigerator, she stopped short to give me an inquisitive once-over. "What's the problem?"

I showed her the lodgings list, ending my update with a dispirited, "Bottom line, Alison Girard is nowhere to be found in Magnolia Grove."

"She could've decided to stay in Charleston while she's conducting her business. It's only forty-eight miles to the south," Maggie speculated.

I angled a curious glance at her. "How'd you know that?"

"I looked it up in my road atlas last night," she supplied. "A hurricane devastated that part of the country not too long ago. Perhaps Alison hasn't called because the phone lines are still down."

"I didn't have a bit of trouble getting through," I said, rejecting the theory. "She could've been in an accident, though. Maybe I should check the hospitals or call the sheriff's office."

"Or maybe you should get away from that phone and come sample Sam's gingerbread persons," my neighbor advised. "Alison will arrive safe, sound and on schedule Saturday morning."

My hopeful sigh seemed to originate from all the way down in the soles of my sneakers.

SAMANTHA'S BIRTHDAY dawned gray and foreboding; by late afternoon, Georgetown was awash in a rainstorm of monumental proportions. It was as though the heavens themselves were conspiring to extinguish the few remaining sparks of hope I had for Alison's return. Even Maggie's humor was affected by the downpour.

"That blasted television weatherman hasn't gotten a forecast right since Caesar was a corporal," she muttered, draping the last of the crepe paper streamers around the archway that led into the dining room. She climbed down from the step stool, her café-au-lait face a study in exasperation. "Samantha will be drawing social security by the time you finish blowing up those balloons, Rachel. I told you we should've rented a helium tank."

"This is much more fun." I released a partially filled balloon, forcing a chuckle as it looped in a schizophrenic track across the room and spluttered in a deflated heap near Sam's crayons. Sam didn't even look up from her sketch pad at my enthusiastic, "Bulls-eye!"

Disheartened by the lack of response, I wandered over to glance at her work. The lone stick figure near the bottom of the page was dwarfed by the ponderous expanse of a dark purple sky.

"I hate rain." The small artist pressed so hard against the newsprint that the waxy cylinder in her fingers snapped in half. She tossed the pieces away, reached for the ubiquitous BeeCee, and clasped him tightly to her chest as she stared out at the dismal landscape.

"It's been an hour since we put the homemade chocolate chip ice cream in the freezer to harden. It must be ready by now." The glance I sent Maggie was a plea for backup.

"Sure, and it's high time we got this show on the road." The elderly woman went for the stash we had hidden in the credenza, returning to deposit the pyramid of beribboned packages on the window seat beside the little girl. "Have you ever seen so much loot, sugarplum?'' she queried, beaming.

Samantha's somber ''Uh-uh'' was all we got. She made no move toward the gifts.

''Open the one from Cricket first. It's the very best of all,'' Mrs. Peace instructed, handing her the present on top.

It was hard for me to suppress my eagerness as Sam dutifully ripped through the lavender tissue. The finished portrait was truly my labor of love. I must have printed that photograph a dozen times before I came up with an enlargement that met my standards. I'd experimented with different paper textures and had finally faded the background into a oval vignette that showcased Alison's ethereal loveliness.

Samantha's reaction was stony silence. She stared down at her mother's face for a long moment, a storm of conflicting emotions gathering in her eyes. Anger finally won the battle. ''I don't want her. She doesn't love me anymore,'' she said through clenched teeth, pushing my gift aside.

''You know that's not true, Sam,'' I soothed, adding with more confidence than I felt, ''I'm sure she'll be here soon.''

''No she won't, and I don't care because I don't love her anymore, either.'' Now sobbing, the child spun away from me. I reached for her arm, but caught BeeCee instead, ripping off his precariously tethered tail.

''I'm so sorry, honey, I didn't mean to hurt him,'' I hastened to assure her, bracing myself against the accusation in her eyes.

My apology fell on deaf ears. Hurling the torso of her stuffed companion aside, Samantha ran into her bedroom, slamming the door behind her.

The pressure of Mrs. Peace's hand on my shoulder stopped me from following. ''Give her a few minutes alone.''

I sagged down on the window seat, bleakness permeating to the very bone. ''What am I going to do, Maggie?''

''Pray,'' was her advice. ''And while you're about that, go fetch a needle and thread. We're going to perform some reconstructive surgery.''

When I returned with my seldom-used sewing kit, I refused Maggie's assistance. Though I was way out of my league, I stuck to the task grimly; repairing the damage gave me something concrete to deal with. "Alison isn't much better at artsy-craftsy stuff than I am," I muttered, removing the safety pins that held BeeCee's stomach seam together. After a couple of uneven sutures, the needle hit an obstacle; in an effort to get it through, I plunged my hand into the wound. My fingers met a curious anomaly, the slickness of plastic beneath the matted batting. "There's something in here besides cotton," I reported, finally tugging free a small sandwich bag.

Inside was a touching assortment of Samantha's treasures—a set of mismatched earrings, a pebble striated with bands of brown and rose, a sheet of notebook paper folded into a tight square. On the latter was drawn the outlines of two small handprints, one labeled Sam, the other Jenny.

The last item in the stash was a real attention-getter, distinctly out of place in the collection of childhood memorabilia: it was a man's watch fob, the length of chain attached to it obviously solid gold.

Maggie cut loose a long, low whistle. "I wonder how Sam came by that?"

"Beats the hell out of me." Frowning, I examined it more closely. The elaborate crest engraved on the fob—a crown enclosed with a diamond-encrusted horseshoe—was a design I'd seen before, though precisely where escaped me at the moment. I also couldn't account for the shudder of revulsion it produced. "This could have belonged to Burdett Compton. As I remember, he always wore a pocket watch," I told Maggie, feeling a twinge of guilt for having gone through Samantha's private treasure trove.

"Well, we can't stitch it up in the dinosaur again. If those stones are genuine, that fob's worth enough to finance Sam's college education," was my neighbor's opinion. "Keep it in a safe place until Alison arrives. She'll know how to handle the situation."

The mass of the ornament was oppressive in my hand, the jewels set in its surface glinting an icy malevolence. As I laid it on the windowsill, my insides turned to aspic and a certainty planted deep in my secret soul blossomed bright and terrible. "She isn't coming back."

"It's way too early to give up hope." Maggie rose to pace a circuit that looped the coffee table. She stopped during the second lap to send me a speculative glance. "We've already scratched any business related to the Comptons as the reason for her trip. Does she have in-laws living in South Carolina?"

"Her husband was from Seattle, and as far as I know, he didn't have any family." I scoured my brain for information about Noah Girard, but the results of the survey were pitifully thin. "She met her husband when she was in grad school at Stanhope College. He was dean of the music department."

Mrs. Peace's brows arched in surprise. "The dean?"

"He was a good twenty-five years older, but the age difference never mattered to her. She once said he was the dearest, gentlest man she'd ever known." I fought back a pang of disloyalty as I added, "It's unlikely that he left property in Magnolia Grove, though, because he wasn't from here. And Alison was really always strapped."

Maggie's "Hmmm" was noncommittal. "There's still a good possibility that she managed to locate Daniel. The logical move is to check long-distance information to see if he's in the Magnolia Grove directory."

I shrugged. "I wouldn't know who to ask for. Alison was young when she was adopted, and by the time we became friends she had either forgotten her original surname or was afraid to mention it, even to me. The Comptons came down hard on her if she talked about her real family."

"There's a special burner in hell reserved for people like that," my neighbor said grimly, resuming her seat beside me.

I nodded in agreement, turning to peer out into the sullen twilight again. Nothing was there but the rain. "The only thing left for me to do is go to South Carolina and find her."

As the words left my mouth I was filled with an eerie malaise. Mainly, I feared something had happened to Alison, but I also felt antipathy for the town itself. The Magnolia Grove I remembered was an antebellum anachronism; for all intents and purposes, the population consisted of Endicotts, Rochambeaus, Hamiltons, Springfields and Ogletharpes, five families with very old money. Everyone else, nearly ten thousand souls the year I left, existed for the gentry to fold, spindle and mutilate at will.

"I was wondering how long it'd take you to come to that conclusion." Maggie's voice broke into my preoccupation. Retrieving her bifocals and a list from the pocket of her apron, she favored me with a smile. "There's a United flight to Charleston that leaves from National Airport early Monday morning. That'll give you all day tomorrow to pull yourself together—"

"You've already checked the airline schedules?" I interrupted incredulously.

"And made reservations," she admitted, then added after a second's hesitation. "The tickets will be waiting for us at the check-in counter."

The plural zipped by so fast I ignored it. "I really appreciate that, Maggie. Would you be willing to look after Samantha while I'm gone?"

She fortified herself with a deep breath, shooting a worried glance toward the closed door of the bedroom. "The way I see it, you've got no choice but to take her with you. The child already feels her mother's abandoned her, and you're the only person she's got left in the world. There's no telling what psychological damage might be done if you were to leave her behind."

Though I was by no means expert on childhood trauma, the scenario sounded very probable. "Be that as it may, I can't possibly look after Sam and search for Alison at the same time," I objected.

"Which is precisely why I'm going with you." She delivered her coup de grace. "Now then, since Magnolia Grove's right by the ocean, it might be nice if we reserved a beach house from one of those realty companies the chamber of commerce recommended. That would be much better for Sam than staying in a hotel."

I dismissed the suggestion with a wave of my hand. "I have no idea how long I'll be gone or what kind of situation I might be facing. If Alison's been hurt, or—" A gigantic lump in my throat kept me from voicing the more gruesome possibilities that whizzed through my brain.

"Rest easy, girl. No unidentified accident victims have turned up in that general area during this past week."

I swallowed hard. "How do you know that?"

"My husband's partner went to live in Charleston when he retired from the D.C. force, and his son is a South Carolina state trooper. I got antsy day before yesterday, so I called and asked them to run a check for me." She grinned, her thin face radiating smugness. "Aren't police computers wonderful?"

"So are you, but I still think it would be better if you and Sam stayed here."

Maggie folded her hands across her chest and donned a long-suffering look. "You wouldn't deny a frail old lady a seaside vacation, would you? This may be my last chance to see the Atlantic."

My mouth flapped open, but since nothing I could say was going to change her mind, I shut it and wrapped my arms around her. "I love you, Maggie."

"The feeling's mutual." She patted my back, then pulled away to nail down the details. "Now then, are we agreed on the beach house? As soon as we locate Alison and help her finish her business, the two of you can improve your tans while you catch up on old times."

"She always loved the beach." I fingered the watch fob on the windowsill, unable to keep my thoughts of Alison from slowly shifting into the past tense.

"YOU STILL GOT my 'posit box, Maggie?" Samantha queried for the fifth time since the plane touched down at Charleston International Airport.

The item in question, a small rosewood jewel case, was the compromise we'd reached in lieu of sewing my godchild's treasures back inside her stuffed toy. To overcome her fear that someone other than herself might gain access to her trove, I'd strung the key on a gold chain and fastened it around her neck.

Maggie straightened after stowing her luggage in the trunk of the rented car and then she patted the bulging sides of her voluminous needlepoint carryall. "My purse is as safe as a vault in the Vatican. As soon as we get to the beach house, we'll find a good place in your room to hide the 'posit box."

Sam's expression was dubious, but she hopped into the rear seat without further comment.

"Are you sure you don't want to sit up front with us?" I asked as I slid behind the steering wheel.

She shook her head, settling the canvas tote that held BeeCee and sundry other childish essentials firmly beside her. "I can see better back here."

My first move was to turn the air conditioner to full blast, but the low-powered unit in the economy special was no match for a South Carolina July. The sun was now at its zenith, brilliant and merciless, and the inert atmosphere draped the landscape in a super-saturated shroud. I felt wilted and drained, though less intimidated by the muggy climate than by the uncertainty of what lay ahead. "I'd forgotten how blasted hot this place can be in the summer," I complained, running my tongue over lips that seemed in imminent danger of shriveling.

"If you think this is bad, you should have been raised in Montgomery, Alabama. My Aunt Hettie used to swear we lived at the third train stop past Hades," Maggie countered serenely. As I blended into the traffic that clogged the airport access lanes, she twisted to caution our tiny passenger. "Buckle up, sugarplum."

"I can't. I have to see if the blue car is coming," Samantha objected.

My glance in the rearview mirror caught her scrambling to a kneeling position beside the left window.

"You're going to have to fasten your seat belt, Sam," I admonished, working to keep a lid on my impatience. "This isn't a good time for your game."

"Is too. Mommy lets me do it when she's driving."

The rising petulance in her tone told me she was prepared to go to the wall on this one. If her safety hadn't been involved, I probably would have let the matter slide. As it was, I pulled over to the curb and cut off the motor.

Before I could marshall a more forceful instruction, Maggie intervened with a gentle, "Come up here and sit between us, pudding. Cricket and I will take the first turn at the game."

Samantha considered the compromise, then, dropping her bag into the front seat, climbed over after it and obediently tethered herself in place.

Handling kids was fairly simple, provided you knew the right buttons to push, I mused as I pulled back into the stream of traffic. And at the rate I was going, I figured I'd get the hang of it just about the same time Samantha graduated high school.

"Now then, Sam, tell me how to play your game," Maggie requested.

The little girl retrieved a box of crayons from her tote and, after studying the assortment, chose a shade between royal and peacock. "The Horsey car is this color, and it's got a white top."

Her specificity belied my assumption that the target involved was one of a generic class of vehicles. There was a strange intensity to her expression. She had the guarded aspect of a fawn alert to the presence of a predator.

Intuition told me there was more at stake here than the first-prize chocolate ice-cream cone. I cut my speed in half. "Do you know what make it is?" I asked uneasily.

"Uh-uh." She paused to sketch a design on a sheet of paper. "But the silver thing on its nose looks like that."

Her drawing was of a circle divided into three equal wedges. A Mercedes-Benz logo.

An irate honking from behind urged me to pick up the pace, and Maggie took up the interrogation. "Why do you call it the Horsey car?"

"Because that's its name." Apparently satisfied that Maggie and I could be trusted with sentry duty, she pulled out a picture book and began thumbing through it.

By now my internal warning system had clicked in. I wasn't crazy about the way the pieces were beginning to fit together, and before we got to Magnolia Grove, I had to have more information. Though I was positive Samantha could give me the answers I needed, I didn't want to spook her with the wrong questions. After a moment's study, I ventured a casual, "When did you and your mommy start playing the game, Sam?"

"When we first went to Maine."

From my brief phone conversation with Alison, I was able to place the time at six months ago.

"I didn't want to leave Lisa and go there, but Mommy told me I'd make friends in the new place, too. She says that every time we move, and I guess she's right, 'cause now Jennifer stays in the apartment right next to ours, and I like her almost as much as Lisa." She chattered on, launching into a disjointed comparison of her playmates.

"Have you lived in a lot of different cities?" Maggie broke in at the first opportunity.

"Uh-huh. Chicago was best, though. Lisa's daddy took us fishing at a big lake, and we found the brown rock that's in my 'posit box." Samantha's bottom lip trembled ever so slightly. "Mommy says pretty soon we're going to find a place we really like and we'll never, ever, have to leave it. We're gonna get a house with a big yard so I can have a kitty, maybe even two of 'em. Mommy likes kitties almost as much as I do."

"I know," I murmured, thinking of the black cat Alison had found when we were in second grade. The Comptons refused to let her keep the pet, so it had stayed at the parsonage with me. I steered onto the ramp leading into Interstate 26 before I got back to the business at hand. "When was the last time you saw the blue-and-white automobile, Sam?"

"In Boston. The Horsey man is very bad. He hit our car in the back. I thought he was going to do it again, but the police drove by and he ran away. That's when we stopped at the motel. Mommy and me fooled him good, though. After we changed our hair, he didn't know who we were."

My blood went through a number of rapid temperature changes before settling on freezing; the deep breath I gulped kept me from swerving off the road. "Why haven't you told me about him before now, Samantha?" I snapped, straining for control.

"Mommy didn't want to worry you. She said she'd s'plain everything when she came back."

"Of all the dumb—"

"Steady, Rachel," Mrs. Peace murmured, lightening her tone to address Samantha. "Since she's been delayed, I'm sure she wouldn't mind if you told us his name and what he looks like, honey."

The child shook her head, mumbling, "I didn't see his face. I don't want to talk about him anymore."

From the tension that stiffened her small shoulders, it was clear that further probing would be counter-productive. Slowing the vehicle to the highway minimum, I relegated the driving to automatic reflex while I tried to make sense of the sinister patchwork that was unfolding.

Someone was tracking Alison Girard, and if her pattern of frequent relocations was any indication, she had been followed for the past two years. But to what purpose? The job she'd had before she left Washington, assistant to a low-level curator at the Freer Art Gallery, was light-years removed from the cloak-and-dagger circuit, and nothing on God's green earth would have induced her to become involved with anything vaguely akin to organized crime. In addition, I knew while she was living in D.C., there hadn't been any romantic relationships, failed or otherwise, that might have caused her to run. The mental inventory ruled out almost everything except the remote possibility that the "horsey" driver tailing her was some well-to-do whacko with a fatal-attraction syndrome.

No matter what the pursuer was after, he'd apparently posed sufficient threat to Alison to run to ground in South Carolina. My mind steadfastly refused to entertain the notion that he had caught up with her, but common sense insisted it was at least possible that he had followed her to the area. In which case, my original plan for this southern junket required substantial revision. Rather than mount an overt search and risk blowing Alison's cover, I'd have to publicize my arrival and wait for her to contact me. The passive strategy didn't suit my style, but for the moment, it was the best I could manage.

I now realized Samantha had been shipped to me strictly or safekeeping, and although bringing her along had been a huge blunder, we'd long since passed the point of no return. The chances of the mysterious Mr. Horsey recognizing the little girl had been lessened by the change in her hair color, but I needed a little extra insurance.

"Let's play another game while we're in Magnolia Grove, Sam," I suggested aloud. "Until we find your mother, it would be lots of fun if you pretended to be my daughter."

Her reluctant "Okay" came with a stipulation. "I can't call you mommy, though, 'cause that's what I call Mommy."

"Cricket will do just fine," I assured her. "And you'll have to remember to say that your name is Samantha McKinnon, and you live in Washington. Think you can do that?"

"Uh-huh. How long do we have to wait before we see Mommy?"

"I'd like to play the new game, too," Maggie hastily interjected, diverting the child's attention.

Samantha smiled and patted Maggie's knee. "I always wanted a grandma just like you, so you can be her."

"Bless your heart for the thought, child, but I don't think the locals will buy that." Maggie planted a kiss on Sam's forehead, sending me a look of secret amusement as she counter-offered, "I'll be the housekeeper, providing your make-believe mama keeps in mind that I don't do windows."

By the time we reached our highway exit, Maggie and I had devised a simple, plausible explanation for our sudden appearance: I would be on a working vacation with my daughter, freelancing a feature photographic layout for *Southern Style* magazine. Equipment wouldn't be a problem because I always traveled with my cameras and a kit for jury-rigging a bare-bones darkroom. The story would provide us the high profile necessary to alert Alison. If the M.G. grapevine was still in working order, word of our visit would zip through the hamlet before our bags were unpacked.

The outskirts of my hometown had changed very little in the seventeen years I'd been away. Clapboard shanties once

inhabited by the "have-nots" had given way to mobil
homes that were jacked up on cinder blocks in hodgepodg
clumps on either side of the narrow blacktop. Despite th
occasional plastic flamingo yard ornament and petunia
planted in white-washed tractor tires, the overall effect wa
still relentless poverty. The view beyond the windshiel
triggered my recollection of the woebegone faces in m
father's congregation—servants, mill hands, tenant farm
ers—all seeking a heavenly reward, since for sure, none wa
forthcoming in Magnolia Grove.

"You must've made a wrong turn somewhere," Maggi
said, pursing her lips in dismay as she surveyed the disma
scenery. "This is nowhere close to what I expected."

"The real Magnolia Grove is a secret the powers that b
aren't particularly anxious to share. This backwater acces
road generally discourages ordinary tourists who acci
dently wander off the beaten path," I explained with
chuckle that didn't come easily. "Don't worry. The cottag
we've reserved fronts the most gorgeous beach on the whol
South Carolina seaboard."

Samantha perked up noticeably. "After we find Mommy
can we go swimming?"

"We can stay in the water until our skin prunes,"
promised, tiptoeing around the prerequisite in the ques
tion.

Maggie's initial misgivings melted into open-mouthed
amazement when we finally hung a right at a scripted sig
marking the beginning of Plantation Boulevard.

"Can't say that I care much for the name, but the stree
is spectacular," she said.

A twinge of civic pride surprised me. "It is rather pretty,'
I agreed, sliding my glance down the tree-shaded, cobble
stone length of the town's main thoroughfare.

The architecture of the buildings that lined the street wa
a fortuitous mélange of Adam, Federal and Regency styles
accented here and there with the cool classicism of Greek
Revival. At every intersection, magnificent displays of ver
bena, impatiens, and moss roses—as tasteful as they wer
exuberant—nodded from wooden planters with the co
quettish grace of well-bred southern belles. Further along

the statue of Colonel Jubel Tobias Springfield, its regularly polished copper splendor unsullied by time or errant sea gulls, still presided over the town square.

The directions I'd been given over the phone by the realty agent eventually led us to Seagate Plaza, an upscale shopping center in the final stages of construction. A pharmacy, a few chi-chi boutiques, sans prices on the items in their windows, and a delicatessen with a special on Beluga caviar were already open and doing a booming business. At my best guess, the combined costs of the automobiles in the parking lot approximated the annual budget of a Third World country. The west end of the complex was absent significant pedestrian or vehicular traffic, but that was hardly surprising since Ogletharpe Properties, Inc., the management company with which I'd made the reservation for the cottage, was currently the lone occupant of the commercial arcade.

As we got out of the car, the afternoon temperature was hovering just below three digits; the humidity wasn't too far behind. A rush of perspiration plastered tendrils of my hair against my forehead and I began to regret my preference for natural fibers. The front of my linen skirt looked as though it had never been anywhere near an iron.

"While you're getting the lease squared away, I'll run over to the drugstore and pick up some sun block," Maggie proposed.

"Good plan," I agreed, gingerly fingering the already tingly skin on the bridge of my nose. "Better lay in a supply of insect repellant, too. The mosquito is South Carolina's state bird."

She chuckled, extending her hand to Samantha. "Come along, sugarplum. We'll see if we can find a beach ball and a sand pail while we're shopping."

The little girl shook her head, securing the strap of her tote bag over her shoulder. "I'd better go with Cricket so she won't get lost."

It didn't take a shrink to figure out she was fearful of another abandonment. She slipped her tiny hand in mine, and I again felt a crushing weight of responsibility for her. But with it came the most incredible surge of love; it occurred to me that I needed Samantha every bit as much as she needed me.

"Will the people in here know where Mommy is?" she queried as we approached the door of the realty office.

"I doubt it, honey. When we were growing up, we lived on the other side of town. She might have gone over there to visit some of our old neighbors."

"On television, policemen always know where lost people are. We could ask them to help us find Mommy," she persisted.

"That's a very good idea. I'll go to the station just as soon as we get settled."

She accepted my promise with a resigned sigh and preceded me through the door.

The realty company's platinum-blond receptionist viewed my heat-disheveled appearance with an expression generally reserved for lower-order amphibians, then she all but laughed at my request for a lease. After a cursory glance at the log in front of her, she informed me that there was no record of my reservation. The agent I'd supposedly spoken with was not in the office.

"I'm not responsible for your screw-ups. Let me speak to your superior," I demanded, matching her tone icicle for icicle.

She shrugged. "Mrs. Vickers's office is down the hall. Your little girl will have to stay in the waiting area, though. That's company policy."

I was on the verge of telling her precisely where she could put her organizational rules, but of the agencies I had contacted, Ogletharpe was the only one with available listings in a price range I could afford. At the moment, I needed lodging more than an outlet for my temper.

"I won't be long, Sam. You can read BeeCee a story," I suggested, motioning to a couch by the window.

The little girl trotted obediently to her seat, appropriating a double handful of lemon drops from a crystal bowl as she passed the coffee table.

Still stewing over the receptionist's ill-concealed contempt, I stalked off in the direction she pointed.

Lula Vickers, as the discreet plaque on the office door proclaimed, was a well-upholstered woman who looked to be in her forties. Her expression was as rigid as the lacquered coils of her iron-gray upsweep. Preparing myself for a major hassle, I launched into an explanation of the problem.

"I authorized your agent to put the deposit for the cottage on my credit card, and I believe that constitutes a valid contract," was my final shot.

Mrs. Vickers tapped her fingers against the desk blotter, studying me through narrowed eyes. I wasn't easily intimidated, but I found her steady surveillance strangely disconcerting. I tugged anxiously at my earlobe, a long-time habit whenever I was backed into a corner.

At my involuntary gesture the expression on her face immediately zipped into incredulity. "Little Rachel Bodine!" She bounced from her seat and rounded the corner of the desk, adding as she enveloped me in a Shalimar-scented hug, "Lord, girl, you're the best thing I've seen in a month of Tuesdays. You probably don't recognize me with all this weight I've put on, but I'll bet you remember the purple passion nail polish."

A thin trickle of recollection grew to a flood. "Lula Sue Dawson," I breathed, returning my one-time baby-sitter's embrace with more than a little affection. Though I'd been barely five when she gave me my first manicure, I'd hung on to the thrill of it for a lot of years. Luby, as I'd called her then, had been my idol, the prettiest, most popular girl at Jubel T. Springfield High School.

Beaming, she ushered me to a chair, then pressed a button on her intercom. "I'll do the paperwork on this rental myself, Becky. Have the keys, a map to the Pelican Cay beach house, and one of our gold-star guest packets ready for Ms. McKinnon when she comes out," she said. The lease she handed me a few minutes later was for a rate considerably less than the one I'd expected to pay, but Lula overrode my attempt to have it corrected. "Don't bother to sign it now. I'll have someone come over and pick it up after you've had a chance to go through all the fine print. Right now, we've got a ton of things to catch up on. Is your mama still in Arizona?''

"She died ten years ago." I swallowed a bitterness that refused to leave me. "To tell you the truth, I think she was glad to go. She never got over losing Papa."

"Everyone in Magnolia Grove thought the world of Reverend Bodine, especially the teenagers. He kept quite a few kids from dropping out of school—me for one—and he always found a spare minute to listen to everyone's problems."

Except mine.

Resentment sneaked up to blindside me, and I wondered how long it had lain dormant beneath the layers of my consciousness. Reverend Gideon Bodine had been a loving husband, an exemplary father, but his work was his life, and the needs of the congregation had always come first. Mama had accepted that with grace, grateful for the time he'd chosen to share with her. But I still held him accountable.

"I never would've tried for a college scholarship if it hadn't been for your father's encouragement," Lula said. She was interrupted by the ringing of the phone.

I rose. "Thanks for everything, Luby. I know you must have tons to do, so I won't take up any more of your time."

"Call me when you get settled. I'll make you the best country dinner you've ever laid a tooth on," she invited, reluctantly picking up the receiver to resume her work.

When I reached the waiting room, the blond receptionist was cordial, almost fawning as she handed me the keys and a gilt-sealed vellum envelope. "You'll be in one of our best properties. It's got a breathtaking view," she assured me.

"Where's my daughter?" I cut her off, staring toward the now-vacant couch. Motherhood—even the temporary, surrogate brand that had been accorded me—apparently came with a built-in mechanism for detecting trouble, and my new equipment was buzzing like nobody's business.

Becky's glance skittered nervously over the waiting area. "She was playing by the window when I went to refill the coffeepot. I only left her alone for a minute."

I was through the front door before she could finish her effusive apology. The immediate vicinity of Ogletharpe's was completely deserted, but my thin hope was that Sam had gotten tired of waiting and had gone to find Maggie. I shaded by eyes against the afternoon sun, squinting over at the opposite side of the center, but Samantha wasn't among the shoppers clustered beside the entrance to the drugstore. I had taken a couple of steps in that direction when a sixth sense turned me around.

She was some thirty yards away, not far from the line of thick shrubbery that ringed the back of the parking lot. The man with whom she was holding an animated conversation was tall, well over six feet, I gauged. His face was shadowed by the bill of a New York Mets cap, and he was dressed in tight jeans, a faded muscle shirt and leather boots. It was the sort of outfit I generally associated with redneck bikers.

Before I could open my mouth to call out a warning to Samantha, he took her hand. Still chatting, they walked slowly in the direction of two cars that were parked on the other side of a construction barrier.

One of them was a blue car—a high-priced German import.

Chapter Three

Panic pumped at least a quart of high-octane adrenaline into my bloodstream, but I tightened my throat against the impulse to scream. Instinct warned that I would have a better chance against the would-be abductor if I caught him unaware. I kicked off my high-heeled pumps and started to run.

When I had cut the distance between me and my quarry to a few scant yards, my stockinged foot came down hard on a jagged stone. The pain that zipped along my calf must have forced a gasp through my clenched teeth, because the man turned to face me. Surprise, and what appeared to be disappointment, slackened his jaw. Releasing his grip on Samantha's fingers, he raised his arms in an open-handed gesture of surrender. In that same instant, I hurled my body through space.

Hitting him was like running into a stone wall: I was fairly certain the blow had done more damage to my shoulder than to his midsection. I could feel his muscles brace against me, but the momentum of my desperate dive still took him down. I landed spread-eagled atop of him, and though the impact squeezed most of the breath from my lungs, I managed the wheezy command, "Go get in the car and lock the doors, Samantha."

Instead of obeying, she squatted beside us, her expression a mixture of confusion and concern. "D.J.'s my new friend. Please don't hurt him, Cricket."

"Do as I tell you—now!" I scolded, fumbling for a grip on the kidnapper's motionless arms as the child pelted away.

At my best guess, the man who now lay pinned beneath me tipped the scales at one-eighty-something, and not an ounce of that was fat. Since he had at least a seventy-pound advantage on me, I wondered why he wasn't putting up any resistance. Point of fact, if it hadn't been for the rhythm of his breathing, I wouldn't have known he was alive. Concluding that I'd knocked him unconscious, I lifted my head to peek at his face.

Though his features weren't notable—the nose was a shade broad and the square jaw hinted at obstinacy—their general arrangement was on the up side of pleasant. He didn't fit my preconceived notions of a pervert, but who could tell by looks? Just as I finished the instant inventory, his lashes lifted.

"Nice tackle—I take it you're Samantha's missing mother."

The gently spoken observation, plus the realization that he'd been playing possum, caught me off guard. I gaped at him, momentarily at a loss for words.

"If any of my neighbors were to see us like this, my reputation would be shot to hell. Think maybe you could let me up now, Ms. McKinnon?" was his polite request.

The lazy sensuality in his grin prompted a surge of embarrassment that heated the nape of my neck. I scrambled to my feet. "Who are you?"

Maintaining his prone position, he answered, "Jericho Quaid, M.D., P.C., OB, PED. The alphabet soup means I dabbled with a lot of medical specialties before I found out I was happiest being an old-fashioned family practitioner."

He swiveled his hips just enough to permit him access to his back pocket. When he retrieved his wallet, his movements further strained the denim of his Levi's, accentuating the contours and power of his thighs. Right about then, my simmering blush rolled into a full-fledged boil, but if Jericho Quaid noticed the by-product of my covert surveillance, he didn't let on. He rose to his feet and handed me a driver's license and verification of his membership in the American Medical Association.

In my current state of mind, I wouldn't have accepted a reference signed by St. Peter. I returned his identification with a tight-lipped "Where were you taking my little girl?"

Before he had a chance to answer, a drop-dead gorgeous redhead wearing a jumpsuit that would have gotten her arrested for indecent exposure in some jurisdictions, undulated across the parking lot toward the Mercedes. "Don't forget to stop by my booth at the festival Saturday, Jerry," she called out. Her smile lapsed into a speculative sneer as she switched her attention from him to me, but apparently discounting me as any serious competition, she got into her vehicle and pulled away.

I breathed a trifle easier. The remaining car, Dr. Quaid's, I presumed, was a vintage model Ford that in its salad days had been brown. Its hood, obviously a junkyard replacement, was yellow, and dents in the right front fender had been repaired with blotches of pink body filler. The haphazard combination was homey and oddly touching. "Where were you taking Samantha?" I repeated, reducing my tone from strident to merely stern.

"To the police station. I suggested that we check with the security guard in the mall first, but she insisted that her mommy was lost somewhere else in Magnolia Grove. And she didn't seem to know whether her father was in heaven or California," he reported, his expression curious.

"My husband and I are divorced," I blurted before I could stop myself. Blushing at the inanity of the remark, I plugged any other incipient holes in my cover story with a hasty, "Sam tends to get mixed up when she's excited."

He stooped to retrieve his hat, running his fingers through the mahogany mop of his hair before he settled the cap in place. "I wish she'd mentioned the fact that her mother could hit like a linebacker. Have you ever considered a career with the Redskins?"

There was a large dollop of the South in both his diction and delivery, all the more reason to downgrade his position on my list of suspects. So far, all the information I had on Alison's pursuer pegged him as a Washingtonian. Be that as it may, I still found Dr. Quaid's cavalier attitude irritating.

"There's nothing funny about this situation. Count yourself lucky that I don't carry a pistol," I advised him coldly.

"I can guess what must've been going through your mind, Ms. McKinnon, and I'm sorry to be the cause of your concern." The humor had vanished from his face, replaced by something I couldn't read. "Samantha is a very special child, and for what it's worth, I'd sooner lose my right arm than to see any harm come to her."

He had talked to Sam for a scant ten minutes, yet his assertion had the emotional ring of a lifelong commitment. Wary again, I caught and held his glance, searching for any hint of duplicity. I was totally unprepared for what I found.

His eyes were extraordinary—the translucent, amber-warmed gray of a winter twilight—and they contained an inexplicable sadness. He returned my scrutiny with candor, his gaze shifting through curiosity to what seemed like recognition, and finally settling into a timeless wonder. Smiling, he reached to brush the curve of my cheek with his fingers, a gesture, which to my complete amazement, I found as natural and right as the sunrise. At the touch, I felt a harmony, a homecoming, as though I'd rediscovered an important portion of my soul that I hadn't even known was missing.

The contact lasted no more than the space of a heartbeat, but it left me confused and shaken. It must have had a similar effect on Jericho Quaid, because he shoved his hand in his pocket, reddening as he took a step backward.

"I hope you and Samantha will have a pleasant stay in Magnolia Grove," he said, adding with the barest trace of a grin, "My office is at the corner of Plantation and Palmetto, two blocks south of Springfield Park. Feel free to stop by if you need a physician—or a tackling dummy."

"Sam and I are very healthy, Dr. Quaid, and contact sports aren't really my forte." To smooth the ungracious edge from my response, I stuck on a gentler, "I do appreciate your assistance, though. I'm sorry I misjudged you."

He touched the bill of his cap. "No problem."

As he turned to leave, Samantha bounced up, dragging our ersatz housekeeper in her wake. "This is Mrs. Peace," the little girl said. "She's the best cook in the whole world."

"My pleasure, Mrs. Peace."

She shook his proffered hand, and as she scanned his face, her expression slowly changed from mistrust to endorsement. "Maggie will do just fine," she supplied with a smile.

Samantha tugged at his sleeve, hardly able to contain her excitement. "We're going to the beach after we finish lunch. Wanna go with us?"

No ifs, ands or buts about it, Jericho Quaid had to be written out of this script immediately. The scenario was already complicated enough without adding extraneous distractions. "The doctor is very busy, honey. He has to look after his patients," I interjected before he could respond.

Frowning dissatisfaction, Sam hugged her stuffed toy and neatly circumnavigated me with an ingenuous, "I think BeeCee's catching a cold, D.J. After you finish taking care of the sick people, will you come to our house and listen to his chest?"

"He just has a touch of wigglitis. Give him three kisses every hour and he'll be okay," the doctor prescribed, squatting beside Sam to tousle her hair. "I probably won't get to talk to you again before you leave, but I sure am glad I met you."

"Me too." She stretched to hug his neck, adding a soft, "Bye, D.J. Be sure to watch for the moon."

His arms tightened around her briefly, then he pulled back to study her face. "Why?"

"So you won't forget me. Mommy says my really-for-true friends never leave me, even if I can't be with them. And every time they see the moon, they'll know I'm thinking about them."

"Your mommy is a very smart lady." Quaid brushed her forehead with his lips, then gently disengaged himself from the embrace. When he rose to his feet, his eyes were shadowed, distant. Nodding a silent acknowledgement that was mostly aimed at Maggie, he spun on his heel and strode away. His head turned in my direction as he backed his car from its parking space, and although I was fairly certain he noticed my diffident wave, he didn't respond. The slight, whether intentional or not, stung a whole lot more than it should have.

BEEP. "Ms. McKINNON, this is Willa in Dr. Garner's office. It's been six months since your last dental checkup. Please call so we can get you on our schedule as soon as possible." *Beep.* "Hello, homeowner. I'm Tom, your telecomputer friend from Allweather Aluminum, Inc. Is peeling paint a problem? Are you disgusted by damage from dripping—"

"Take ten, Tom," I snapped, frustrated that my remote-control rerun of the messages on my answering machine at home had contained no word from Alison. The numeric sequences I keyed into the kitchen telephone console zapped Allweather's alliteration into electronic oblivion, then insured that all my future calls would be forwarded to South Carolina. I hung up the phone and glanced around.

The cottage—a decided misnomer for a place with a Jacuzzi, three bedrooms, four baths and more televisions than I cared to count—was equipped with every gadget known to mankind. The watchword of Pelican Cay Resorts Extraordinaire was seclusion with convenience; each of the twenty or so villas in the complex had its own slice of the pristine beach and enough privacy to satisfy a Howard Hughes, yet the heart of beautiful, downtown Magnolia Grove was only a fifteen-minute walk away. Thanks to the intervention of Lula Sue Dawson Vickers, Reverend Bodine's baby girl was living in high cotton.

"It seems to me that Samantha really took the scolding you gave her to heart. Don't you think confining her to her room for the rest of the afternoon is overkill?" Maggie broke into my internal review of our good fortune.

"To my mind, teaching kids not to go anywhere with strangers is lesson number one on the parent agenda," I answered stubbornly.

"You're a hundred percent right, and I think Sam already knows it. But for some reason, she considers Dr. Quaid a friend, not a stranger." She retrieved a folded sheet of paper from her pocket and handed it to me. "This is what our little Picasso was drawing when I went in to check on her.''

The crayon sketch was a radical departure from the others Samantha had done in the ten days she'd been with me; its primary colors were bright, its sky dominated by a happy-face sun. The picture featured two stick figures holding hands, one twice the height of the other and wearing a baseball cap. It didn't take too big a stretch to deduce that they represented Sam and Jericho Quaid. While her previous self-portraits had been drawn with brown, corkscrew curls, she now had Alice in Wonderland hair. Why that particular difference, I wondered? Was it an indication that she felt protected by his presence? Safe enough to return to her true identity?

"Sam really took a shine to him, and it was clear that the feeling was mutual," Maggie observed, spearing me with a sly glance. "What do you think of him?"

"He's okay."

Her response was a hybrid of a snort and a chuckle. "Okay, my foot. The man's a natural hunk. I haven't seen a set of buns like that since—"

"I'm not the least bit interested in Dr. Quaid's assets, Maggie." I cut her off firmly.

To avoid further discussion of a potentially sticky topic, I opened the gold-star guest packet and began flipping through the glossy brochure inside. Halfway to the back, I chanced on an advertisement for Fairfax Icons Unlimited, a photography studio on Plantation Boulevard. My attention immediately homed in on the logo, a recumbent figure eight divided in half by a horizontal line. "Five will get you ten this is Wallace Fairfax's place. He always used that symbol to mark his books," I mused aloud.

"I never bet without knowing all the particulars. Who's Wallace Fairfax?"

"My seventh-grade homeroom teacher. He was also adviser to the Shutterbugs, the school photography club. His wife, Marietta, gave piano lessons." Ephemeral images from nearly twenty years before, at first as ambiguous and one-dimensional as underdeveloped negatives, began to form in my mind. I propped my elbows on the countertop, and resting my chin on my hands, forced a sharper focus.

"The whole world went haywire for me at the beginning of that year," I continued. "Papa had to give up the pulpit after his stroke, and we moved from the parsonage into a house on Pickett Court. It was a real dump, but it was the best we could manage at the time. The worse part was that old Viola wouldn't let Alison set foot in our new neighborhood, and our place was too far from hers for me to walk. For a while, we hardly ever saw each other."

"Didn't you go to the same school?"

"No. The Comptons had stuck her in True Faith Academy, a private school in the next county. She detested it." I fought a losing battle against the bitterness of the recollection. "We finally figured out a way to get together, though. The Shutterbugs met at the Fairfax's house at two o'clock every Saturday afternoon. I joined the club, and Alison conned her mother into letting her take piano lessons from Marietta at the same time. Afterward, we'd have half an hour to spend with each other before Viola picked up Alison. If Wallace wasn't using his darkroom, we'd go there to hang out. It was a great place to gossip and commiserate over the big B."

"Which was?"

"Breasts. We were certain we were doomed to go through life without them. I saved all my money, and that Christmas I bought Alison a training bra. She gave me a Brownie Hawkeye camera. Mr. Fairfax helped her choose it."

"It would be nice if you gave him a call. I'm sure he'd be tickled to hear from you after all these years," Maggie suggested.

"I doubt he'd know me. Shutterbug was the most popular club in school, and I didn't do anything particularly outstanding when I was a member." I straightened up, suddenly aware that my trip through the past had led me to something important. "But he would remember Alison. She was so good at the piano that Marietta offered to give her extra lessons. Burdett Compton didn't care, as long as it didn't cost him anything, and Viola loved to brag about her talented daughter. That next summer, Alison practically lived with the Fairfaxes. She and Marietta grew very close."

"If that's so, there's a good chance she would've contacted them when she got to town. She may even be staying with them," Maggie concluded, handing me the telephone directory.

There was no answer when I called the residential number listed for Wallace Fairfax. After twelve rings, I hung up and scooped the car keys from the counter. "It's four thirty-five now, and this ad says the studio is open until five. I'm going to see if I can catch him there," I told Maggie.

As I walked out onto the lanai, the sun sailed low on the western horizon and a soft breeze blew in from the ocean. I breathed in the tang of salt-touched air, now feeling curiously buoyant, almost light-headed. The search was finally revving into high gear. But my elation was short-lived. Two short paces from the rented car, it was replaced by the creepy intuition that someone was watching me.

The nearest of the neighboring villas was some fifty yards down the beach, and if the scaffolding and paint cans on the deserted patio were any indication, it wouldn't be ready for rental for some time. Hunching my shoulders against a cargo of angst, I swiveled to study the sand dune that rose to the right of the driveway. A thick growth of sea oats clumped along its crest would have provided excellent cover for an unseen observer, but except for the ripple of wind through the supple grass, the only motion I could detect was that of a gull above the top of the hill. After a few minutes of fruitless study, I accorded my skittishness to paranoia.

Still, a shadow of doubt needled me into going back to alert Maggie to the possibility of trouble, and apprehension stuck close to me as I returned to the car and left the complex. When I merged from the Pelican Cay access road onto Camellia Drive, a four-lane artery that shunted traffic around the marina, the eerie prickling at the nape of my neck increased precipitously.

Since I had no idea what to expect, watching the vehicles behind me was an exercise in futility, but I did it, anyway. The compulsion to look in the rearview mirror interrupted my concentration, and I urged the Nissan along in fits and

tarts. My erratic progress must have annoyed the driver of
he BMW that was following me. The driver pulled into the
eft lane and shot past with a protracted blast from her horn.
t was then that I noticed the aging, piebald Ford sedan two
ar-lengths to my rear.

Jericho Quaid.

Stress does strange things to the human brain: an out-
andish plot, starring the physician in the role of a hilltop
Peeping Tom, immediately popped into my head. But what
arthly reason could he have had for keeping me under sur-
eillance?

It was a logical question, so my immediate impulse was to
top and ask. Unfortunately, when I aimed for the brake,
ny foot hit the accelerator, instead. The Nissan took off
vith a lurch that snapped the seat belt tightly across my
chest. At the same time, the multicolored rattletrap hung a
ight and chugged off down Twenty-third Street.

I was two seconds from going after the doctor when
:ommon sense kicked back in. Camellia Drive was a major
horoughfare in a very small town, I told myself, and it
vouldn't be unusual that a busy physician would choose to
ise it. That we'd been in the same place at the same time was
iothing more than coincidence.

"You're the planet's biggest goofus, McKinnon," I mut-
ered, thanking the patron saint of paranoid idiots for
sparing me another embarrassing confrontation with Jericho Quaid. Given my earlier performance in the parking lot,
the man would have considered me certifiable if I'd charged
ıp and accused him of spying on me.

Road work at the intersection of Camellia and Plantation slowed traffic to a crawl, so it was nearly five when I
reached Fairfax Icons Unlimited. The closest vacant parking space was in front of a bicycle shop four blocks from the
studio, and by the time I'd covered most of the distance
back, my former teacher was walking away from the front
door of his business.

"Hold up, Mr. Fairfax," I hailed.

He turned, his expression registering recognition and
astonishment as I jogged the final few paces between us.

"Rachel, you look marvelous. What a nice surprise."

"It's great to see you again," I responded, trying not to react to the changes I saw in him. His eyes and the set of his shoulders were old, weary, and he was so much thinner than he'd been seventeen years before that he almost seemed shrunken. His gaze darted past me as though he were searching for an avenue of escape.

"I realize that you're probably anxious to get home," I apologized, "but I'm not going to be in town for very long, and I was hoping you'd have a few minutes to chat with me."

For a moment I thought he would refuse, then his lips relaxed into a fledgling smile. "I always have time for my Shutterbugs, particularly one who's gone on to become a professional," he said as he escorted me to the studio and unlocked the door. "Nine or ten years back, I saw some of your work, truly magnificent studies of Native American children, in a national monthly. I was going to call the editor for your address so I could write and compliment you, but I let the opportunity slip away and I haven't run across your byline since."

"I got married just after those pictures were published, and I started using McKinnon, my husband's name."

"I'll watch for it from now on." He flicked on the lights, flooding the interior in a warm, seamless glow. "Are you still on the staff of the magazine?"

"No, I'm currently freelancing for *Southern Style*," I explained briefly. I was mentally struggling with the issue of how much of the real story to tell him when the phone on a desk at the far side of the room started to ring.

"Look around if you'd care to. I'll cut this as short as possible," Wallace promised. He scurried to answer the summons.

The gallery area of the studio was elegant, yet deliberately unobtrusive, its raw-silk wall coverings and plush carpeting the color of Devon cream. Wallace Fairfax's photographs, life-sized portraits of Magnolia Grove's moneyed elite, could have been used as textbook examples of composition and attention to detail. Every square centimeter of his subjects' skin was flawless, their eyes jewellike in depth and clarity. But his artful airbrush had erased more than crow's feet: the regal faces held all the character and animation of wax mannequins.

When I'd completed the circuit of the exhibition, my former teacher cradled the receiver and waved me to a Louis Quinze chair beside his desk. "Will you join me in a glass of cognac?"

The invitation surprised me. To my best recollection, he didn't drink. Although brandy ranked dead last on my list of preferred beverages, I didn't want to appear ungracious. "Just a thimbleful. I'm driving."

He retrieved a crystal decanter and two whisper-thin snifters from a tray on his desk; the portion he poured for himself nearly filled the goblet. Settling back in his chair, he favored me with abstracted curiosity. "What brings you back home after all this time, Rachel?"

Two factors made me abandon my cover story: in the first place, if my fatal attraction theory was correct, the danger to Alison was from an outsider, not a resident of Magnolia Grove. And secondly, if there was anyone in this town I trusted, it was Wallace Fairfax. Since I needed his help in the worst way, straight to the point seemed the best route to take.

"I'm looking for Alison Compton Girard. She sent her daughter, Samantha, to stay with me while she came down here on business and I haven't heard from her since." The fragile stem of my glass was in imminent danger from the tightening pressure of my fingers, so I set my untouched drink on the small table to my right. "I was wondering if she might have contacted you and your wife when she arrived. She's always been very fond of Mrs. Fairfax, and—"

"Marietta is in a Savannah nursing home," he interrupted dully, polishing off most of his cognac in a couple of swallows. Pushing the snifter aside, he swiveled to stare at a sixteen-by-twenty enlargement that hung beside the desk, a candid of his wife kneeling in a bed of pansies. "I took that snapshot of her just before she…" Wallace clamped his lips tight on the rest of the sentence, either unwilling or unable to finish.

The photograph was a refreshing contrast to the stifling perfection of his other portraits. Marietta Fairfax was a frumpy dumpling of a woman—her wispy hair was an improbable orange, the arrangement of her features at kindest assessment, plain—but his lens had captured a gentle joy in her eyes, her aura of sweet serenity, translating her flaws into something close to beauty.

In the old days, the couple had been extremely devoted, one never far from the touch of the other, and it was obvious from the bleakness that shadowed Wallace's face that he hadn't adjusted to their separation. Feeling like an intruder, I averted my gaze. "I'm so sorry. How long has she been ill?"

"Five-and-a-half years. Most weekends when I visit she doesn't recognize me, but she's happier when I'm there and so am I. In spite of everything, she still needs me, and I wouldn't miss a single second of the time we have left together." Pulling himself from his private pain with apparent difficulty, he turned his gaze to meet mine. His eyes were now opaque, unreadable, and his tone became brisk. "All of that is beside the point, though. I'm afraid I can't be of much assistance in your search for Alison. The last time I saw her was in Columbia, South Carolina, not long after her baby was born. Marietta and I were invited to the christening at the Stanhope College chapel."

"Does Alison know that Mrs. Fairfax is ill?"

"One of the neighbors who was helping out at the house when Marietta first went into the hospital took a long-distance call from Alison. She didn't leave a number, though, and she wasn't sufficiently interested in my wife's condition to phone again," he said with a trace of acrimony.

The firm set of his jaw told me the interview was over, but as I rose from my chair, I took a stab at prolonging it. "I don't mean to be a nuisance, but can you think of anyone else she might've contacted when she arrived in town?"

He shook his head. "Given the way she used to hate Magnolia Grove, it's hard to imagine her returning of her own volition." Leaving his seat, he moved to stand beside me, regarding me with a sympathetic gaze. "My guess is she wanted time away from her daughter and she's using you as a convenient baby-sitter."

"She wouldn't put her own needs above being with her child." Swallowing my anger at the charge he'd leveled, I plunged on. "Alison sent Samantha to me because someone's been chasing them."

"Is that what she told you?"

"No, but she dyed Sam's hair to disguise her, and from what I've been able to piece together—"

"It pains me to say this, Rachel, but the Alison I knew wasn't emotionally stable. She's always had an overactive imagination. The way she got wrapped up in her premonitions when she was a teenager used to worry Marietta no end," Wallace said, cutting me off. "If she's on the run again, it's from her own internal demons."

"Again?" I echoed.

"She has a long history of disappearing when situations are too tough for her to handle. In her final year of high school, she ran away from home repeatedly, and after she left during the summer following, her parents refused to take her back. She stayed with us for a month or two. Marietta arranged a tuition scholarship for her at Stanhope College in Columbia, and we offered to pay the rest of her expenses, but she preferred to do it on her own. It took her two extra years to finish because she kept dropping out to work. Even though she never came back to Magnolia Grove during all that time, Marietta kept in close touch with her. When she got married, we thought she was pretty well straightened out, but then her husband committed suicide and she took off from Columbia without so much as a goodbye."

"Are you sure Noah Girard killed himself? I thought he died of a heart attack." In truth, that was my own assumption. Alison and I hadn't actually discussed the cause of her husband's death.

His eyes held a mixture of resignation and sadness. "Positive. As I understand it, the Stanhope administration looked askance on a marriage between a dean of his years and one of his students, and there was also some talk about her seeing other men. The pressure of the situation obviously proved too much for him because he locked himself in his office and put a bullet through his temple."

The space around me took on a surrealistic cast; I blinked rapidly to restore my equilibrium. "Alison would never have betrayed her husband's trust. She loved him," I protested.

"So she insisted, but the line between reality and fantasy wasn't always clear to her. She tried her best to convince Marietta that there was foul play involved in Noah's death, even though all of the evidence was to the contrary. A few days after the funeral, she and the baby disappeared without a trace. Marietta never got over losing them." Mr. Fairfax cast an anxious glance at his watch, emitting the softest of sighs. "May I walk you to your car now, Rachel? I hope you won't think me rude, but I have quite a few things to attend to before I leave for Savannah in the morning."

"I'm sorry for taking up so much of your time," I said, trailing him to the entrance. As he locked the front door of the studio behind us, I ventured a final plea for assistance. "Can we talk again when you get back? As you can tell, I know next to nothing about things that happened to Alison during the fifteen years we were separated. If you could fill in some more of the gaps for me, I might be able to get a handle on what's happened to her."

"Nothing's happened to her. She'll show up as soon as she's worked through her problems. At least that used to be the way she operated." Fairfax stepped closer, grasping my arm. "Leave here, Rachel, today if possible. Believe me, it would be best for both you and the child if you went back to Washington and waited."

The words emerged taut, hard-edged, and the sudden harshness that contorted his face could have been either anger or fear. Whatever the emotion that gripped him, it died as quickly as it was born. Releasing his hold on me, he jammed his hands in his pockets and hurried away.

The episode left a bitterness in my mouth, a combination of disappointment that Wallace Fairfax hadn't been more supportive of my cause, and resentment of what I regarded to be a cynical, unfair assessment of Alison. Given her hasty departure from D.C., I was hard-pressed to refute his charge that she had a penchant for running away, but she was far from the unbalanced flake he'd made her out to be. As a kid, I'd considered my friend's psychic abilities a gift, no more abnormal than a talent for music or a knack for numbers, and early on I'd learned to rely on the accuracy of her predictions. As an adult, though, I was forced at least to entertain the possibility that her eerie intuitions might now be slanting her perspective of reality.

In the grand scheme of things, I was worse off than I'd been before I'd talked to Fairfax; instead of answers, I'd only dredged up more questions. And as though that weren't discouraging enough, I was beginning to have hefty misgivings over the way I was handling the entire situation. If I'd had the mother wit God gave a cabbage, I would have filed a missing person's report and let the authorities handle the legwork. Instead, I had dragged Maggie and Sam over six hundred miles on what was looking more and more like a fool's errand. Thus far, we hadn't a shred of concrete evidence that Alison had actually come to Magnolia Grove.

As I trudged back toward my car, the majority of the entrepreneurs along Plantation Boulevard were in the process of closing shop for the day. Come hell or high water, the town's sidewalks were always rolled up tight by 5:30 p.m. The first couple of greetings that came my way startled me; it had slipped my mind that in M.G., it was de rigueur for strangers and homefolk alike to acknowledge one another's existence in passing. Oddly enough, the small amenity gave me a lift, and before long, I was "How doing" with the best of them. By the time I reached the grizzled merchant who was securing the awnings on the bicycle shop, I'd worked up enough panache to add, "Been hot enough for you today?" to my repertoire.

"Worse summer we've had in nigh twenty years. Bad for my business, too. Don't many folks wanna pedal around in weather like this," he responded with a gap-toothed grin. "You wouldn't be interested in a ten-speed, would you? I'll cut you a good deal."

A refusal was halfway to my lips when it occurred to me that I was very interested. I could give Samantha her coveted birthday bicycle. Although it wouldn't mean as much to her as one from Alison, learning to ride might divert her attention from her loneliness. "Do you have a pint-sized girl's model with training wheels?'' I queried. ''A purple one?''

His expression registered incredulity. ''Matter of fact, I got hold of one like that just last week. Come on in and I'll show it to you.''

As I stood at the counter waiting for the proprietor—T. W. Hawkins, the nameplate beside the cash register read—to fetch the bicycle from the storeroom, I stewed over the details of my parting conversation with Fairfax. Something about it was out of kilter, and the feeling that I was overlooking a crucial element was as persistent as a swarm of August gnats.

''Will this do?'' Mr. Hawkins pushed in a tiny two-wheeler.

My mouth rounded into an O of bliss. The bike's gleaming finish was a regal amethyst, accented with thin lavender racing stripes along the fenders, and the bulb horn on the handlebar produced a merry, two-note toot. Add the stuffed-dinosaur-sized wicker basket in front, and voilà—Samantha's dream machine.

I pulled out a credit card and plopped it on the counter without a second's hesitation. ''Mr. Hawkins, that bike is so perfect it's almost a miracle. You have no idea how happy I am to find it.''

''Works out right for me, too. I thought I was going to have to take a loss on the little sucker.'' He began writing the receipt, stopping in the middle to add a companionable, ''We usually don't sell children's cycles—had to one-day special that one from Charleston—and the customer never picked it up. Some people are so inconsiderate.''

''Isn't it the truth,'' I agreed, wanting him to finish so I could be on my way.

''I didn't ask for a deposit because the lady was so dead set on getting it that I figured she was bound to come back. I guess her little girl's birthday wasn't the big deal that she made it out to be.''

An electric tingle traversed from the base of my spine to the nape of my neck. ''When did she come in?'' I asked carefully.

"Last Monday. Or it could've been Tuesday. No, must've been Monday, because I ate at the diner. My wife doesn't cook on Monday night because her sewing circle meets—"

"Please, Mr. Hawkins, could you describe the woman for me?" The timing fit perfectly with my newborn suspicion that Alison might have ordered the bicycle. My knees went so rubbery at the prospect of a solid clue that I leaned against the counter for support.

"Let's see now...." He scratched his head for what seemed like an eternity. "She was smaller than you, but her hair was about the color of yours. Can't say much about her face—she was wearing big shades."

"What about her voice?"

"Sounded 'bout like everybody else's down here." He pushed the slip and a pen across the Formica surface, his expression curious. "Think you might know her?"

"No," I said more sharply than I'd intended. Tempering the tone with a forced smile, I amended, "But I'd hate to deprive her daughter of such a special gift. If she comes back for the bike, would you please have her get in touch with me? Tell her I'm certain we'll be able to work something out if we can only get together."

If the woman in question were Alison, she would get the message immediately; if not, I was going to have a hell of a time trying to wiggle out of returning the bike. I was all out of business cards, so I scribbled my name and the phone number at the cottage on a scrap of paper.

"That's real nice of you. I was tellin' my wife just the other day that what this old world needs is more kind people." He tucked the paper in the register. "Hang on, I'll help you stow the cycle in your car."

"I can manage. Thanks for everything, Mr. Hawkins."

As I wheeled Samantha's present to the rear of my car, I couldn't believe my luck. The statistical probability of what had just happened was roughly the same as my winning a million-dollar lottery. The moves that led me to the bicycle—seeing Mr. Fairfax's ad in the brochure, having to park in this particular space, initiating a conversation with Mr. Hawkins—were an incredible string of coincidences, I mused.

The thought toggled an internal switch, and a fragment of trivia from my college days flashed into my brain. Some German poet had written that there was no such thing as chance. "What to us seems merest accident springs from the deepest source of destiny," I finished the quotation aloud.

According to that philosophy, whoever had drawn the blueprint for my life had penciled in a super-abundance of obstacles. The latest was opening the trunk of the car. When I inserted the key in the lock, it refused to turn and no amount of jiggling could remove it.

"Stupid car," I muttered, slamming my fist against it.

"I've had lots of experience with stupid cars. Let me give it a try," a resonant voice spoke up from behind.

"I'd appreciate it." Surprise sliced off my gratitude when I turned to discover that the offer had been made by Jericho Quaid. My former wariness returned full blast. "What are you doing here?"

"My office is across the street." He gestured in the direction of a green-shuttered Victorian house, then glanced at the bike. "That's sporty. I'm sure Samantha will love it."

"If I ever get it home." I twisted the key impatiently and this time it moved. The lid of the trunk swung upward easily.

He had already lifted the bicycle, so I reluctantly stepped aside to let him stow it in the car. My "Thanks" was as tight as his "Don't mention it" was casual.

Pleasantries out of the way, I proceeded to the more important item on my agenda. Even at the risk of appearing nutty, I had to clear up my suspicions. "I saw your car behind me on Camellia Drive. Were you following me?"

"Yep."

I was startled by the unhesitating admission, but I pressed on. "And by any chance, did you happen to be on a hill beside number eight, Pelican Cay Circle, this afternoon?"

"Uh-huh."

"Were you called to the bedside of a sick sea gull, or is lurking your hobby?" I snapped.

His gaze didn't waver. "I wasn't lurking, I was trying to work up enough nerve to come knock on your door. I wanted to talk to you about what happened at the shopping center.''

I could feel a rush of blood gathering in my cheeks. Candor was an infrequent ploy in the man-woman situations I'd been party to, and his use of the tactic had me thoroughly off balance. ''I've already apologized for tackling you. Unless you're planning to file charges, that's the end of it, Dr. Quaid.''

''Jericho,'' he corrected me, reaching to tuck a flyaway strand of my hair behind my ear. His blunt fingers were as light as the brush of a butterfly's wing. ''Do you believe in serendipity?''

''Happy accidents have never been my long suit. I subscribe to the fairy godmother school of thought.'' The absurd rejoinder came out before I could censor it.

''Guardian angels have always been my thing. Would you care to compare philosophies over a cup of coffee?''

The invitation barely got through. I was lost somewhere in the uncharted clarity of his eyes. ''Coffee?'' I parroted vaguely.

''The brown stuff with caffeine. I always keep a pot plugged in over at the office. If that doesn't tempt you, I've also got a pitcher of lemonade in the icebox.'' He smiled, the expression ingenuous, boyish. ''That's the yellow stuff with pulp and seeds floating around in it.''

The laughter his gentle teasing provoked felt clean and fresh in my throat.

''S'cuse me, Miz McKinnon, I forgot to get your address on the sales slip,'' Hawkins interrupted. ''And I can't fully make it out from the credit card receipt.'' He skidded a knowing glance between me and Jericho as he walked up to hand me his copy of the sales receipt. ''I wouldn't trouble you, but the missus keeps the books, and she's mighty picky about details.''

''No problem. Do you want my D.C. address or the one here in Magnolia Grove?''

''Jot down both, if you don't mind.''

I complied and returned the paper.

''I swan, you sound like you've got Southern roots. I wouldn't have known you were from Washington if you hadn't said so," he observed, turning to amble back to his store with a cheery, "Good luck to you, now."

I stared at Hawkins's retreating back. I realized that Fairfax had told me to go back to Washington, yet I had never once mentioned where I lived. The only way he could have known was for Alison to have told him.

"Rachel?" Jericho touched my shoulder diffidently. His brow was furrowed with puzzlement and concern. "Is something wrong? You look pale."

"I'm fine."

I shrugged off his hand, but he followed me around to the driver's side of the car. I slid under the wheel and closed the door, but before I could start the motor, he leaned down to the window. "If you don't like lemonade, I could squeeze you some orange juice."

"I've got to go now."

"Will you at least give me a rain check? We really need to talk."

"I don't share that opinion, Dr. Quaid, and I'd appreciate it very much if you'd stop following me." I packed all the ice I could muster into the rejection. My first responsibility was to Alison and Samantha, and I would not, could not, let anything or anybody interfere with that.

"I won't bother you again, but I'm only a phone call away if you need me." He stepped back, and as I turned on the ignition, I thought I heard him add a soft, "Watch for the moon, Rachel."

Chapter Four

Why had Wallace Fairfax stonewalled me? The only reason I could think of was that Alison had sworn him to secrecy. Even at that, it didn't make sense that her interdiction would have applied to me. She had to realize I'd be concerned, and although she might not want me to know where she was, she would have at least given him permission to tell me she was okay. Unless, of course, she wasn't. The more I thought about it, the less his insistence that I leave Magnolia Grove seemed like prosaic advice. Had he been trying to warn me? And if so, against what?

Since I hadn't been able to catch him before he left for Savannah, the questions continued to dog me through the weekend, and as though they weren't troublesome enough, I had to contend with the other big item on my worry list: what to do about Jericho Quaid.

A cold shower and a dose of common sense were my standard prescriptions for curing errant physical attractions—there was no space in my life plan for transient itches—but the affinity I'd experienced with Jericho was totally resistant to therapy. Through the wee hours of the coming Saturday morning, I examined it inside-out, upside-down and hindparts-before, and when sleep finally zonked me at dawn, I still hadn't a clue to what the mystical gestalt between us was, or how to get over it.

It was close to ten when an exaggerated and patently phony sneeze cut through the haze that encased me. I opened bleary eyes to find Samantha beside my bed. "How long have you been standing there?'' I mumbled, squeezing my lids shut against the glare coming through the window.

Small fingers gently pried my eyes open again. ''A gazillion hours. I'm not s'posed to wake you up, so I'm being very quiet.'' She bounced from foot to foot. ''Since you're not sleepy anymore, you can come out and play with me and Arvy.''

For reasons known only to the internal workings of the seven-year-old mind, she had named her new bicycle Aardvark Bumpity—Arvy for short—and from the moment I hauled the shiny machine from the trunk of the car, she'd set about learning to ride with all the determination of a pro training for the Tour de France. Maggie and I had been pressed into service to lead her through laps around the patio until darkness forced us inside.

''Be with you in a minute,'' I sighed, dragging myself from the bed.

A brisk shower and the smell of fresh-brewed coffee dissipated most of the fog in my head, and by the time I'd thrown on shorts and a T-shirt, I felt reasonably human again.

As I wandered into the kitchen, Maggie greeted me with a cheery, ''Did you know that Pelican Cay has a bicycle trail? The brochure says it runs from here to Springfield Square, and there's a playground at the other end.''

Sam was fairly dancing with excitement. ''Riding around the back porch is baby stuff. I need to practice on a real street. Can we go, Cricket?''

''Okay. I'll have my coffee while Maggie's getting dressed,'' I agreed, homing in on the percolator.

''My knees are feeling arthritic this morning, and I wouldn't want to slow you down,'' my elderly friend objected, limping to a seat at the counter.

As far as I knew, her legs were in better shape than mine. I also didn't miss the tips of her best Naturalizers peeping from under the hem of her long housecoat. That, plus the dash of lipstick she was wearing, told me she was up to something. ''Maybe you should go back to bed,'' I said innocently.

"I never was one to pamper myself. While you're out, I'll do a little grocery shopping, maybe look around for an A.M.E. Baptist church so I can go to service tomorrow. You don't mind if I take the car, do you?"

I suppressed a groan. Besides being blessed with a heavy foot, her favorite pastime was collecting parking tickets. "Help yourself—just don't get arrested."

"C'mon, Cricket, let's go," Samantha insisted, tugging at my arm. "You can have your coffee when we get back."

"Slave driver." I leaned down to plant a kiss atop her curls, then dashed to retrieve my camera bag. Though I'd just enrolled in "Parent 101," I knew that a beginner's bike ride was transcendent in the hierarchy of childhood firsts; Alison might miss the actual event, but thanks to my trusty Nikon, she would have a photographic record of every single second.

The bike trail, a flat, shell-paved path meandering through a stand of pine that bordered the resort, was unexpectedly crowded, given that the mercury was already heading through the upper eighties. To keep Samantha from disrupting the flow of traffic, I jogged alongside her bike, one hand on the handlebar, the other on the back of the seat. At the pace we had to go, it took half an hour for what should have been a fifteen-minute trip.

When we finally reached the Square, an eight-block quadrangle that fronted Plantation Boulevard, Samantha's patience was on a short leash. "I want to ride by myself, and bicycles aren't s'posed to have four tires. Can't you take off the two little ones on the back, Cricket?"

"Not just yet. They're there to keep you from tipping over while you're learning to balance by yourself."

She dismounted, and crossing her arms over her chest, scowled her displeasure. "Arvy and me don't like 'em."

The combination of heat and frustration beaded my forehead with perspiration; the last thing I needed was a confrontation with a cranky child, so I knelt to inspect the bike. Blessedly, Arvy's manufacturer had left me room to negotiate. After raising the adjustable training wheels to the intermediate level, I stood up with a firm, "That's the best I can do without a screwdriver."

Sam accepted the compromise with a sunny smile and climbed aboard again. The south side of the park had been cordoned off for an open-air festival, so I wheeled her to an isolated spot at the rear of the Square before I let her go.

Her solo progress was rocky, the course angling every which way but straight ahead, the cycle skidding first on one training wheel then the other. After a couple of yards the force of gravity overcame her determination and Arvy tipped over. I managed to catch Samantha before she hit the ground, but my lower body took a few licks in the process. Five attempts and as many failures later, I was praying that her enthusiasm would give out before my shins.

"This is hard," she said dismally, gritting her teeth as she prepared to remount for a sixth go at it.

"It takes work, but you'll get the hang of it." Afraid that her discouragement might change to defeat, I offered a graceful out. "My mouth is so dry I'm practically spitting dust. Let's walk across the way to get some sodas before the next go-round. We might even be able to buy a helium balloon to tie on Arvy's basket."

She considered the offer solemnly. "A purple one?"

"What else?"

The festival—the Annual Celebration of the Low Country's Heritage and Arts, the banners announced—was presided over by a gaggle of costumed junior leaguers: there was enough crinoline floating around to outfit the cast of G.W.T.W.-Part II. At the base of Jubel T. Springfield's statue, a string quartet played a montage of minuets. Bunting-draped booths set up beside the walkways held lavish displays of antebellum memorabilia. With nothing so mundane as a cold-drink vendor in evidence, Sam and I had to make do with plastic goblets of Ogletharpe Nectar, a minty, citrus spritz that my godchild pronounced, "Not near as good as Kool-Aid."

The uniform of the day for adult patrons was apparently casual chic, and I attracted more than my share of frosty stares from crowds milling around the booths. It was as if the label Poor White Trash—a phrase I heard frequently during the bad old days—had been stenciled across the front of my baggy T-shirt. The difference between past and present, though, was that their rejection had lost its power to harm; I wouldn't have traded places with one of those supercilious snobs for all the gold in Fort Knox.

Still, I saw no value in subjecting Samantha to overt rejection; murmuring a promise to hunt for her balloon elsewhere, I turned to push Arvy toward Plantation. In the process, I blocked a narrow path, and a petite, silver-haired woman stopped to wait patiently.

Her bearing made her appear regal, taller than her scant five-foot height, and the creamy silk jumpsuit she was wearing whispered "Paris original."

The name Amelia Springfield came to my mind without much urging. She was the only one of the Magnolia Grove elite I thought of with anything close to attachment. She had always been extremely kind to my mother; over the years, the two had kept up an intermittent correspondence, and she had phoned several times during Mama's final illness.

Acting on pure impulse, I stepped forward and extended my hand. "You probably don't remember me, Mrs. Springfield, but I wanted to say how nice it is to see you again. I'm—"

"Rachel Bodine—or I should say, Mrs. McKinnon," she supplied without missing a beat. Rather than shaking my hand, she clasped me in a brief embrace, then moved back to study me with a pleased smile. "Just look at you—all grown up and lovely as a South Carolina morning. I heard that you're staying out at Pelican Cay, and I was hoping we'd run into each other."

My faith in the grapevine had apparently been justified. I absently wondered what else the uncontested empress of Magnolia Grove might know about me. Her next words saved me the trouble of speculating.

"I understand you're here on an assignment for *Southern Style* magazine. We're all so delighted to count a professional photojournalist as one of our own," she said warmly. "And to tell you the truth, you couldn't have come at a better time. Our regular photographer—you remember Wallace Fairfax, don't you?—is out of town, and he apparently forgot his promise to send an assistant to cover the event. If you take shots of the festival, the historical com-

mittee will double the fee that would've been paid to Fairfax.''

The request had the undertones of a command. ''The
black-and-white film I'm using now won't do your gala
justice, Mrs. Springfield, and unfortunately, it's all I
brought with me,'' I said firmly, not about to get shang-
haied into the job.

Her face momentarily tightened. She handled the refusal
with a brief ''I understand,'' then moved her attention to
Samantha. ''Are you enjoying the celebration, little one?''

''It'd be a lot better if there was a hot dog man,'' was
Sam's considered opinion.

''I'll pass that along to the planning committee,'' Mrs.
Springfield promised with a throaty chuckle. A good deal
of the imperiousness faded from her expression. ''Aren't
you just precious?''

''Uh-uh. I'm Samantha, but you can call me Sam if you
want to.'' She pulled her stuffed toy from the bicycle basket
and presented it for inspection. ''This is BeeCee.''

Though the socialite's blue eyes twinkled, her expression
didn't betray her amusement. ''Pleased to make your ac-
quaintance, sir,'' she said gravely, shaking a tattered paw.
''When my son was a little boy he had quite a collection of
dinosaurs, but none of them was as handsome as yours,
Sam.''

The mention of the Springfield scion resurrected a hoard
of butterflies that had hibernated in my innards for seventeen years. He had been the secret passion of every pubes-
cent female within a fifty-mile radius of Magnolia Grove, a
golden teenaged hero with a perfect face and even better
body. And to ice the cake, he was a genuinely nice guy. The
recollection pushed me to ask, ''What's Michael up to these
days?''

I was ill-prepared for the pain the trivial question elicited
and the sudden mist that glazed her eyes.

''He was killed in an automobile accident quite some time
ago,'' she responded softly.

It was one of those horrible moments when everything I
could think of to say was wrong. I dropped my gaze to the
sidewalk, and if I could've found a large-enough crack, I

would have oozed into it. To my surprise and relief, Samantha came to the rescue.

"You don't need to be sad. Mommy says heaven's a really neat place," she said, reaching to pat the woman's hand. "That's where my daddy lives and guess what? I bet he plays baseball with your little boy and reads him stories every night before he goes to sleep."

"I'm sure you're right, sweetheart, and thank you for telling me that. You've made me feel better than I have in a very long time." There was a catch in Amelia's voice, and for an instant, she appeared to be struggling with her emotions. But when she turned back to me, she was composed and smiling. Fortunately, she didn't mention my supposedly dead husband. "You're obviously a wonderful mother, Rachel, but then, I'd expect as much of a Bodine. Would you and Samantha come to the house for tea this coming Tuesday? I'd like to show her Michael's collection."

There were possibly hundreds of people in Magnolia Grove who would have exchanged their firstborn and all hope of redemption for a chance to visit Springfield Manor. I, on the other hand, would've paid big bucks to avoid it. Getting entangled in M.G.'s social structure wasn't my idea of a good time. It might also prove dangerous.

Before I could think of a diplomatic way to decline the invitation, Samantha accepted it. "I like chocolate milk better than tea, and can Maggie come, too? She's our best friend in the whole world."

"I wouldn't dream of having the party without her," was the gracious response. Amelia turned back to me, her expression apologetic. "I realize my attempt to press you into service today was presumptuous, Rachel. This affair must seem ostentatious and inconsequential to you, but it will benefit Mothers Against Drunk Driving, for obvious reasons, a cause that's very dear to my heart. I'd be more than grateful for any assistance you could provide."

There was very little for me to say besides, "I'll bring a set of proofs on Tuesday."

"I was sure I could count on you. Would you like for me to entertain Samantha while you're photographing?" she asked.

I steeled myself against the wistful appeal in her eyes. "Thanks, but we work as a team."

"I understand completely. If she were my daughter, I'd find it very hard to let her out of my sight." Mrs. Springfield pressed my fingers briefly. "You can leave the bicycle with Skinner, my driver, if you like. He's waiting by a tan Rolls on the west side of the square."

What Amelia wants, Amelia gets, I mused as she moved away through the crowd. Retrieving my camera from the bag slung over my shoulder, I grinned at Sam. "C'mon, partner, let's park Arvy so we can do our job."

Though the little girl wasn't exactly thrilled with the arrangement, she relinquished her bike at the chauffeur's promise to polish the frame while we were gone. For the next half hour, we worked an amazingly cooperative crowd of gentry. If any of them still considered us out of place, it no longer showed on their faces. At nearly every booth, the hoop-skirted belle in charge plied Samantha with some small treat. Amelia had obviously passed a good word on us.

I was almost enjoying the shoot until I zoomed my lens into a close-up of an exhibit at the periphery of the action. The redhead I'd seen at Seagate shopping center—now a Scarlett O'Hara wannabe wearing at least fifty yards of lime-green organdy—was standing beside a display of antique crystal, batting her lashes a mile a minute at Jericho Quaid. When I tightened my focus on the doctor, he seemed inordinately attentive to Miss Scarlett's décolletage.

Speared by an irrational irritation, I captured the moment then slapped on my lens cap. "That's a wrap, Sam. Time for us to hit the road again." I herded her away from the festival before she could catch a glimpse of the physician.

True to his promise, the Springfield's chauffeur had shined Arvy to a high luster. Refusing the tip I offered, he slid behind the steering wheel of the Rolls and promptly dropped off to sleep. I was hoping for a hasty retreat back along the bike trail, but Samantha was already climbing in the saddle again.

"Okay, a couple more tries and we pack it in for the day," I said firmly as I pushed her to the center of a grassy, deserted area at the rear of the park.

She only needed one. This time when I let go of the seat, Arvy rolled straight and true on two wheels.

"I'm doing it!" Sam squealed.

"Way to go, short stuff. Try to guide it around in a circle while I get some pictures."

To my delight, she was able to follow the instruction. I slung the strap of the camera around my neck, and, setting the auto advance, panned to catch the action.

Samantha was really getting into the ride. As her confidence grew, the choppy churning of her small legs gradually smoothed to a controlled rhythm that propelled the bicycle at an increasing rate of speed.

I was transfixed by the images I was getting: the little girl's bottom lip nipped in by concentration, her eyes brimming with wonder. There wasn't a doubt in my mind that the sequence would be the best I'd ever shot.

If I hadn't been so absorbed with documenting Sam's accomplishment, I might have noticed that the radius of her loops was increasing. As it was, she had widened the distance between us to some fifteen yards before I began to get uneasy.

"Slow down," I called.

Trotting toward her, I increased the zoom ratio on my lens, filling the viewfinder with her face. She turned her head abruptly stopping the motion at three-quarters profile. As she stared past me, her mouth dropped open in a startled O, her skin now so pale that the freckles on the bridge of her nose were as prominent as cinnamon sprinkled on whipped cream.

Reflex made me swing the camera around to follow the line of her frightened gaze. The scene in the frame was the street that bounded the west side of the Square. It was deserted, except for a blue-and-white luxury sedan headed up from Plantation. The ominous implications of what I saw hit instantaneously and, without my bidding, my finger tripped the automatic shutter release. The camera only gave me three shots before the film reached the end of the roll.

Moving at a good clip, the vehicle made a left at the next intersection and was quickly blocked from view by the high hedge that surrounded a house on the corner.

In real time, the sequence took fifteen seconds tops, but that was far too long for my attention to be diverted from my charge. When I pivoted, she was pedaling away as fast as her little legs would allow.

"Samantha—no!" I yelled, taking off at a dead run as she rolled onto the street and turned north. I was petrified when I realized her obvious intent: she was going after the blue car.

There was neither vehicular nor pedestrian traffic along the stretch, but just as I reached the curb the sound of heavy footfalls came from behind. Jericho Quaid pulled even with me, his long strides easily outpacing mine. Without breaking stride, he tossed me the bag I'd left in the park as he passed. The gap between him and Sam decreased at an awesome rate, but when he was an arm's length away from the bike, its front wheel hit an irregularity in the pavement.

The next few seconds came to me in a jerky stop-action series, each still more brilliant and terrible than the one before. The rear of the bicycle raised above ground level at a forty-five degree angle; the child suspended over the handlebars, arms outstretched as though she were flying, and the taut desperation of Jericho's final lunge.

Although he absorbed some of the impact of Sam's fall, she bounced off his chest, forward momentum skidding her across the pavement and into a collision with the curb. When I got to her, she was as crumpled and motionless as a broken doll.

"Don't move her," the physician commanded.

He shoved me aside and knelt beside Samantha, his fingers gently probing her scalp. At his touch, the tightly shut eyelids popped open and she let out a lusty wail. It was the most beautiful sound I'd heard in my entire life.

Screaming bloody murder, Samantha ignored Jericho's, "Lie still, honeybunch," and scrambled up to plaster her arms around his neck. He rose to a standing position, cradling her as though she were an infant.

When I saw the angry abrasions on her legs and the blood streaming down her arm, the earth under me seemed to buckle. "We've got to get her to a hospital," I gasped, blinking to dispel the bright spots dancing in front of my eyes.

"She's probably more frightened than anything else. My office isn't far from here, so we'll take her there, unless you'd prefer to have another physician examine her." His voice was tight, a shade next to hostile.

Sam's sobbing immediately rose another decibel.

"She'll be more comfortable with you," I assured him.

He'd already started to stride off before the words left my mouth. Hurriedly stuffing the dinosaur and my bag into the bicycle basket, I trailed him along an alleyway for a couple of blocks to the rear entrance of the Victorian that housed his practice.

On the way through the kitchen and into the examining room, Jericho kept up a steady stream of silly jokes and animal imitations. By the time he had stripped off Samantha's ripped, dirt-streaked playsuit and started cleansing the debris from her injuries, her sobs were interspersed with wobbly giggles. To my intense relief, most of the wounds were superficial. The one exception was a deep gash on her shoulder.

"I could use a little help here, Mrs. McKinnon. Do you think you're up to it?" He dropped a red-soaked wad of gauze into a metal tray and reached for what I assumed to be suturing equipment.

I swallowed the sudden sourness in my mouth, willing my knees to stop knocking together. "Shouldn't I be sterile or something?"

"I'd be the last to recommend that." Jericho glanced across the examining table at me, the barest hint of mischief in his eyes. It was gone as quickly as it came, and his tone resumed a brisk professionalism. "Just hold her still and try to stay out of my way."

When he approached Samantha with the needle, she clutched my fingers and squeezed her lids tightly shut. "It's gonna hurt, but I won't cry."

"Crying's good for you," he said companionably. "I do it all the time."

She peeped at him from under her lashes. "You do?"

"Sure enough. It keeps my eyeballs nice and clean." He lightly touched the tip of her nose, and without looking at me, added, "Even your brave, strong mommy cries once in a while, doesn't she?"

"Uh-huh. Like the night before we took the bus ride. She thought I was sleep, and put her face in the pillow, but I heard her, anyway," Samantha confided. "I think she's sad because she misses my daddy."

I sucked in a deep breath to block the anguish radiating through my chest: the thought of Alison suffering her secret sorrows alone was as difficult to bear as seeing her daughter lying injured in the street.

Jericho lifted his gaze again; it now held compassion and what appeared to be disappointment. "Sorry. I didn't mean to pry."

He had obviously assumed that Sam was referring to me, and it hit me that he must believe I was grieving over my divorce. Though I was sorely tempted to set the record straight, I limited myself to a terse nod.

He quickly returned to the task at hand, putting stitches in Samantha's arm with such gentle expertise that he only elicited a few "Ouch's." Surgery completed, he retrieved a gaily printed smock from the stand beside the table and slipped it over her head.

"I'm fresh out of Ninja Turtle gowns, so Mickey Mouse will have to do until your mommy gets you home," he apologized as he lifted her into his arms. "Now comes the good part. You get to meet my friend and faithful feline companion, Citronella. I named her that because she chases bugs."

Feeling excluded from the camaraderie between them, I followed as he carried her into an airy, sun-filled room stocked with toys and enough books on the floor-to-ceiling shelves to open a children's library. When he deposited Sam on a cushioned window seat, the room's other occupant, a rotund calico cat, mewed approval and promptly settled her head on the child's lap.

Sam's expression was sheer bliss. "She's fatter than Garfield!"

"That's because she's been eating for five. While you two are getting acquainted, your mother and I are going to have a chat," Jericho informed her.

As he ushered me to a chair across the room, the smile on his face segued into detachment. "This won't take long, and when we're finished, I'll give you a lift home."

"I'd appreciate that if it wouldn't inconvenience you," I said, matching his impersonal tone.

Without responding, he settled himself on the near corner of the desk and picked up a pen and clipboard. "As far as I can tell, Samantha didn't sustain any head injuries, but I want you to watch her closely for the next twenty-four hours. If she seems unusually sleepy or lethargic, you're to call me immediately," he directed, scribbling a mile a minute. "I assume she received all the necessary vaccinations during infancy. Has she had a DPT booster series?"

"Pardon?"

"Diptheria, pertussis and tetanus," he interpreted, frowning. "I don't need an exact date. Just get me into the right ballpark."

"It was probably before she was enrolled in kindergarten." I hazarded a guess, hazy on the protocol for such events.

"That sounds about right. Most school districts require certification of inoculation." He made a notation, then threw me another curve. "Is she allergic to any type of antibiotic?"

The palms of my hands were beginning to sweat. "Not that I know of. Why do you ask?"

He stopped writing to study me intently. The look may have been simply curious, but I read it as suspicious. "I don't anticipate a problem with infection, but if there is one, I wouldn't want to prescribe the wrong medication. If you'll give me the name of your pediatrician in D.C., I can phone for a consult."

"I don't know—I mean, she's of Czechoslovakian descent, and I'll have to look in my address book for the exact spelling. Besides, she's on vacation right now." I was left dangling at the end of the stupid string of lies, wishing desperately that I could confide in him. Dropping my gaze to my lap, I continued in a muffled tone, "I'm trying my damnedest to take proper care of Samantha, Dr. Quaid, but I guess I'm not doing a very good job of it. When I think that my negligence might have cost..." I stopped to steal a glance at Sam, now happily engrossed with the cat, and for the life of me, I couldn't finish the sentence.

The tautness slowly ebbed from Jericho's face.

"If people could watch their kids every single second, fairy godmothers and guardian angels would have to go out of business." He leaned forward to capture my hand, massaging it gently between his own. "I suspect this accident did more damage to you than it did to Sam. She's fine, honestly, and if it will make you feel better, I'll stay for a while after I take you home. 'Course, you'll have to feed me, but I'm not picky—bologna and crackers are what I'm used to."

I smiled in spite of myself, and suddenly I felt two tons lighter. "Maggie will probably go out and bag a fatted calf." I would have elaborated on the menu if the phone hadn't chosen that moment to interrupt.

Jericho disengaged his fingers from mine and picked up the receiver before the second ring. His side of the rapid-fire conversation sounded ominous in tone, and as he hung up, a deepening furrow bisected his brow. "One of my patients at the Goose Creek clinic isn't doing well. I need to get over there as quickly as possible, so we'd better head out now," he said, reaching for a medical bag that was placed beside the desk.

"You go on. Maggie can pick us up. Is there anything special I should do when we leave?"

"The security keypad on the nurse's desk in the waiting room controls access to the office. The front door opens when you press the red button, and it automatically locks behind you. I'm not sure when I'll be back, but I'll phone you to see how things are going," he promised, detouring to plant a kiss on Samantha's forehead. His farewell to me, an abstracted, "If it's not too much trouble, would you throw some dry cat food into Citronella's bowl before you go?" came just as he reached the exit.

"Can we take her home with us, D.J.? She'll be lonesome if we leave her here by herself," Sam begged.

He consented with a smile and a hurried, "Fine with me if your mother doesn't object."

After the door closed behind him, my feeling of abandonment increased by leaps and bounds, and it didn't lift my spirits any when Maggie failed to answer the phone. I left a message on the machine at the villa, then, forlorn and a touch overwhelmed, wandered over to deal with Samantha's recent sally into independence. "You know it was wrong for you to go out into the street, don't you?" I scolded gently.

"Uh-huh. Are you gonna punish me?"

"No, but I think it will be better if you ride Arvy on the patio from now on. And if you see that car again, I want you to stay as far away from it as possible."

"Okay," she said, after some time. Her face brightened. "When D.J. comes back, I'll tell him all about it so he can beat the bad man up and make him say where Mommy is."

"You'll do no such thing, young lady. You aren't supposed to tell Dr. Quaid or anyone else why we're here."

She studied my face for a long moment, then moistened the tip of her finger with her tongue and solemnly crossed her heart. "Okay, but maybe he could help us."

"He's very busy, and it wouldn't be fair to ask him." I sat down and slipped my arm around her, finishing with a firm, "You'll have to trust me enough to let me handle this my own way. I promise I'll find your mommy."

"How?"

Since I hadn't anticipated the question, fielding it was awkward. "Well, the first thing I have to do is develop the pictures I took of the Horsey car. You can help if you'd like," I said, launching into a diversionary lecture on the joys of processing film.

By the time I got to the procedure for mixing the stop bath, Sam's eyes were glazed with boredom. "That sounds like fun, but you'd better do it by yourself. I wouldn't want to make you mess up," she interrupted politely, scrambling away to join the cat at the sill. After a moment of studying the view beyond the window, she commanded, "Look,

Citronella, that lady who's coming up the front walk is Maggie.''

The animal yawned disinterest, and leaping from the window seat, left the room for parts unknown.

Barely a minute had elapsed since I'd phoned, so it stood to reason that Maggie, dressed to the nines in her navy linen, had no idea we were waiting for her. I met her at the front door. "What are you doing here?''

"I was in the neighborhood, so I dropped by to see if Dr. Quaid could prescribe something for these creaky old knees of mine. What's your excuse?'' she countered, grinning sheepishly. She looked past me to Sam and the humor drained from her face. "Lord-a-mercy! What happened to my baby?''

"I'll fill you in later, and when we get home, we're going to have a nice, long chat about your arthritis,'' I informed her, gently shooing Sam outside. "You two go ahead to the car. I've got to get the bicycle.''

"We have to take Citronella,'' the little girl prompted.

Right on cue, the cat streaked through the waiting room. I managed to capture her a second before she reached the door. "I think it would be better if she stayed here. I'll make sure she has plenty of food and water,'' I assured Sam, closing the door before she could mount a stiff objection.

If the animal's indignant yowls were any indication, she was none too pleased at having her escape thwarted. When I set her on the floor, she stalked along behind me all the way to the kitchen, protesting mightily while I located the kibble, not an easy task since it was stashed behind a towering stack of books on the table. One volume, a weighty tome on esoteric body parts, lay open to a lurid illustration of some internal organ in the final stages of a multisyllabic disease.

"Your housemate takes his profession much too seriously if he reads that stuff while he's eating,'' I confided with a shudder, kneeling to pour a generous portion of tuna-flavored crunchies in a bowl beside the refrigerator.

The pregnant Citronella ignored the cat food, launching herself upward and into my arms. I rubbed the fur on the side of her bulging abdomen, the quickening inside strange and wonderful to my fingers; in that instant, there was a kinship between us, an attachment that was purely female. When I attempted to put her down, she engaged her claw tips in the fabric of my shirt.

"You've really got your heart set on going home with me and Sam, haven't you?"

She stretched to scour the point of my chin with her tongue, then, settling heavily against my chest, turned on her purr motor. The move melted my resistance in nothing flat.

"Okay, you talked me into it. We'd better leave the big guy a note to confirm the arrangement."

Shifting her furry bulk to my left arm, I rose to my feet and pulled a yellow pad from beneath the medical reference book. The writing on the upper third of the top sheet was in the cramped, unintelligible shorthand usually scrawled on a prescription. After a blank space, a phone number and the name Meredith Fisher were block-printed in red; my mind's eye supplied the missing title, Senior Photography Coordinator, *Southern Style* magazine.

I stared at the pad for a long moment before the shock of the discovery was replaced by an escalating anger. Obviously, Jericho Quaid had been checking up on me.

Chapter Five

The equipment in my portalab kit, supplemented with miscellaneous items filched from the kitchen, was more than adequate for basic darkroom procedures, and for a person who had once processed a week-long shoot's worth of Ektachrome in the closet of a Mexican motel, jury-rigging a light-proof work space in the downstairs powder room of the villa was a mere bagatelle. Sans an enlarger, my prints would all come out roughly twice the area of a postage stamp, but I couldn't worry about size at this stage of the game. If push shoved too hard, I would simply present Amelia Springfield with negatives and a page of proofs on Tuesday. Since I had no intention of charging her for the job, she would have small reason to complain.

As I developed the four rolls of film I'd taken that morning, worry that I might somehow screw up the only tangible evidence of the Horsey car's existence changed work I usually enjoyed into tedious drudgery. I found myself clocking each procedure to the split second, compulsively nit-picky about the proportions and temperatures of my chemicals. By the time contact sheets of the images I'd taken in the park had been transferred from a bath of fixer solution to the final water rinse, the muscles in my neck and shoulders were taut to the twanging point.

"It's nearly seven, Rachel, and you've been cooped up in there for over an hour. How's it coming?" Maggie's muffled query came through from the hall.

Toggling the switch on the wall, I squinted until my pupils adjusted from the amber glow of the battery-operated safelight to the fluorescent brightness of the overhead fixture. "I'll be done in five more minutes. Come keep me company while I finish washing the prints."

I halfway expected her to refuse the invitation. When we got back from town, she had busied herself with Samantha, partially, I suspected, to avoid the subject of her visit to Jericho's office. After a few seconds, the door inched open and she stuck her head through, the expression on her face carefully neutral.

"Is Sam still watching television?" I queried casually, tweezing the contact sheets from the basin and depositing them on a towel-padded tray.

"She was falling asleep in front of the set, so I put her to bed. I promised her I'd leave the cordless phone on her nightstand, in case her mother calls, but I can't find it. Did you bring it in here?"

"Yep. While I was waiting for the negatives to dry I tracked down Meredith Fisher. Quaid hasn't contacted her yet, but she said she'd corroborate my cover story. Plus, she's going to alert me the minute he or anyone else starts meddling in my business." The bulletin was laced with a healthy dose of rancor; the doctor's ostensible plan to invade my privacy had already added him to my hit list, and by breaking his promise to call, he'd moved himself perilously close to the number-one spot.

"I can't see much wrong with him being interested in your work," she said, quickly switching to, "I've got a pan of cocoa simmering on the stove. Soon as I take the phone to Samantha, I'll bring you a cup."

"I'll get it myself. There's no reason I can't dry the prints in the kitchen," I called after her retreating back.

I was putting together the things I'd need to finish the job when Citronella padded into the makeshift darkroom to rub against my ankles.

"I can't wait to get your nosy housemate's reaction to the note I left him," I said grumpily as she followed me into the kitchen.

While the marshmallows melted in my cocoa, I spread the contact sheets atop the table in the breakfast nook. Maggie came in to kibitz as I directed a gentle flow of cool air from the blow dryer over the glossy surfaces of the prints.

"It's hard to make out details in those little bitty pictures," she observed, adjusting the reading glasses perched on her nose. "Show me the page that has the frames you shot of the car. I want to see what the sneaky son of a misbegotten muskrat looks like."

I grinned at the creative epithet, and, abandoning the dryer in favor of a magnifying glass, scanned slowly along the inch-high rows of connected photographs on the sheet I had marked as those from the last roll. When I reached the series chronicling the wobbly solo bike ride, Maggie's fingers tightened on my arm.

"That isn't just Samantha, you know. You've captured the best of what it is to be a child," she said softly.

Though I appreciated the compliment, I was too caught up in a recall of the actual sequence to respond. Moving the glass slowly across close-ups of Sam, I shivered as frame by frame, the joy in her expression collapsed into dread.

Unfortunately, my touch had deserted me when I'd spun to take the last three photos. Not only were they out of focus, but since I'd been shooting into the sun, quite a bit of the detail had been obliterated by glare.

"Is there any way you can sharpen the contrast? If we could get a fix on the license plate, we'd be able to run a make on the owner through the department of motor vehicles."

"Overexposing some of the areas while I'm printing may bump up the detail. First thing Monday morning, I'll take the negatives to Icons Unlimited. Since I substituted for Wallace Fairfax's assistant on the festival shoot, the least he can do is let me use his enlarger."

Maggie rose from her seat beside me, moving over to the counter to fetch a fresh supply of miniature marshmallows. "When you talk with him, ask more questions about his wife."

"What good would they do?"

"Talking about her might relax his guard a little, and you never know when you might pick up something useful. My husband, rest his sweet soul, used to say that there was no such thing as throwaway information in an investigation. When Leon was on a case, he'd try his best to get into everybody's head—victims and witnesses as well as his suspects."

"I assume you wanted to interview Jericho Quaid because you think he fits into one of those categories." I interrupted what was sure to be a lengthy discourse on D.C. police procedures.

Her mouth opened and closed a couple of times before it took on an embarrassed set. "My guess is he's an innocent bystander. I'm not really sure why I went to his office this morning. It just seemed like the right thing to do at the time," she finally answered. "You may not have noticed, but Samantha has been a lot less troubled since he came on the scene. Early this morning I overheard her telling her dinosaur how much she wanted D.J. to come play with her."

"So you thought you'd pass along the invitation," I concluded, not bothering to hide my annoyance.

She regarded me levelly. "Where's the harm in that? It's obvious to me that he cares for the child and has her best interests at heart. And besides, it's equally clear that you two are attracted to each other. Why are you so hell-bent on brushing him off?"

Denying the charge would have been useless, and in addition to that, I wasn't in the habit of lying to her. "Self-preservation, I suppose. I hardly know the man, but the closer he gets, the harder it becomes for me to run away."

"Why even bother? I consider myself a pretty fair judge of men, and I'd say he's one of the good ones—sensitive, warm, responsible, dedicated—"

"Bingo. You just said the secret word. I'll lay you odds that medicine is now and always will be the number one priority in Jericho's life." Restlessness urged me from my chair, and sweeping the contact sheets into a stack, I continued, "I've had it up to the gizzard with dedicated men, Maggie. My father was totally devoted to his congregation—he was probably the closest thing to a saint that

Magnolia Grove will ever see—and my ex-husband was the most committed public defender in Tucson. But sterling characters notwithstanding, both of them were so fixated on their work that they had neither time nor energy left over for the people who loved them most. If I ever get involved again—and that's a very big if—it will be to a nine-to-fiver who worries more about our crabgrass than his career."

She poured the remains of her cocoa into the sink and rinsed out the cup, countering with a dry, "I suppose you're prepared to pack your cameras in mothballs and turn your darkroom into a sewing center. Or do you expect to leave Mr. Right at home scraping waxy yellow build-up off the kitchen linoleum while you go traipsing off to take your pictures?"

"I didn't say my plan was perfect," I grumbled, "but I'm the only one who can patch up the holes in it."

"Sorry. I won't interfere again."

If the rigidity of her posture was any indication, Maggie's temper was fast approaching critical mass, and I knew from experience that my best chance of averting a meltdown was to give her space and solitude while she sorted through her pique.

"You're dead on target about Wallace Fairfax. In fact, it might be useful for me to nose around town and see what I can find out about him. As soon as I check on Sam, I think I'll drive into town and see what I can dig up."

"Go on about your business. I'll take care of the baby." Maggie wheeled to march away. At the archway leading from the kitchen, she snapped a tight-lipped, "Unless you don't trust my judgment about that, either."

"I not only trust you, I depend on you, and..." Since my reassurance was playing to her retreating back, I swallowed the rest of the sentence. Although I had no intention of investigating Wallace Fairfax at the moment, I'd backed myself into a corner. Thinking that a little air might clear my head, I trekked glumly into the living room to retrieve my purse and keys. Just as I shut the front door behind me I thought I heard the phone ring, but I ignored it.

HEADING WEST on Camellia Drive, the vast majority of traffic was queued in the right lane, a patient phalanx of panel trucks, station wagons and pickups that inched its length onto the tradesman's road serving Plantation Harbor Country Club. Most of the occupants of the vehicles were liveried in maroon and buff, which told me that in an hour or so, they would be bowing, scraping and generally sucking up to the over-jeweled and under-mannered rich folk who belonged to the club.

"Thank God I got out of this town," I mumbled, pulling into the passing lane to leave the convoy behind. Had my mother and I stayed, I might very well have ended up in a maid's uniform, with fallen arches. The only other non-agricultural option was forty-eight hours a week of breathing cotton lint in Ogletharpe Textile Mill.

In the grip of a morbid urge to drive through the old neighborhood, I hung a left at the next intersection and headed cross town, aimlessly playing out what a life in Magnolia Grove might have held for me, which was not a lot. On my first day as a freshman at Jubel T. Springfield High, the guidance councillor had taken one look at the low C average I'd accumulated through middle school and promptly shunted me into a vocational track—homemaking and food services, no less. From there, the very best I could have hoped for was a tract house with a killer mortgage, a bunch of kids and, coincidentally, a husband with a name like Gomer. In the worse-case scenario, Gomer would have divided his time between the unemployment office and the Boll Weevil Bar and Grill while the crumb-crushers and I made do in the trailer camp.

But on the flip side of the coin, if I hadn't moved to Tucson, Alison wouldn't have had to go through the pain of adolescence alone, we wouldn't have missed fifteen years of friendship, and at this very minute, my Gomer and all of his shotgun-toting relatives would be standing squarely between her and the driver of the blue car.

The thought created a heaviness the size of Cleveland in my chest, and if it hadn't been for an ominous flashing from the oil gauge on the dashboard, I might have given in to the sudden pressure of tears behind my eyelids. As it was, I nipped my lower lip between my teeth and pulled into the first service station I spotted.

"No biggie, she's running a quart low," a mechanic diagnosed after a cursory inspection of the dipstick. "Normally I'd recommend top grade, but since this here's only a rental buggy, putting in regular would save you a little change."

His folksy familiarity threw me for a second. Was I supposed to know him?

"Thanks for the tip." My glance flicked to the Z.Z.Z. embroidered on the pocket of his coveralls, and "Zebulon Zack Zwisler" slid out of my memory bank, followed closely by a nickname he'd been tagged with in school. "Sleepy! It's terrific to see you again. How's your family?"

His long face reflected pleasure. "Real good, knock on wood. My sister Zena and me sent the old folks to the Poconos for their golden anniversary. Pop came back strutting like a rooster, and Mom hasn't stopped blushing yet." Running his fingers through the scant remains of what once had been a shock of carroty curls, he confided, "Cousin Selena told my wife she'd heard from Lula Vickers that you were back home, and the whole clan's been teasing me ever since."

"About what?"

Sleepy popped a nozzle into the top of an oilcan and drained the sluggish liquid into the crank case, his grin expanding. "The major crush I had on you in seventh grade."

I chuckled at the unexpected confession. "Is that why you slipped a dead jellyfish in my lunch bag?"

"It got your attention, didn't it? The main reason I joined the Shutterbugs was so I could hang around you. Remember the time you accidentally dumped fixer acid all over my brand-new sneaks?"

I didn't, but I nodded anyway. "Beanbag Shoffner claimed you had a thing for Alison Compton. Did the two of you ever get together when you were teenagers?" I improvised, my intent to pave the way for an indirect interrogation.

"Not hardly. You know the kids from True Faith Academy didn't mix with us Springfield rednecks. Besides, Burdett kept her tethered on a short leash. I don't think she ever went out with anybody," he said, pitching the now empty oilcan into a trash barrel beside the gas pump. "I haven't seen Alison in years. Wonder whatever became of her?"

"I wish I knew." At his curious glance, I made my tone casual. "Are you still taking pictures?"

"I lost interest in cameras when you left town, and anyway, Shutterbugs went downhill after Mr. Fairfax left Jubel T. to be headmaster at Palmetto." He slammed the hood of the car shut, his eyes suddenly solemn. "If you get a chance, you might want to drop in on ole Wally before you leave. You were always one of his favorites, and seeing you might give him a boost. He's had a tough row to hoe since his wife was attacked."

I stared at him, slack-jawed. "Attacked?"

"Some thug in Charleston beat her up and left her for dead in an alley. She stayed in a coma for nearly six months, and when she finally came to she wasn't right in the head. The way I hear it, she's pretty much a vegetable now."

The muscles of my stomach knotted against a rising queasiness. I had assumed the problem was Alzheimer's, but a deliberate assault was even more ghastly. "How could anyone do such a horrible thing?"

"For the twenty-five thousand dollars she had just gotten from Charleston Equitable. The cops said the mugger probably hung around the savings and loan looking for victims. You want to hear the strange part? The Fairfaxes had been socking back money to buy a retirement place in Florida, but Marietta emptied the account without telling Wally she was going to do it. Nobody in town could figure out what she needed it for, but the word is—"

The rest of the speculation was lost in the tortured clatter from a minivan that lurched up to the far pump. Glad for the interruption, I clasped my arms over my chest, wishing Sleepy hadn't gotten into the story. The Fairfaxes had always been private people, and it troubled me no end that after nearly six years their personal tragedy was still grist for the M.G. gossip mill.

"Yo, Zwisler, this rebuilt engine you stuck me with ain't worth spit. Get your sorry butt over here and take a look at it." The driver of the RV stuck his head through the window of the cab to grumble.

Sleepy flipped a good-natured "Hold on, Otis," in the other man's direction, then walked around the car to open the door for me.

"How much do I owe you?" I asked, sliding behind the wheel to reach for the purse I'd left on the passenger's seat.

"Oil's on the house. Call it payback for the way I used to tease you. If I'd known then that you were going to grow up to be the best-looking female on the East Coast, that jellyfish would've been a chocolate Valentine." He tapped the side of the door in farewell, whistling as he sauntered off to tend to Otis.

The ingenuous compliment touched me in a way I wasn't prepared for. It softened the determined edges of the antipathy I'd nursed so long. As I pulled away from the station, it came to me that before puberty and Pickett Court, I had dearly loved Magnolia Grove.

My drive to the outskirts of town was eccentric, the streets I followed chosen haphazardly. Or so I thought. It wasn't until I hit Blackstock Road—a rutted, tarmac byway that copied the course of Poogan's Creek—that I realized my itinerary wasn't random. I was tracing routes Alison and I had taken when we were children.

It was a little past eight when I parked the car at the beginning of what had been the driveway to my home place, but the July dusk was bright with bands of crimson left over from sunset. The air was heavy, and so motionless that it magnified the distant push-pull sound of ocean waves into a muffled roar. As I picked my way along the weed-choked track, I was inundated by phantom sensations and disconnected flashes from other summer evenings—the sweet crunch of homemade peppermint-stick ice cream, the tickle of a firefly's wings against my cupped palm, the rhythmic creak of the metal glider on the front porch.

All that was left of the home where I'd spent my first ten years was a pile of rubble. It had been taken out, I supposed, by one of the vicious tropical storms that periodi-

cally raked the Carolina coast. But Mama's camellia, an
obstinate bunch of twigs that in spite of her constant coax-
ing never gave her more than a couple of scrawny buds, had
grown to a six-foot glory of pink blossoms and luxuriant
foliage. Though my vision blurred momentarily, the anguish that usually accompanied recollections of my mother
was displaced by a strange serenity. She knew, I was certain, that all of her tender loving care had finally paid off. I
broke off one of the flowers and stuck it into my hair, smiling as I turned away from the bush.

Go look for the playhouse.

The words were so clear in my mind it seemed I'd spoken
them out loud, and without a second thought, I circled the
debris, heading into the stand of pine that backed my home
place. It had been a long while since I'd had to deal with
rural isolation, and the skittery rustlings coming from the
underbrush should have made me twitchy. Instead, I found
myself savoring the solitude and the springy cushion of
needles under the soles of my tennis shoes.

The live oak in which Caleb Soames, Mount Tabor
Presbyterian's volunteer sexton, had built a secret retreat for
me and Alison was some fifty yards due north of the manse.
As I stood staring up through the moss-draped branches at
the playhouse, the man's blunt features and ready smile
formed a perfect hologram in my head.

It was Caleb, I remembered, who had taught me how to
choose the sweetest, ripest blackberries from among the
brambles, baited my fishing hooks and surprised me with a
necklace of polished acorns. In a whole lot of ways, he had
been closer to me than my own father. At the very least, he'd
always been available when I needed someone to talk to. *As
soon as I have a moment to spare, I'll try to find him,* I
promised myself.

The ladder Caleb had nailed to the trunk of the tree was
still in place, and a bit of cautious testing proved that the
rungs closest to the ground were sturdy enough to hold my
weight. I was three-quarters of the way up when one of the
wooden crosspieces splintered under the pressure of my
fingers and common sense finally caught up with me.

"Have you lost your mind, McKinnon?" I croaked, plastering myself against the rough bark of the tree. I peered nervously at the ground, which now seemed an alarmingly far distance below.

The same internal voice that had launched me into this fool's errand insisted that I was much too close to my goal to retreat now, to say nothing of the fact that I could just as easily lose my footing going down as up. Neither argument was totally persuasive, but I gritted my teeth and resumed the climb. The handrail that encircled the plank foundation above was wobbly to the touch, so I avoided it, hanging on to an over-arching branch of the tree while I hoisted myself onto the platform. Heart beating harder from apprehension than exertion, I edged across the porch to the lean-to, giving the front a couple of healthy kicks to announce my arrival to any assorted fuzzies who might have set up housekeeping. With no untoward squawks, flutters or slithers forthcoming, I gingerly pushed open the weathered door. The floor of the playhouse was a five-by-seven foot rectangle, the slanted ceiling barely high enough for me to stand upright. The large, paneless window set in the western wall admitted light enough to see by, and as I picked out details in the lilliputian space, the years stripped away as easily as layers from an onion.

Some of Alison's treasures—seashells, a chipped Barbie mug, a panty-hose egg decorated with glue and glitter—were aligned on the shelf that ran the short length of the room. My only contribution, a wax replica of the Statue of Liberty, had been the centerpiece of a cherished ritual. Whenever something particularly good happened, we would celebrate by lighting the torch while we shared a Snickers bar.

The throat lozenge tin propped beside the candle still contained our cache of kitchen matches, and to my surprise, one of them ignited when I struck it against the rough face of the wall. "It sure hasn't been a Lady Liberty day, Alison, but maybe this will change my luck," I said and sighed aloud, holding the flame to the wick. It caught immediately, and the flicker quickly expanded to a steady glow. Although the worry I carried didn't lighten one scintilla, I began to feel a lot less lonely.

I also got a better look at my surroundings. The screening Caleb had stretched over the window had long since rotted away, and although the place should have been filled with debris blown in by the wind, there wasn't so much as a dead leaf on the floor. The anomaly raised the short hairs at the nape of my neck. Absent a broom-wielding leprechaun, the only conclusion I could come to was that someone else had been in the treehouse recently. And if that someone had been Alison, there might very well be a trace of her still here.

"Please, let me find it," I whispered, moving the light slowly along the length of the shelf. As far as I could tell, there were no new additions to the treasure trove. I slumped heavily against the wall, disappointment turning the taste in my mouth bitter. Since the room was empty of furnishings, there was nowhere else to search.

Except for the hidey-hollow.

My head jerked back as though I'd been slapped. How could I possibly have forgotten the niche concealed beneath the flooring? It had been our most secret of places, a repository so sacrosanct we'd only used it once. The day I left for Tucson, we had plaited snippets of our hair together and interred them as a forever pledge of friendship.

One stride took me the length of the playhouse, and I dropped to my knees, trembling as I set down the candle. A drop of melted wax splattered on my wrist, but I scarcely felt the sting.

"Second row of planks from the window wall, third from the side." I repeated the secret combination, ripping loose the designated floorboard.

Instead of the braid of hair, I found half of a Snickers bar. Beneath the candy was a page that had been ripped from the Magnolia Grove telephone book. The listing underlined in red at the beginning of the third column was for D. Jericho Quaid, M.D.

I stopped breathing. The jumble in my head was frenzied and disoriented. There was no sensation except cold in the rest of my body. Tucking the candy and the remnant of paper in my shirt pocket, I picked up the candle.

Outside the sky had deepened to a rich, clear lapis, and a full moon, entangled in a webbing of cirrus clouds, lent an eerie shimmer to the windless night. Given the wobbly condition of my knees, it would have been stupid to try to negotiate the ladder. I plopped down near the edge of the platform, and setting the wax statue beside me, stared into the wavering flame while I tried to make sense of what I'd found. But without a rule book, there was no way for me to tell who was "it" or which base was home in this game. Running in the wrong direction could very well be disastrous.

"Rachel?" The low-pitched voice that drifted up to me was strained, ragged.

I dropped my gaze. Oddly enough, I was neither surprised nor apprehensive when I saw the man standing in the clearing below. Bracing myself against the tree, I closed my eyes and followed my instinct. "Come on up, Jericho. It's time we had that talk."

The thirty seconds it took him to climb the ladder seemed more like thirty minutes, primarily because when he was on the second or third rung, a connection abruptly clicked in my head. The candy and the listing Alison had left in the hidey-hollow were neither meant to warn me away from Quaid nor to prompt me to ask for his help. They were simply her way of celebrating a marvelous discovery with me. She had finally located her brother.

As he hauled himself up to sit beside me I studied him obliquely, finding confirmation for my hunch in the line of his jaw and the outward angle of his ears.

"When I called the villa to see how Sam was doing, Maggie told me you'd gone for a drive. I circled around town until I spotted you leaving the gas station," he explained, surreptitiously checking out the surroundings. "I blinked my headlights, but you didn't seem to notice."

"There was a lot of stuff going on in my head." Since no easy way to approach the subject came to mind, I went for the straight hit. "Your first name is Daniel, isn't it?"

"Yes, but I hardly ever use it." He brushed the subject away with an impatient wave of his hand. "Our conversations have an annoying habit of ending before I put in my two cents' worth, so I'd appreciate it if you'd let me kick this one off."

The unyielding set of his jaw indicated that an objection would neither be welcome nor tolerated. "Be my guest."

He removed his baseball cap and raked his fingers through his hair, obviously uncomfortable. "Since you wrote the note about Citronella under Meredith Fisher's phone number, you obviously realize I intended to call her. But I'd like you to know my interest in you isn't personal."

"That's a relief," I said dryly.

He ignored the comment. "Do you know what an intra-ventricular septal defect is?"

"No, but I'm sure you're about to tell me."

"It's a congenital problem. A baby is sometimes born with a hole in the wall that separates its right and left ventricles, and when the heart contracts, venous and arterial blood is intermixed," he explained obligingly. "Judging from the faint scarring on Samantha's chest, I'd say surgery to correct the condition was performed when she was between one and three years old."

It was a good two minutes before I could force an "Oh, my God," through my numb lips. "Give me the bottom line in plain English. Is she okay now?"

"She's one of the healthiest kids I've seen. If you're concerned, I can run some tests, but I'll need her real mother's permission." The gauntlet was laid down gently, but with no room for compromise. "Rachel, I'm willing to bet my soul that Sam is my niece."

"You'd win." My gaze locked with his. "Just out of curiosity, when did you first suspect?"

"The minute I laid eyes on her. Even with her hair dyed, she's the spitting image of my little sister at that age. And I knew for sure when she told me to watch for the moon. I made up that story the day Alison and I were separated. It was the only thing that would make her stop crying."

The distress on Jericho's face was deeply hurtful to me. Without conscious thought, I reached to touch his cheek.

He caught my fingers and held them tightly. "I know how much you love Sam, and even if I could prove she's related to me, I wouldn't try to claim her. I just need to know where Alison is and that she's all right."

"So do I." I disengaged my hand from his and, dropping it helplessly into my lap, began the story of the past two weeks. It was halting, disjointed at first, but as I talked, a growing relief pushed the words out in a torrent. I gave him chapter and verse, the pitifully few facts I knew fleshed out with my assumptions, suspicions and all the fears that had taken root in the secret recesses of my soul. The only information I censored was Wallace Fairfax's assessment of Alison's instability. Since I gave it no credence, I saw no point in passing it along. When I was finished, the planes of his face were so hard they might well have been carved from granite.

"If she knows I'm here, why hasn't she tried to call me?"

"A lot has happened since the two of you were separated. Maybe she's not quite sure how you'll react. Or maybe—"

When I stopped short of the obvious—that Alison might not be in a position to contact anyone—Jericho wordlessly pulled me to him. I relaxed against his chest, counting the measured pace of his heartbeat, perfectly content to be still. After a while, he tipped my face upward, his lips brushing my temple, my cheek, then the line of my chin.

"We'll find her," he whispered. The reassurance and then the soft stroking of his tongue were honey on my mouth. Taking his comfort, I gave back mine, both of us stronger, better, for the sharing. There was warmth, not heat, in the embrace, and the tightening of our arms around each other was less a demand for passion than a promise of safe haven. For the moment, that was more than enough.

"I can't wait to tell Sam she's got a new uncle," I murmured into the hollow of his neck.

Jericho straightened up, putting a tiny, but troublesome, distance between us.

"It might be less traumatic for her if we let Alison break the news." That didn't make much sense to me, but then, who was I to argue with a doctor? He rose to his feet, extending his hand to help me up. "I've got a sleeping bag in the car, and if you don't mind, I think I'll camp out in the playhouse just in case she shows up."

"She won't come back here again." I didn't know how I knew that, but it felt as certain to me as holy writ. "There are other places where we used to play, but it would be better if we waited until morning to search them."

"I'll pick you up tomorrow at first light and we'll go over every inch of the area," he promised.

The weary attitude of his body told me he'd absorbed all he could handle for now. "Good plan," I agreed, screening regret that I'd be going back to the villa alone from my voice. I stooped to pick up the guttering candle. "Before we go, though, there's one more thing we have to do. Give me your hat."

He complied and followed me into the playhouse, practically bending double to get into the cramped space. I knelt to pull up the floorboard again, and after depositing the cap and the blossom from Mama's camellia bush in the hidey-hollow, retrieved the Snickers bar I'd stuck in the pocket of my shirt.

"Skoal," I said, carefully breaking it into two equal parts and handing one to Jericho.

He examined it dubiously. "Do you always make toasts with linty chocolate bars?"

I polished off my portion in one bite. "Only on Lady Liberty days."

Chapter Six

Although my alarm clock was set for 5:00 a.m., I was up and bathed long before it rang. My initial wardrobe choice for the daybreak sortie was a lemon cotton pullover and matching walking shorts, but as I slipped the top over my freshly shampooed head, an overly vivid recollection of the tree-house kiss made me mistrust my motivation for the selection. I quickly decided that it was one thing to be swept away by the unexpected discovery of an ally, quite another to deliberately push the feeling past simple gratitude. While I wasn't about to shower away perfume that cost a bundle per squirt, I changed tops and scrubbed off most of the makeup I had applied. I skinned my hair back into a utilitarian ponytail before I went into the kitchen to wait for Jericho.

Maggie, who had beaten my time by at least half an hour, already had the microwave buzzing and the blender whirring. The force-feeding syndrome was a sure sign her matchmaker glands were in hyperactive phase—the more pots on the stove, the more severe the attack. Currently, every available burner was occupied.

"If Jericho and I eat breakfast, we'll lose time," I objected.

"There's not much point to getting an early start if you run out of steam five minutes later. Besides, most of what I'm preparing is for dinner. I'll bet that man can't remember the last time he had a home-cooked meal." She dumped a cup of flour into her mixing bowl then turned to regard my outfit sourly. "Your yellow sweater is a lot more becoming than that baggy sweatshirt."

"It's also sleeveless. The woods around Poogan's Creek are crawling with chiggers, ticks and other assorted nasties. I'd rather be bug-free than cute." I laid the subject to rest and, filching a rasher of bacon from the crispy mound beside the coffeemaker, tackled a more pressing one. "Maybe I should wake Sam before I leave. I don't want her to think I've abandoned her."

"Citronella and I will keep her busy until you two get back." Maggie tore a paper towel from the roll on the counter and polished her glasses, a troubled furrow bisecting her brow. "You know, I really believe it's a mistake not to tell her that she and Jericho are related."

"So do I, but that's his call," I said pointedly. As I peered through the window at the beginnings of a hazy Sunday sunrise, the sight of the multicolored jalopy pulling into the driveway raised my pulse level a few notches.

Maggie moved behind me to unfasten my barrette and fluff my hair around my shoulders. "You surely worked hard at looking plain this morning, girl. Those lips could do with a little rouging," she scolded, pinching color into my cheeks.

I retrieved a tube of lipstick from the canvas hip pouch belted around my waist and applied a haphazard dash of coral to my mouth. But when I opened the door to admit Jericho, the abstracted aloofness of his expression made me sorry I'd gone to the trouble.

A scent of soap and spicy-fresh cologne preceded him. Although his face was clean-shaven, lines were deeply etched around the corners of his eyes and mouth. He stopped just inside the doorway, his brief "Morning" to me at least ten degrees cooler than the greeting he sent my elderly friend.

"You look tired, son. Come have some coffee." Maggie fussed over him.

"Thanks, but I've already had more than my quota of caffeine for the morning." The boyish grin that softened the refusal faded as he turned to me. "I guess we ought to get going, Rachel."

"I want to look in on Sam before we leave. Would you like to come with me?"

He hesitated before he nodded, avoiding my gaze as he followed me along the hallway to Samantha's room. Citronella met us at the doorway, twining herself briefly around Jericho's legs, then padding back to leap on the bed. By the proprietary way she settled her furry bulk on the pillow, it was evident that she had switched allegiances.

As usual, the lamp by the bed was burning. My small charge was still apprehensive of the dark, but at least her dreams seemed less troubled now than they had been when she first came to me. She was sleeping soundly, her small body in an attitude of boneless, total relaxation, her mouth touched by the suggestion of a smile. Jericho moved over to the nightstand, and as he stared down at the framed portrait of Alison, his features were tight with a mixture of wonder and anguish. After a protracted moment, he shifted his attention to the little girl, bending to rearrange the coverlet she had kicked away.

Her eyelids fluttered open.

"Hello, sunshine," he murmured, brushing a kiss on her cheek.

"Did you come to take Citronella?" She groped around the pillow until she found the cat's tail. It was clear from her grip that she was not about to give up custody.

"Nope. She can stay with you for the rest of the time you're here, if Cricket says it's all right."

"We have to go out for a little while, pumpkin. When we get back, I'll take you swimming." I moved to her side.

"Okay." She yawned and closed her eyes, rolling over on her stomach with a fuzzy "See you later, Uncle D.J."

He shot me a startled, accusatory glance, then left the room.

I picked up the stuffed dinosaur that had fallen to the floor beside the bed, propping it next to the little girl with a sigh. The day was skidding downhill, and there didn't seem much I could do to stop it. On my way past the dresser, I snagged one of Samantha's hair ribbons and glumly restored my ponytail.

When I returned to the kitchen, Maggie pressed a Baggie filled with blueberry muffins into my hand. "The two of you will need a little snack to hold you until dinner," she insisted, shepherding us through the back door.

"Let's take my car," I suggested after a dubious glance at his car.

"Fine with me. I'll drive." As he slid behind the wheel, his jaw was fast solidifying into stony. "What's our itinerary?"

"Let's hit Mount Tabor Presbyterian first. While my father was pastor there, Alison and I spent a lot of time in the graveyard behind the church." I lowered the visor against the strengthening incandescence of sunup. "After that, we can work our way back to the treehouse. The parsonage was built on the far side of the property, but it's only a ten-minute walk through the woods."

"Shall I go the same route I did last night?"

"It'll be quicker if you take Cotton Mill Run. There used to be a bar and grill called The Boll Weevil two miles before the turnoff to the church," I directed. "There's probably not much left of Mount Tabor. The congregation disbanded nearly twenty years ago."

Without comment, he jammed the transmission into reverse and backed my car from the driveway. It wasn't until he negotiated the eastward onto Camellia Drive that he finally spoke again. "I shouldn't have kissed you last night, Rachel. I hope you didn't take it personally."

There were a number of things I'd expected him to say, but that wasn't one of them.

"Heaven forbid," I shot back, feeling annoyed.

"That didn't come out like I meant it. You're a beautiful woman, and you touch me very deeply." The admission had the dispassionate ring of a commercial endorsement, its romantic content further diluted by the addendum, "The attraction between us doesn't make sense, though, and even if it did, I'm not sure I would act on it at this point in my life."

"Thank you so much for clearing that up. As I recall, you weren't the only one doing the kissing, but I'm certainly not going to apologize for my half. At the time, it was how I felt and what I needed." I couldn't tell whether my indignation stemmed from disappointment or from having come to the exact same conclusions independently. "What we did was to seal a collaboration contract, no more, no less, no strings attached. And not to worry, I won't go Victorian on you—even though you were easy, I still respect you this morning."

The sound he emitted was somewhere between a snort and a chuckle. "You're pretty feisty for a preacher's daughter."

"People who're raised on fire and brimstone usually grow up to be hellraisers," I countered coolly. "While we're setting the ground rules for this alliance, you should know that I don't intend to interfere with your relationship with Samantha. Maggie and I didn't tell her you're her uncle."

Jericho glanced over to study my face for a few seconds. Apparently the results of the inspection were satisfactory because his expression went from skeptical to confused. "Then who did?"

Ninety-nine percent of me argued that Sam had overheard some of the extended discussion Maggie and I had had the night before, but the remaining hundredth held out for a more esoteric explanation. I went with the minority opinion. "Nobody. My guess is that she just sensed that there's a special bond between you. I believe she inherited a lot more than looks from her mother."

A light switched on behind his eyes. He smiled at me for the first time that morning. "I'd forgotten all about the pinto beans."

"Excuse me?"

"A store in Sumpter—that's where we used to live—had a 'guess the number of beans' contest. First prize was a transistor radio, which I wanted more than salvation, so I invested two weeks' allowance in dried pintos and a gallon jar," he recalled, chuckling. "Alison was just learning to write numbers, and she kept bugging me to let her practice while I was counting. I gave her one of my entry blanks just to shut her up, and she scribbled 1,568 on it."

"And you won the radio."

"I would have if I'd turned in the entry blank," he said wryly. "I take it she's zapped you with her premonitions, too."

An instant replay of the prediction in the churchyard raised a major flush to my face. "Yes, but she surely missed the mark on one of them."

"What did she tell you?"

"That my husband and I would live happily ever after." Not about to tell him that the two of us were supposed to marry, I engaged in some selective reporting. "Do you have any of the family talent?"

"Sort of, but it's nothing very dramatic. When Alison was born, I got this weird feeling inside, almost as though a cardiac monitor had been switched on. The linkage between us isn't strong enough for me to know where she is or what's happening to her, but I've always been able to sense her life force."

My breath caught in my throat. "Do you still feel it?"

"Stronger than ever."

That was the most comforting thing I'd heard yet. "If you don't mind my asking, what happened to your parents?"

"Mom died when Alison was three, and a couple of years later, Pop was killed in an accident at the sawmill where he worked. Alison was adopted almost immediately, and I went through a couple of foster homes before I decided I'd do better on my own. I didn't get back to Sumpter until after I pulled my doctor act together, but I couldn't locate her because the records were sealed," he reported in a flat monotone. "I found out from one of our old neighbors that she'd been adopted by a couple who lived somewhere on the South Carolina coast, and I've been searching the area for her ever since."

"If you didn't know exactly where she was, how did you come to settle here?"

"It's the midpoint of the eastern shore, and there was a practice for sale in town at the time," he explained with a shrug. "I feel better knowing she found you when she first came here. Did you keep in touch after you left Magnolia Grove?"

"I wrote to her, but she told me later that the Compton intercepted my letters. She was already living in D.C. whe I moved there. We both like Oriental art, and we just hap pened to run into each other at the Freer Gallery."

Jericho smiled. "Serendipity strikes again."

"Either that or her ESP." Retrieving one of Maggie' muffins from the bag on my lap, I presented him with half "This isn't quite as good as a Snickers, but it'll have to do Here's to your internal heart monitor."

He slowed the car, and freeing his hand from the steering wheel, cupped it around mine. "And to the Quaids's bes friend."

THE BOLL WEEVIL still marked the beginning of Cotton Mill Run, but that was the only thing that made the once familiar route recognizable to me. Every tree, bush and blade of grass on the left side of the road had been bull dozed away, leaving behind a raw stretch of red earth; the growth to the right was much denser, taller than I remem bered. The scene had the aspect of a man who'd shaved off half his mustache.

"What on earth are they doing to this place?" squawked, outraged by the insult to what had been a bu colic sanctuary for deer and migratory birds.

"There's no more room for expansion at the present site of the textile mill, so Ogletharpe is relocating here. The project is on hold because he wasn't able to buy the Poo gan's Creek tract," Jericho explained.

"Thank God for small favors. Who owns it now?"

He shrugged. "The paper trail stops at a holding com pany, and even Ogletharpe's lawyers can't trace the princi ples."

"What big money wants, big money eventually gets," I griped, rapidly losing interest in the whole affair. Good Lord willing, I would be out of this backwater pit stop in very short order, and I'd never have to see, hear of or think about Magnolia Grove, South Carolina, for the rest of my natu ral life.

"We've gone two miles past the Weevil. Where's the turnoff to the church?" he asked, slowing the Nissan to a crawl.

I leaned forward to peer through the window, finally spotting a break in the compacted timberland on my side of the car. "There it is—I think."

The unruly growth between the dual ruts of the trail choked off access by car; we parked on the shoulder of the road and began to muscle our way along the path that wound into Mount Tabor Grove. It was tough going at first: a snarl of brambles clawed my clothes and lashed spiky tendrils across my face with no warning or mercy. Although the sun was now well above the horizon, a thick cover of leaves and Spanish moss draped from overhanging branches turned the track into a murky tunnel.

"I'll go first," Jericho insisted.

I moved aside with a relieved "Be my guest." This was hardly the time to assert my feminist leanings.

Fifty yards in, the underbrush diminished to passable and Jericho held back the last of the tangle for me. The clearing into which I stepped was carpeted with a riot of knotgrass, milkweed and thistle; in its center, the church of my childhood, vacant-eyed and weathered to a nameless shade of gray, still lifted its steeple into the serenity of Sunday morning.

"This is a very special place for you, isn't it, Rachel?" His gentle question was more a statement of fact.

I nodded. "My great grandfather was one of Mount Tabor's first elders, and Papa took over the pulpit when I was three or four," I responded, warmed by an unanticipated rush of homecoming. "While I'm here, I guess I should check out my piece of the real estate."

Surprise peaked Jericho's brows. "You own land here?"

"Not legally, but I've at least got squatters' rights." I took his arm, explaining as we trekked around the side of the dilapidated structure toward the cemetery, "It was a Bodine tradition that babies were assigned spaces in the family plot on christening day. When I came along, all the choice spots were taken, and they squeezed me in between Aunt Esther and her second cousin twice removed. I never intend to exercise my option, though. Those two old biddies detested each other, and I can't see spending the rest of eternity refereeing their squabbles.''

''Why waste a perfectly good parking space? Just take along a box of Snickers and declare a truce.''

He treated the tip of my nose to a playful tweak, then reached to undo a bramble that had caught in my hair. The twig came loose and so did the ribbon that tied my ponytail; my thick mane flopped in an undisciplined mass around my shoulders.

His indrawn breath was quick, barely audible, and need darkened his eyes to smoky. He traced the line of my cheek, his fingers whisper-light as they wandered to the nape of my neck and lost themselves in the weight of my hair. The touch set off an involuntary tremor in my legs.

I captured his hand and returned it to his side. ''That isn't in the contract,'' I objected, my voice gone husky on me.

The hunger in his gaze was replaced by amusement. ''Granted, but there's no prohibition against compliments. You're one lovely lady, Rachel Bodine McKinnon—inside and out.''

I was both pleased and embarrassed. ''You're not bad yourself. Now that that's settled, you can meet the clan.''

The chaos in the front section of the cemetery—there were smashed headstones and litter was scattered helter-skelter among encroaching clumps of vegetation—made me dread what I might see when we reached my family's resting place. To my amazement, what we discovered was a circle cordoned off with white-washed bricks. Weed-free Bodine graves fanned out from the willow that had been planted over a century before; though the markers were tilted from the settling of the earth, a lot of them were still standing.

My only living kin on the Bodine side migrated to Chicago in the mid sixties, and given the estrangement that precipitated the move, it was highly unlikely that they had assumed responsibility for upkeep of the family plot. Amending my mental ''to do'' list to include finding and thanking the anonymous caretaker, I took a deep breath and started around the perimeter of the circle.

"There's Aunt Naomi and her twin sister, Ruth, Cousin Solomon and Uncle Moses," I said, ticking them off as we walked.

"Sounds like an Old Testament roll call. If I remember my scripture correctly, the name Rachel comes from Genesis."

"Chapter twenty-nine, verse six. Auntie Esther wanted to stick me with Hephzibah, but cooler heads prevailed. I'm a repeat—the first Rachel Bodine was my grandmother."

"Where is she buried?"

"In the VIP section on the north side of the tree. Granny was an invalid during her last year, and Alison and I nearly nursed the poor woman to distraction. We thought we were entertaining her, but I suspect it was the other way around. After she died, we'd bring Kool-Aid and paper cups to the grave and pretend we were having a tea party with her. It was one of Alison's favorite games."

"Tell me about it. The last Christmas we were together, she got china for her dollhouse, and all afternoon she followed me around with two of those little bitty cups filled with some god-awful brew she'd concocted. I got so desperate that I hid the dishes and told her the Grinch stole them. I don't think she believed me, though," he admitted, his smile not quite masking the pain in his eyes.

"Probably not. She could always spot a lie a mile away."

"That's one reason I stopped telling them. Next time I pass a toy store, I'm going to buy my sister a replacement tea set just to set the record straight." He slipped a companionable arm around my shoulder, pointing to a double headstone diametrically opposite from where we were standing. "Who were the lovers?"

The monument in question, two intersecting hearts carved from polished salmon marble, was a startling contrast to the weathered slabs and simple crosses that marked the other graves.

"I've never seen it before. Maybe some other family is using the plot now. That could be the reason it's so well kept," I speculated, moving across to investigate.

A large spray of faded plastic carnations obscured the engraving on the memorial. Pushing the flowers aside, I read the epitaph. "Reverend Gideon Bodine and His Cherished Wife Sarah—In Their Love, Together Forever."

Dropping to my knees in front of the polished stone, I gulped in air to ease a fierce ache in my chest.

"Your parents?" Jericho asked softly.

I bobbed my head up and down, then shook it from side to side, swallowing convulsively before I could untangle the contradiction. "That's who they were, but my mother's grave is in Tucson and my father's ashes are buried with her. She always intended to have a stone put up here for him but—"

A loud, metallic click from behind us interrupted the remainder of the explanation.

"Y'all have exactly ten seconds to clear out of here. After that, you're risking a backside full of buckshot."

My head swiveled in the direction of the gravelly warning. The erstwhile sexton of Mount Tabor church peered nearsightedly at us from the other end of a twenty-gauge shotgun.

"Brother Caleb," I breathed incredulously, scrambling to my feet.

The elderly man lowered his weapon and scanned me from head to toe, his scowl slowly changing to delight. "You can't be my little Cricket."

"Not so little anymore, but still making a lot of noise," I said, hurrying to meet him. "I can't tell you how happy I am to see you again."

"That makes two of us who're pleased. Bless God for bringing you home, child," he said, clasping the hand I extended.

His grip was like steel. My mental calculation put Caleb Soames's age at past seventy. Time had robbed him of some of his bulk and most of his hair, but the quiet dignity I remembered still graced his mahogany face. There wasn't a doubt in my mind that it was he who had cared for my family's burial ground.

"The memorial is lovely, Brother Caleb. Mama and Papa would be so proud to know you've honored them."

"I wish I could've given them more than a chunk of stone," was his gruff response. "Mrs. Springfield placed a nice tribute in the *Gazette* when your mother passed, and it grieved me to read it. Sarah and Gideon were two of the finest people who ever walked this earth. I thought it only fitting that the love they had for each other be acknowledged."

If there were words eloquent enough to express my gratitude, I couldn't find them. The gentle pressure of the old man's hand on my shoulder told me he understood the message in my silence.

Turning his attention to Jericho, Caleb flashed a sheepish grin. "Sorry for the double-barrel greeting, Doc. Last week a bunch of teenagers ran a car in here and messed up this place something terrible. I spent my whole day off putting it back in order. So now, whenever I can get away from work long enough to make the trip out here, I come patrolling."

"Did you report the damage to the police?" Jericho asked.

"No point to it. You know as well as I do that Sheriff Tillman would lose his job if he so much as looked cross-eyed at those prep school brats."

"How do you know the vandals go to Palmetto?" I continued the interrogation, disturbed by the idea of the myopic old man standing sentry. Armed or not, he was no match for a bunch of wild kids.

"I found a class ring on the north side of the willow. It wasn't there a couple of weeks ago when I trimmed the grass around Granny Rachel's plot, so it's a cinch one of the young'uns dropped it," Caleb reported.

The location of the find set my newly developed detective's antenna quivering. "Are you sure it wasn't a True Faith Academy ring, Brother Caleb?"

"Positive. Why do you ask?"

I trusted Caleb Soames now as I had in my childhood. He was as much responsible for who I'd grown to be as my own father, and it never for a moment occurred to me to lie to him.

"I thought perhaps Alison Compton might have left it as a clue for me. Jericho is her brother, and we have reason to believe she's here in Magnolia Grove," I explained, following up with an abbreviated version of the search that omitted its more sinister aspects. I didn't see much point in alarming the oldster unnecessarily.

"As I remember, Alison stayed with the Fairfax's some years back. After she finished whatever business she was tending here, she may have gone on to Florence to visit Marietta," Caleb said.

"Florence?" I repeated, stiffening. "Wallace told me his wife was in Savannah."

"I heard tell she was in the Willow View rest home in Florence while she was in her coma, but I could be mistaken or Wally might've moved her. Most of the doings in Magnolia Grove pass right on by me. Mr. Albert's been poorly for some time now, so I've stayed pretty close to the house." A rueful grimace twisted his mouth as he added, "Speaking of which, it's time I got on back. He raises Cain if his breakfast is late."

"You're still with Mr. Albert Hamilton?" I was barely able to screen disappointment from the question. While I wasn't surprised that Caleb would continue to work past retirement, it didn't seem fair that he was stuck in the same job. I'd once heard it said that his reclusive, wheelchair-bound employer had more money in his vault than God and less kindness in his heart than the devil.

"The old geezer keeps me company, and taking care of him gives me something useful to do while I'm waiting for the Grim Reaper. That's more than most people my age can lay claim to."

The opportunity to repay Maggie's matchmaking machinations in kind was too good to resist. "If you haven't made plans for your next day off, why don't you come for supper?" I invited, supplying him with the Pelican Cay address. "I'd like for you to meet Alison's daughter, Samantha, and my friend, Margaret Peace."

Caleb smiled his pleasure. "I can make it this coming Wednesday if that suits you." With a wink and a teasing "Even dollars I'll see you there, too, Doc," he shouldered his shotgun and walked away whistling.

"I'd sure hate for the man to lose his money," Jericho said, pulling his features into a wistful droop.

"You're about as subtle as a steamroller. Consider yourself invited, sawbones."

Shelving my amusement, I turned toward my grandmother's plot. After a good ten minutes of searching the area on my hands and knees I had to admit defeat. "This is a waste of time. Either Alison hasn't been here or Caleb cleaned away anything she might have left."

"So, what's our next move?"

"Short of sifting through every dead leaf and gopher hole between here and the treehouse, I'm fresh out of ideas," I sighed. "Let's go back to the villa and have a real breakfast. I always think better on a full stomach."

He tousled my hair playfully, grinning his approval. "You're a woman after my own heart."

Not yet, but I'm giving it a lot of consideration. The errant thought popped into my mind. I promptly banished it back to its lurking place, but as Jericho and I headed back through the unkempt section of the graveyard, I put a little lateral distance between us. "I suppose we could check out the Florence nursing home, although I doubt anything would come of it. I can't see why Wallace would lie about his wife being in Savannah."

"Maybe he doesn't want you to visit her."

"That doesn't make sense. From what Zeb Zwisler said, Marietta couldn't tell me a thing."

"Still, I've got a feeling she's a piece of the puzzle, and before we can solve it, we have to find out where she fits. First thing tomorrow morning, we're going to have a serious discussion with her husband," he said grimly.

"I'll be at your office by 8:45, so we can catch him the minute he opens the studio."

As we rounded the corner of the church, I slowed to scan its crumbing facade. "I'd like to look inside."

"So would I. It reminds me of St. Matthews in Sumpter."

The area directly adjacent to the foundation was carpeted with the creeping green of kudzu. I tiptoed gingerly through the ankle-deep weeds to the open arch of the entrance and peered at the interior. A good many of the clapboards were missing and most of the pine flooring in the nave was gone; sunlight streamed in through a gaping hole in the roof.

"Better not go any further. There's bound to be a lot of termite damage, and the whole structure could collapse at the slightest vibration," Jericho cautioned.

Caught up in an unbearably sweet nostalgia, I scarcely heard the warning. My memory reglazed the circular window above the chancel with jewel-toned glass, brought back the shellacked pews and peopled them with fan-waving, throat-clearing parishioners.

From behind, Jericho circled my shoulders with his arms, resting his chin on the top of my head. "I'll bet you were a cute kid. You probably wore patent-leather Mary Janes and pink organdy to Sunday school."

"Corrective oxfords and a pleated jumper. And I was a gawky klutz with the knobbiest knees you'd ever want to see," I said, leaning back into the strength of him. "Frills were your sister's thing. Viola Compton didn't provide much in the way of affection, but she dressed Alison like a princess. She bought her a pinafore with forget-me-nots embroidered along the ruffles and a wide satin sash."

A soft sighing—the freshening of the wind through the rotting timbers or perhaps the complaint of a dove whose nesting we'd disturbed—distracted me from the description. The sound was anguished, hopeless, the last breath of a dying dream, and it intensified until there was no room left for warmth in the sanctuary. All at once, I felt Alison's presence, her despair, her fear... she had surely been in the spot where I now stood. And I knew deep in my soul it was here that the hunter had cornered his prey. Shivering uncontrollably, I lifted my gaze to the splintered rafters. A thunderhead scudded across the face of the sky beyond.

"What is it, Rachel?"

Nothing would come from my mouth.

"Talk to me," he insisted.

"The noise—I can't stand it." I wanted to block out the moaning, but I couldn't lift my hands to my ears.

"I don't hear anything," he said, turning me to face him.

Instead of Jericho, I saw a malevolent, hooded figure that came straight from my recurrent nightmare. The fingers that gripped my arms were cruel, terrifying in their power. With what I was sure was the last of my strength, I jerked away and stumbled through the doorway of the church.

The sky overhead was clear, the air sun-drenched and still. The tranquillity of the morning only served to fuel my panic. How could I have seen clouds when there were none? I started to run, drawing in rapid drafts of air that never seemed to reach my lungs. When Jericho caught up with me, I was near the center of the grove.

"Take it easy, Rachel. I'm here for you," he reassured.

I slowed to a walk then stopped, feeling drained, brittle and afraid that the slightest touch would shatter me into a million pieces.

He reached for me, then dropped his hand, as though sensing my fragility. "What happened?"

The gentleness in his eyes steadied me. "I have no idea," I finally answered.

Logic told me the evil I'd sensed had no more substance than my quicksilver glimpses of the past, and though the dread that held me captive gradually ebbed away, it left a residue of darkness and confusion in its wake. When I turned to stare at Mount Tabor Presbyterian, I could be certain of only one thing. The church of my childhood was lost to me forever.

Chapter Seven

The white-clad receptionist seated behind the desk, a perky brunette whose smile showed off an amazing collection of metal braces, surveyed me with open curiosity as I walked into Jericho's waiting room the next morning.

"You must be Ms. McKinnon. Dr. Quaid said you'd be in at 8:45. I'm Carrie Barstow," she said, rising to extend her left hand.

It didn't take a rocket scientist to tell that the main purpose of the southpaw greeting was to show off the Hope-sized cubic zirconia she was wearing.

"Nice to meet you. What a beautiful ring," I said to oblige.

"Isn't it? I think CZs are ever so much better than real stones. You get a lot more shine for your money. My fiancé and I saw this one while we were watching cable and—"

"The shopping channels have such wonderful bargains," I cut in hastily. "I wouldn't want to keep you from your work. May I see Dr. Quaid now?"

"He had to go out on an emergency, but he said to tell you he'll phone you at home." Eyes widening, she added a conspiratorial, "Sheriff Tillman called this morning. One of his deputies found a corpse over at the Camelot Court development."

My internal temperature dipped toward freezing. "Was it a woman?" I forced myself to ask.

"Must've been a man. I heard Dr. Quaid tell the sheriff not to move *him*. Magnolia Grove doesn't have an official coroner, you know, and Dr. Quaid is the only physician in town who'll do the job for free. Most of the others are fancy specialists. There haven't been that many suspicious deaths, maybe two or three since Dr. Quaid's been here, but I think the town council should pay him for his time, don't you?''

I didn't have an opinion one way or the other, but I nodded agreement. "Do you have any idea when he'll be back?''

The nurse shrugged. "There'll probably be lots of forms to fill out. My guess is he'll be gone for a couple of hours, so I've already rescheduled all of his morning appointments. You're welcome to wait if you like.''

"Thanks, but I'd better be on my way. When Dr. Quaid returns, please tell him I've gone to the meeting alone and that I'll get in touch with him later.''

"Will do,'' Carrie promised absently, tuning the small set on her desk to a shopping channel. She was already lost to the glittering world of diamonoids before I reached the door.

Some of the irritation that tightened my lips as I marched down the front steps was a holdover from Sunday. On our way home from the church, the CB radio in Jericho's heap summoned him back to his patient at the Goose Creek clinic. He'd barely had time to dump me at the villa and promise his niece another phone call—which never materialized—before he was off and running. The way things were shaping up, his contribution to the search for Alison would be at best minimal.

"So who needs him?'' I fumed, jerking my car door open to slide behind the wheel. The short answer was Rachel McKinnon, although it galled me to admit it.

My disposition wasn't sweetened any by the Closed Until Further Notice sign that was taped to the inside of Icons Unlimited's front window. I was willing to swear that it hadn't been there Sunday afternoon when Maggie, Sam and I had passed on our way to a nearby movie theater, so it stood to reason that Fairfax had put it up sometime after six. That meant he'd returned from Savannah.

Consulting the directory in the phone booth on the corner boosted my aggravation level another notch. Wallace's home phone number was busy when I called, and I wasn't familiar with the street in the listing. He had obviously moved since I was last in Magnolia Grove. Frustrated, but a long way from daunted, I snagged the first passerby, an adolescent who was dressed like an unmade bed.

"Can you tell me how to get to Avalon Terrace?" I queried after I managed to wrest his attention from the Walkman plugged into his ears.

He chewed the wad of gum in his mouth a full minute before he came out with a rapid-fire "Three lights down, hang a left, go straight until you get to the Six-twelve on Galahad, turn right and you can't miss it."

"Much obliged." I thanked his retreating back.

Intent on remembering the directions, I only gave the sideview mirror a cursory glance as I started to pull out of my parking space in front of the studio. I heard a screech of brakes and the blast of a horn behind me.

"Sorry about that." I stuck my head out to apologize.

The driver who pulled alongside me could easily have made the cover of *GQ*. He had a Clark Kent cowlick, piercing blue eyes, aquiline nose and a chin dented by the requisite off-center dimple. The perfect face was rescued from monotony by an overly generous mouth that, at the moment, was contorted with fury. "If you can't drive that piece of trash, you'd better keep it off the road," he snarled before he sped away.

My usual reaction to incivility was righteous indignation. As it was, my muscles stiffened with a creeping paralysis as I gaped at the rear of the blue-and-white car. The vanity plate on the back told me how Samantha had chosen a name for the vehicle: it read HORSE II. When I saw that the license had been issued by the State of South Carolina, the "fatal attraction" theory I'd constructed to explain why the man had been tailing Alison collapsed faster than a trailer in a tornado. She hadn't run to Magnolia Grove to avoid danger. She'd deliberately thrown herself into the teeth of it. Her own words supported the new supposition. When I'd asked on the phone what she hoped to find here, her response had been, "Freedom."

Although the prudent move would have been to have the plate traced through the department of motor vehicles, my current mind-set demanded instantaneous action. My initial immobility had given way to a severe case of the shakes, and I had to waste a precious minute whipping my nerves into shape to drive. By the time I was out of the space and on the trail, my quarry was three blocks away.

My guardian angel must have been on the job while I zigged and zagged my way through the morning traffic on Plantation to close the gap. My reflexes weren't in top form and my brain was in even worse condition, but determination not to lose him kept me going. I hadn't the vaguest notion what to do when and if I caught him.

The sum total of what I knew about stalking suspects came from watching made-for-TV detective movies, most of which involved the tailer keeping a discreet distance and a couple of other vehicles between himself and the tailee. The ploy worked fairly well until I got stuck behind a slow-moving panel truck. When I finally got the chance to move into the passing lane, the blue car was turning right at an intersection dead ahead. Following suit would have entailed cutting in front of the truck, a risk that neither I nor my budget compact were equipped to handle. The best I could do was keep going until I could make a U-turn, a feat that cost me fifteen minutes and a lot of teeth grinding.

When I got back to Foundation Avenue, my target destination, the car had long since disappeared. The street was flanked on either side by six-foot-high wrought-iron fences, behind which were gardens that rivaled any the White House had to offer. A quarter of a mile along, the stretch of concrete terminated in a circle with only one other exit, a broad driveway closed off to traffic by a pair of ornamental gates. Beyond them I could see a complex that looked to be constructed entirely of dark-tinted glass. The only clue to its purpose was a sign posted on the sentry box by the entrance that read Private Property—Access to CANTER by Pass Only. The obvious connection between the acronym and the license plate on the blue car prompted me to join the line of four cars waiting for admission through the gates.

Whatever the organization's function, getting in was a tough ticket. A uniformed man shooed two of the vehicles away in short order; a third was reluctantly admitted after its driver presented a sheaf of papers and put up a five-minute argument. The hiatus gave me chance to dredge up the information I had on the car. It wasn't much, but by the time the security guard demanded my pass, I had the faint glimmer of a plan.

"I don't have one, officer, but my name is Hilda May Jeffers and I've simply got to get in. It's a real emergency." I arranged my face into what I hoped was distressed sincerity. "I was trying to park on Plantation this morning—the space was a bit snug, but I thought I could make it—well, anyway, there was this blue-and-white car—"

"Could you get to the point?" the guard interrupted impatiently.

"Did a car like that come in here a little while ago?"

"Sure did. It's part of the executive fleet."

"I hit it," I blurted out, surprising myself with the quick lie. "At least, I think I did, because I heard this horrible scraping noise. I was going to leave a note on the windshield, but I had to go into the bookstore and borrow a pen. The car was pulling away when I came out, so I followed it. If you won't let me in to talk to the driver, could you at least give me his name and number so I can call?"

"It could be any one of a dozen people." Removing his mirrored aviator shades, he leaned down to favor me with a sympathetic glance, adding in a low tone, "My advice is to forget about it and let the consortium's insurance company foot the bill."

"My conscience wouldn't give me a minute's peace if I didn't at least look to see if I did any damage."

Either my pleading or the honking from the automobile behind convinced him. "You should talk to Mr. Green, the manager of the motor pool. He's in the front office of the third building on the left past the fountain. I'll call ahead to let him know you're coming." Hitting the switch that controlled the gates, he waved me in with a cordial, "Have a good one, Miz Jeffers. It's real nice to know there are still honest people in the world."

Although the compliment made me cringe, guilt was a small price to pay for access to Alison's pursuer. My triumph at breaching the CANTER security system vanished when I pulled into the lot beside the designated building. HORSE I, II, III and IV were parked in adjacent spaces.

The proliferation of identical automobiles was a decidedly nasty development, but cutting the right one from the herd need not prove a problem, I mused. Given Samantha's account of the encounter in Boston, the vehicle that slammed into Alison's car had to have sustained damage in front. Hoping against hope it hadn't been repaired since its return, I left my compact to surreptitiously examine the fleet. To my disgust, all four cars were showroom perfect.

"Scratch one easy solution," I grumbled, heading for my prearranged meeting with the motor pool dispatcher.

Mr. Green, a grim-visaged bear of a man with a penchant for foul-smelling cigars, kept his attention fixed on his computer screen as I walked up to his desk. "I'm listening, Ms. Jeffers, but I'm a busy man. Don't take all day with this."

The story I gave him was essentially the same as the version I'd used for the guard, except that I set back the time of my alleged fender bending.

"Why are you just now coming forward with this information?" He slanted a suspicious stare at me.

Sensing that my ethical act wouldn't play well on this stage, I hung my head. "Leaving the scene of an accident is a felony, and I was afraid I'd be prosecuted. I thought I might get a break if I admitted it now, though."

"Hmmmm." He inhaled a toke from his stogie, emitting a noxious cloud of smoke. "What number was on the license plate of the vehicle you hit?"

I had no solid basis for the choice, but the offense behavior of the driver I'd encountered on Plantation prompted a firm "Two."

Green's rapid computer search of the maintenance records showed that II was the wrong HORSE. "Two was brought in for routine detailing fifteen or twenty minutes ago. There's no mention here of any dents or scratches," he informed me.

"It could have been HORSE I. I was so nervous I could hardly see straight," I supplied, planning to use that excuse to get me through all four cars if need be.

He leaned forward to peer at the terminal, puffing harder with every line that popped up on the screen. "Number one just came back from the shop this morning. It went in with a smashed headlight, twisted bumper and a dent in the right front quarter panel. Total cost of the repairs was—". He punched a sequence of keys then growled a figure that made me blanch.

"That's more than my husband, George, makes in three months." I gulped realizing that I might've dug myself a deep hole. If he demanded payment, I would be forced to admit I was lying about the whole deal.

"Body work on these babies doesn't come cheap. You couldn't have been responsible, though. The damage occurred out of state."

Jackpot.

"It must've been a pretty bad accident. I hope no one was hurt. Who was driving?" I pressed, hoping to squeeze more information from the kernel he'd unwittingly given me.

"One of CANTER's vice presidents. No one else is allowed to take the HORSE cars." Dismissing me with a wave of his cigar, he turned back to his computer.

The plot had not only thickened, it had widened and deepened into an impossible morass. Was Alison's executive pursuer acting on his own or on CANTER's behalf? In either case, he obviously had mega resources and clout at his disposal, and that meant that Alison was in very big trouble. Jericho and I had to get to Fairfax as soon as possible. Once he realized the seriousness of the situation, he couldn't possibly refuse to tell us what, if anything, he knew.

"Was there something else you wanted?" Green's irascible query broke into my speculations.

"Is there a public phone here?"

"Closest one is in administration. That's the building to your right as you leave here."

The instruction hardly left his mouth before I was heading for the door.

The huge lobby of CANTER's main building was a study in eclectic ostentation. A Calder mobile was suspended from the cathedral ceiling, museum-quality oriental vases were displayed in a showcase on the far wall, and Hepplewhite occasional chairs were scattered around the ecru broadloom in chatty groupings.

What do you expect from an organization that sports a company fleet of top-of-the line cars? I thought, making the required entry in the visitors' log under the watchful eye of the Carolina peach who presided over the front desk. In my haste to get to a bank of pay phones by the elevator, I signed my real name instead of the Jeffers alias.

Before I could change it, the receptionist offered a cordial, "Have a pleasant stay at CANTER, Ms. McKinnon."

Except for the dubious pleasure of ogling the decor, the only thing I got from my trip to the phone booth was more frustration. Jericho hadn't yet returned from his medical examiner gig and Fairfax's line was still busy. Since the directions to Wallace's place that the kid on the street had given me were by now an irretrievable mush in my mind, I hurried back to the desk in search of a new set.

"Getting to Avalon Terrace from here can be tricky. I'd better draw you a map," the receptionist offered.

"Thanks a lot. I'd also like any material you have on CANTER's functions and organizational structure if it's not too much trouble."

"No trouble a'tall. As information specialist, my job is to help our visitors in every way possible." She presented me with a glossy brochure from a stack on the counter, then began sketching a grid on a heavy sheet of vellum.

CANTER, the cover of the publication enlightened me, was the acronym for the Consortium for the Advancement of Natural, Technological and Environmental Research— Magnolia Grove's Partnership with the Future. Two-thirds of the way through the convoluted bureaucratese on the fly sheet, I finally determined that the place was a think tank, and I was starting on the roster of outside consultants, quite a few of whom were retired government bigwigs, when the weighty scent of musk distracted me from my reading. I raised my head just as the driver I had been following strode up to the desk.

His gaze flicked briefly over my face, then he moved away, his expression affable but disinterested. "The Yamihita delegation is due in less than an hour, Tiffany. Is it a go on this end?"

The receptionist snapped to smartly and recited a list of completed preparations, ending with, "I'll triple-check everything as soon as I explain these directions to Ms. McKinnon."

"McKinnon?" I now had his undivided attention. "What a pleasant surprise. I assume that you're here gathering background information for your magazine layout."

Taken aback, I folded the brochure and stuck it in my purse, responding with a wary, "You're very astute, Mr.—"

"Barrett Endicott III, CANTER's senior vice president in charge of public relations. I'm also a member of the Magnolia Grove Heritage Committee, and I'd like to express our gratitude for your work at the festival," he said, extending his hand.

I shook it, stunned to speechlessness. The last time I'd seen Barrett—aka "Triple Barium Enema" to his Palmetto Prep classmates—he had been the designated fall guy for every cruel joke his peers could devise. Even the public school kids had secretly ridiculed him. At Springfield, the slang B.E.-III had been interchangeable with "loser" and "goofus." But some miraculous alchemy had converted three-hundred-plus pounds of blubber into one-eighty of prime muscle, and deepened pale eyes to piercing navy. I was certain that the doctor who'd resculpted his pudding face would go down in AMA annals as the Michelangelo of plastic surgery.

"I missed the activities on Saturday and I'm anxious to see the photographs you took. In fact, I'd like to have a duplicate set of the prints. You may add the additional cost to the committee's bill," the executive informed me.

Though the request was superficially innocuous, its imperious tone set my teeth on edge.

"I won't be submitting a bill, Mr. Endicott. The shoot is my contribution to a worthy cause. My current equipment only allows me to process negatives and contact sheets, and I'll be presenting those to Mrs. Springfield tomorrow afternoon. I suggest that you get in touch with her to arrange for any prints you might require."

I couldn't interpret the glint in his eyes, but it didn't seem to match the Mr. Congeniality smile that lifted the corners of his lips.

"To be sure," he said, glancing down at his Rolex. "I'll be tied up for the rest of the afternoon, but I'm extremely interested in the work you're doing for the magazine. Perhaps you'd care to join me for dinner at the club sometime this week."

All things being equal, I'd rather have gone out with the old B.E.-III than this too-much-improved version. He was a CANTER vice president though, and by definition now one of my prime suspects. It was possible that I could use this date to manipulate him into revealing useful information. "I'll have to check my schedule," I hedged.

"Do that, and be sure to leave your number with Tiffany. I'll call later to arrange the details." He allowed his gaze to slide from my face, lingering lazily over my salient features on its downward journey. When the survey was complete, he inclined his head in an appreciative nod. "I can't tell you how much I look forward to seeing more of you."

With that, Endicott turned on his heel and sauntered away.

My inclination was to pick up the nearest loose object and throw it after him.

Tiffany's eyes narrowed as they followed his progress toward the elevator. "Ninety-eight percent of the women in this building are in love with Mr. Endicott. He's gorgeous, isn't he?"

From the composite of resentments and disdain on her face, I could tell she was among the hold-outs.

"A real work of art. It's a pity current medical technology doesn't include personality transplants."

"Pardon?"

"Just an editorial comment."

Smiling again, she handed me the map. "This way is a little longer than going back to town on Route 18, but it by-passes PHCC. I avoid the country club whenever possible. The traffic in that area can get really sticky," she said pointedly.

"Thanks for everything. CANTER is lucky to have such a helpful and knowledgeable information specialist."

"You forgot to give me your phone number," she prompted as I started away from the desk.

I grinned back at her. "No I didn't."

TIFFANY'S DIRECTIONS got me back into town in less than ten minutes, but there was something about them that nagged me into increasing my speed past the thirty-five mph limit. Two miles past the marina on the south side of town, I turned into a residential area that was on the low end of upscale. The houses, variations on three basic, aluminum-sided models, were comfortably large, but spaced too closely together. In another ten or fifteen years, when spindly, newly planted trees attained some size and homeowners strayed away from the currently tacky color combinations, the neighborhood might attain some character and uniqueness. Right now, it was depressingly redundant.

Cutesy street names were first on the list of things I disliked about housing developments, and this one had a bunch of them—such as Lancelot Landing and Excalibur Way. It wasn't until I passed Merlin Mews that I tuned into the pattern. I was driving through Camelot Court.

I clamped my fingers onto the steering wheel so tightly that my knuckles bleached white. "It's only a coincidence," I reassured myself. But as I turned onto Avalon Terrace, I knew in my heart what I would find. A multicolored VW, a squad car and a hearse from Hargett's Mortuary were parked in front of 3647, the house that belonged to Wallace Fairfax.

The lawn was cordoned off with strips of yellow plastic, and a buzzing group of onlookers—mostly housewives with small children clutched in their arms or clinging to their skirts—was clustered on the sidewalk.

I elbowed my way through Wallace's neighbors, immune to their grumbling and curious stares, but as I ducked under the tape and started up the flagstone path to the front porch, a policeman moved over to block my way.

"I've got to see Dr. Quaid," I insisted, trying to sidestep him.

He grasped my arm gently but firmly. "Sorry, miss. No one's allowed inside but authorized personnel."

"I can either go around you, by you or through you, officer, it's your choice. And unless you shoot me in the back, I'm going into that house."

He returned my determined stare with one of his own, neither of us budging an inch. The confrontation might have gone on indefinitely if Jericho hadn't intervened.

"It's okay, Ken, let her in," he called from the porch.

Although Ken didn't seem thrilled, he hitched his bulk out of my way.

When I reached Jericho's side, he greeted me with a tight "I've been trying to get hold of you since nine-fifteen. Where the hell have you been?"

"It's a long story." I directed an apprehensive peek into the two-car garage attached to the house. There was a blanket-covered form on the cement floor, and the two men standing beside it were deep in conversation. I swallowed to rid my mouth of its metallic dryness. "What happened to Wallace?"

"Suicide. Judging by the condition of the body, I'd say it happened around five this morning."

"I can't believe he would kill himself," I protested. "Marietta needs him. He told me that he wouldn't miss a second of the time they have together."

"Time's run out for both of them. This morning at seven, she was found dead in her room at Ocean Manor—"

"He didn't want to go on living without her," I cut in. The theory barely got past my lips before I spotted the flaw in it. "If he killed himself at five, though, he couldn't possibly have known about Marietta."

Jericho glanced at the cops in the garage. "She was smothered with a pillow, Rachel. The Savannah police claim they have a tight case against Wallace, but for the moment, they're keeping the details under wraps. From what Sheriff Tillman and I have been able to piece together here, Wallace got home around four, sealed the cracks around the garage door, turned on the motor of his car, then laid down with his head near the exhaust pipe. In the note we found beside him, he asked to be forgiven for what he had done."

The huge breath of air I sucked down wouldn't come back out. As my lungs expanded to their limit, my mind produced the image of helium balloons lifting me, floating me away to a place where I wouldn't have to deal with the ghastly particulars of the suicide.

"If you faint, I'm going to slap you," Jericho warned, gripping my shoulders.

The rasp in his voice sliced through the fog gathering in my brain. "You do, and I'll break your arm," I snapped, glaring up at him.

A smile spread its sunshine over his face, melting the icy glint in his eyes. "There's my favorite linebacker."

His approval straightened my shoulders, and a little of the steel snapped back into my spine. "Have you found anything that might link Wallace to Alison's disappearance?"

Jericho frowned. "We only did a quick walk-through in the house. Savannah is sending in a team of detectives, and Tillman doesn't want to disturb the scene before they arrive."

"Once an official investigation is underway, we won't have a chance to do any searching. We've got to think of a way to get in there now."

Before we could formulate a strategy, a beefy, gray-haired man came out of the garage and walked up to his. "You can take off any time you're ready, Doc. The boys and I have things under control," he said, eyeing me suspiciously.

"Sheriff Tillman—Rachel McKinnon," Jericho said. "She's one of Fairfax's former students."

"Pleasure, ma'am." He touched the broad brim of his hat briefly. "I'm going to have to ask you to move back behind the barricade. A crime scene is no place for a lady."

"Unless she happens to be a forensic photographer." I winged it, struck by an inspiration. "I was with the sheriff's office in Rillito, Arizona, during the Desert Slasher murders. Six decapitations in one week, bodies and heads scattered all over the Santa Catalina mountains."

It wasn't exactly a lie—I had served an internship in the sleepy little town during the summer of my junior year in college—but I saw no point in mentioning that the victims had been longhorn steers.

Some of the ruddiness disappeared from Tillman's jowls. "Can't say that I recall that series. Was the perpetrator apprehended?"

"We were on the verge of breaking the case when the Tucson PD horned in and snatched the collar. You know how it goes when jurisdictional politics are involved."

"Big fish gobble up the small ones every time." Jericho bought into my scam. "It'd be a pity to let the Fairfax case get away from you, Sheriff. The wire services will probably pick up the story and that kind of publicity couldn't hurt come election day."

"It'll take the Savannah crew at least a week to process their pictures of the scene, and they may or may not be willing to share them. You need your own set," I pressed. "I'll be happy to volunteer my services."

He shifted from foot to foot, rubbing his chin nervously. "'Preciate that. Won't do for the Georgia boys to think I'm withholding evidence, though, so it's better to keep this amongst the three of us."

"My lips are sealed," Jericho promised with a straight face.

In planning my strategy, I had overlooked one very major obstacle. I'd neglected to bring my camera bag.

"We don't have time," Tillman said, brushing off my proposal to go home and retrieve my equipment. "There's all the gadgets you could possibly need inside, and for sure, ole Wally's not in any shape to object to your using them."

I had to clench my jaw tight to hold back a response to the crass observation, but the surge of anger did serve to keep my mind off the gruesome task that was to come. As we followed Tillman through the front door of the house, Jericho slipped a protective arm around my waist.

"Are you sure you're up to this?" he murmured.

"No, but I'm going to do it, anyway."

The sheriff hadn't understated the amount and variety of photographic devices in Wallace's home studio. Fifteen state-of-the-art cameras were arrayed on the shelves, along with lenses and filters for every conceivable purpose. Feeling like a grave robber, I selected a model closest to my Nikon and connected a strobe attachment.

"It would save time if you'd start selecting the areas you want me to shoot, Sheriff." I wanted him out of the room. "I'll be with you as soon as I find the film."

Jericho took up a position beside me. "I'll help her carry the equipment."

"Don't take all day," he grumbled, plodding out into the hallway.

"We make one helluva team, don't we?" Jericho said, grinning.

I had to drag myself away from the warmth of his eyes. "Let's not congratulate ourselves until we find something," I cautioned, hurrying him into the adjacent darkroom. It was the most complete I'd ever seen. "Wallace spent a small fortune on this layout, and what he dropped setting you up his studio in town could've bankrolled a Third World country. How long has Icons Unlimited been in operation?"

"Two years—three at most."

"Business must be extremely good," I mused aloud, opening the nearest cabinet. It was stacked high with unexposed film. I picked six rolls at random and shoved them into the pocket of my skirt.

"What are we looking for?"

"I was hoping you'd know." I loaded the camera, set the shutter speed and turned to snap miscellaneous shots of the darkroom.

"I suppose this is as good a place to start as any," he said, fanning through contact sheets stacked by the enlarger.

I stopped photographing long enough to pick up a large, lead-lined envelope. "Stuff them in this. We can go over them later." There was only one roll in a bin labeled Newly Exposed. On impulse, I dropped it into the bag before I handed it over to Jericho.

"Why are you taking pictures in here?" Tillman asked from the doorway.

The sudden intrusion jerked me around. At the same instant, I pressed the shutter release. The sheriff reeled backward, blinking from the glare of the strobe.

"She's testing the flash attachment," my partner said smugly.

For the next fifteen minutes I photographed the rooms from every angle I could get. I worked as slowly as possible through the kitchen and toward the exit, my mouth getting progressively dryer with each click of the camera, my dread of walking into the garage so thick it was almost choking me.

"Pictures of the stove won't do me any good," Tillman complained, shooing me through the door. He strode over to the blanket-draped bundle lying by the rear bumper of the car and pulled the covering away.

Wallace Fairfax was doubled into a fetal position, one hand tucked under his head, the other clutching an empty vodka bottle. In death, his open eyes had become filmy, lending them a hopeless resignation that was strangely akin to peace. The crumpled form held no trace of the teacher I'd admired and respected, and the loss was more painful than I'd expected.

Thanks mainly to the steady comfort of Jericho's hand on the small of my back, I was able to fight off the sob that bubbled up in my throat. Purging my mind of all but the mechanics of the job, I focused the camera and began to shoot.

There were no outward signs of a struggle, no scuff marks on the concrete surrounding the body, no untoward bruises on the head or arms. Although I was far from expert at forensic photography, experience and logic dictated that this death was most probably suicide. Evidence notwithstanding, every fiber in me still rejected the proposition that Wallace Fairfax had killed himself, and my belief that he couldn't possibly have murdered the woman he had loved so deeply was even more uncompromising.

When the last frame was taken, I unloaded the film, knelt to remove the bottle from his outstretched hand, and replaced it with his camera. It seemed little enough to do for the man who had given me my career.

Chapter Eight

"This is the biggest car I've ever seen. It's just like Cinderella's pumpkin," Samantha said. She arranged the pale lavender pleats of her skirt into a fan that covered her knees.

Maggie fingered the spray of fresh orchids cascading from a crystal vase on the door panel, her expression sheer bliss. "Better—Cinderella didn't have color TV in her coach."

I fidgeted against the plush upholstery, trying to work up enthusiasm for the limo ride, but had very little success.

Some of my apathy must have transferred to Sam. The hint of a pout pursed her lips. "I wish D.J. was here. Why can't he come see us today?"

"Because his office hours are from two to nine this evening." I had explained this at least three times since breakfast. More for my benefit than hers, I tacked on a determined "But we're going to have so much fun at tea that we'll hardly miss him. Isn't that right, Maggie?"

"You bet." Her response sounded a trifle strained. She glanced toward the glass partition that separated us from the front seat. Apparently satisfied that the chauffeur couldn't overhear, she added conspiratorially, "Yesterday I was talking to a woman at the supermarket, and she said the Springfields live in a genuine English castle. Is that true, Rachel?"

"Actually, it's French. Jubel T. had it shipped over from Périgueux, and his slaves reassembled it stone by stone. The only thing that's missing is a moat." The tidbit was drawn from a fifth-grade history lesson. Although my teacher's knowledge of Paul Revere had been fuzzy, she'd drilled us daily on the past glories of Magnolia Grove.

Sam clutched BeeCee, her eyes wide with excitement. "I betcha dragons live in the basement," she said, launching into a stream of castle trivia gleaned from the Brothers Grimm.

I tuned out in the middle of Rapunzel, fiddling with the folder of proof sheets in my lap and wishing I could have thought of a polite way to weasel out of the invitation to tea. The prospect of spending an afternoon at Château Printemps filled me with uneasiness, a holdover from the old days when I accompanied my mother, Amelia's favorite local seamstress, to the Springfield estate for fittings. We always went to the servants' entrance in back, where a maid would whisk us through the kitchen to the day chamber, an oppressive room with too much furniture and too little light. I'd never known what lay beyond, and since it seemed highly possible that trapdoors and chain-wielding spooks would be part of the decor, I'd never attempted to find out.

Besides being reluctant to squander precious time on a tea party, I was bone-weary, the legacy of a sleepless night spent rerunning the events of Monday. The Savannah squad had arrived not five minutes after I'd stashed the lead-lined bag and rolls of exposed film in the trunk of my car. As I'd predicted, they had slammed the lid on the case and shooed the Magnolia Grove PD and company away from the scene. What I had needed after that was a quiet corner, a stiff drink and Jericho's undivided attention—not necessarily in that order—but since he had an office full of patients to tend to, I'd spent the bulk of the afternoon in Charleston buying used equipment to expand my darkroom. It wasn't until he called at ten that evening that I'd given him the full story of my experience at CANTER. In my view, collaborating by telephone was a jackleg way to conduct an investigation.

"We're here, Cricket." Sam interrupted my internal tirade.

I heaved a gusty sigh and arranged my features into what I hoped would pass for pleasant.

Amelia Springfield was waiting for us in the library, a mahogany-paneled room with brocade drapes that blocked a good deal of the light coming in through the windows. She seemed frail, almost ethereal, in comparison to the massive leather chair in which she was seated.

Rising to greet me with a kiss on the cheek, she acknowledged my introduction of Mrs. Peace with a cordial handshake, and in a skinny minute, the two had established themselves as "Amelia" and "Margaret." It was obvious, though, that Sam was the main event of our hostess's afternoon. Amelia complimented her dress, paid respects to BeeCee and asked after Arvy, all without sounding either condescending or artificial—a nifty balance, in my book. But with the amenities completed and my folder of photographic contact sheets duly delivered and admired, the conversation sagged. I was racking my brain for a way to reestablish the pace when Maggie jumped into the breach.

"That's a fine piece of art, Amelia," she commented, gesturing toward a painting above the stone fireplace. "The composition and brush strokes remind me of an Albrecht Dürer."

I angled a surprised glance in her direction. My neighbor had wide-ranging interests, but I hadn't known German Renaissance artists to be among them. While I couldn't disagree with her technical assessment of the work, I found both its Gothic mood and emotional content deeply disturbing. General Springfield dominated the portrait, both literally and figuratively, his left hand placed on his young son's shoulder in an attitude of control rather than affection. To me, the set of Michael's face appeared defeated and more than a little lost.

"My husband, Clayton, is particularly fond of Dürer, and he reviewed quite a number of portfolios before he found an artist who could approximate the style." She moved to gaze up at the picture, her voice becoming subdued. "Michael was only eight when this portrait was painted, and although the sittings were long, he held his pose without once complaining."

That didn't exactly surprise me. The General was holding a riding crop in his right hand.

Amelia turned back to us, her face pale but carefully composed. "Perhaps you all might like to take a walk through the gardens. The floribundas are especially lovely this year."

My tolerance for estate tours and social chitchat was running extremely low, particularly since roses, my least favorite plant on the face of the earth, were to be involved. Sneaking a fast peek past at the grandfather clock to her left, I repressed a sigh. Only seven minutes of teatime had passed and the balance stretched ahead interminably.

Samantha, who had gotten restless during the art critique, was now openly fidgety. "When can we look at the dinosaurs? BeeCee wants to see if he can find any of his relatives."

At her request, some of the color returned to Amelia's cheeks. "Now that you mention it, I think one of the triceratops may have Washington connections. Family trees are much more interesting than flowers. Let's go see if we can trace BeeCee's."

Samantha skipped over to award our hostess custody of the plush animal then took her hand, and as the two of them led the way from the library, they chatted with the ease of good friends. The spacious salon into which Amelia Springfield ushered us was brightly illuminated by recessed spotlights, its only furniture a small Victorian chair set in the exact center of the marble floor. Although the ambience was markedly different from the cluttered gloom of the library, it was equally stifling in its own way. The room was a memorial to Michael Springfield. Every stage of his growth was chronicled in silver-framed photographs, his awards and trophies were preserved in glass cases and his personal belongings were arrayed on the floor-to-ceiling shelves. As we followed his mother to a grouping of toys at the beginning of the exhibit, I couldn't shake the creepy feeling that we were invading Michael's privacy.

"Your BeeCee looks most like a stegosaur to me." Amelia set the stuffed animal atop a display case filled with miniature replicas of prehistoric denizens. She selected a picture encyclopedia from the shelf above and opened it carefully, almost reverently, to an appropriate drawing. "See? They both have triangular plates standing up along the middle of their backs."

"That's neat. Can I read it?" Sam asked eagerly.

Amelia hesitated, then knelt to present the book to her. "As often as you like. It belongs to you, now."

"I'm gonna take very good care of it." The little girl planted a kiss on her patron's cheek, and without further ado, plopped cross-legged onto the floor to peruse her gift.

Amelia rose to her feet, a glimmer of moisture in her eyes. "Samantha has lovely manners, Rachel," she murmured. "It's obvious she's getting a lot of quality time and attention. Does she usually accompany you on your assignments?"

"Whenever possible," I hedged.

"Travel is so wonderful for children. I first took Michael to Paris when he was six months old. He was a delightful baby—active, of course, but so sweet-tempered. He never gave me one minute's trouble." Breaking off abruptly, she walked over to realign a picture on the near wall.

Maggie and I exchanged an uneasy glance.

"He certainly was a handsome boy." My neighbor breached the gathering silence. "And from the looks of all these trophies, he must have been a star athlete."

"Michael excelled at everything he did. He graduated college summa cum laude and was working toward a doctorate in archaeology. Antiquities were his absolute passion, you know. As a matter of fact, he spent eleven months supervising a dig near Cuzco." Her focus was fixed in our direction, but her attention seemed light-years away. "My son came back from Peru a week before his thirtieth birthday. We had celebrated early because I was going to New York to attend a Broadway opening. The accident happened while I was on my way home, so I never got another chance to tell him how much I loved him."

"I'm sure he knew." Although it was a trite comfort to offer, it was the only one I could think of at the moment.

Amelia straightened her shoulders and smiled brightly. "You'll have to forgive me! I do rattle on sometimes. Now then, ladies, shall we go have our cocoa party?"

"Yaaay," Sam cheered, scrambling up post haste.

A porcelain service and an elaborate assortment of pastries had been arranged for us atop a low glass table on the west veranda, and as I perched on the nearest wicker chair, a few of the kinks in my nerves began to loosen. Getting out of the house would have been a relief of magnificent proportions if it hadn't been for the roses massed on two sides of the flagstone porch. The breeze was so filled with their cloying scent that it almost felt solid in my nose. To combat a creeping nausea, I cut the usual depth of my breathing in half and concentrated on the muted tolling of bells that drifted in from the west of the house.

"Has one of the churches in town put in a carillon, Amelia?" I asked, mainly to get an innocuous conversation going. While chatting about Magnolia Grove would be deadly dull, it beat being inundated with Michael stories by a country mile.

"The chimes you hear come from a chapel that Clayton's father had built in the early twenties. I can show you through it, if you like, but in my opinion, it isn't one of the more attractive features of the estate."

"It's so pleasant here on the veranda, I'm reluctant to move," I hastened to assure her. Covertly pressing my fingers against a throbbing in my right temple, I inwardly calculated our earliest graceful departure time. Not only was I uncomfortable, but none of this was bringing me any closer to finding Alison.

"That will be all, Parks." Amelia dismissed the uniformed butler who hovered in the background. Settling at the head of the table in a swirl of silk, she poured the first cup of cocoa and beckoned to Samantha. "Would you like to help me serve, dear?"

Sam bounced up eagerly, then turned to me. "I'll be real careful. Is it okay?"

I cringed. Although the china on the tray looked as if it might shatter under the weight of a whisper, I wasn't about to undermine her confidence, so I murmured my permission. My elderly neighbor seconded the decision with an approving nod, but I noticed that her fingers were crossed.

When the beverage deliveries went off without a hitch, I allowed myself to relax. Samantha was halfway around the table with a small serving plate of petits fours when the thud of heavy footsteps came from the dayroom adjacent to the veranda. "Amelia!" The voice was irate extremely.

Mrs. Springfield took a dainty sip from her cup, not turning so much as one hair. Since there was no chance she hadn't heard, I assumed she was ignoring the summons. Scant seconds later, a livid Clayton Springfield strode through the open French doors.

"This time you've gone too far, you bi—" He broke off the expletive abruptly. A dull flush stained his neck as he scanned the terrace. Inclining his head to acknowledge our presence, he modulated his voice to a courteous drawl. "Forgive the intrusion, Amelia. I didn't realize you were entertaining."

She rose, beaming as though he had handed her a bouquet of roses. "This is Margaret Peace, darling, and, of course you remember Rachel Bodine McKinnon."

He swept a disinterested glance over Maggie, dismissing her without so much as a nod before he turned his attention to me. "You're very like your mother, my dear," he said, regarding me steadily.

His eyes, so pale they were of no discernible color, were the coldest I've ever seen, the smile on his lips too thin to mask an underlying cruelty.

"I take that as a very great compliment, sir," I said, matching his saccharine inflection.

"And this precious child is Rachel's daughter Samantha," Amelia said. "She and our Michael share a love of dinosaurs."

That she should speak of her son in the present tense struck me as exceedingly odd, but I had very little time to wonder at the anomaly. Clayton walked across the terrace to stare down at Sam, his ersatz civility fast disappearing.

"Put that plate on the table." His tone was two shades past deadly.

She gaped up at him, dumbstruck and ashen.

"Now!" he thundered.

Any red-blooded, American child who was scared half out of her wits would have dropped the china, and Samantha was no exception. As the plate smashed against the flagstones, one of the pastries splattered pink icing all over the toes of Clayton's spit-polished riding boots. His face became mottled with fury and the sound that came from his throat reminded me of an animal's snarl.

Maggie was out of her seat in an instant, but I beat her to Sam by a heartbeat. As I wrapped an arm around my charge's shoulders, she pressed against me, trembling but dry-eyed.

"It was an accident. I'll be glad to pay for the damage," I said with all the dignity I could muster—not a lot, since most of my energy was being diverted into holding my temper.

"I doubt you'll earn enough in the next year to reimburse me. There are only two-hundred-fifty sets of that particular porcelain pattern still in existence, and until today, mine was one of the few complete ones. I'd suggest that you either teach your destructive brat not to touch other people's possessions or keep her tethered on a very short leash." With a final withering inspection of Samantha, he executed a snappy half turn and stalked past Amelia. "I'll deal with you later," he said before he headed off through the garden.

Maggie's gaze bored holes in the General's retreating back. I'm not sure what reaction I expected from Amelia, but it certainly wasn't the blank serenity she presented.

"Clayton tends to get overwrought now and again. I'm sure when he's calmed down, he'll come to apologize for his little outburst." She rang a silver bell. When the butler appeared, she commanded him to set another tea in the salon.

I couldn't tell whether she was insensitive, or just out of touch with reality, but her motivation didn't really concern me. "I think it best that we leave." I said none too politely.

Maggie had already retrieved BeeCee and our respective purses and was standing within a pace of the door.

Our hostess's shoulders lifted in a delicate shrug. "As you wish. Parks, have Skinner—"

"The car is waiting in front even as we speak, madam." The butler cut through his employer's order. Favoring Sam with a sympathetic glance, he glided back into the house.

"Parks is a jewel," Amelia announced to nobody in particular. Retrieving the dinosaur encyclopedia from the wicker couch, she walked over and held it toward Samantha. "You mustn't forget this, sweetheart."

Sam's face was as wistful as it was sad. She ran a finger over the cover, then reluctantly pushed the volume away. "That mean man might yell at you again if you give your little boy's book to me. Thanks for letting me read it, though, and I'm sorry I broke your dish," she said in a very small voice. Releasing her grip on my hand, she ran to join Maggie.

Amelia's composure crumbled, and for an instant I caught a glimpse of the person inside. I saw humiliation, torment and above all, loneliness. "I haven't the strength to stand up to Clayton. Please forgive me, Rachel," she whispered.

"There's nothing to forgive." On impulse, I leaned forward to kiss her cheek, in small part to salute the woman who had shown my mother kindness, but mostly because I felt sorry for her. As I turned away I wouldn't have changed places with her for all the prestige, power and money on earth.

"I CAN'T FIND Citronella," Samantha reported anxiously, padding shoeless into my room to investigate the space under my bed. When that search proved fruitless, she scrambled to the closet and tugged at the empty luggage I'd stacked on the floor.

"She's probably hiding in the clothes hamper." I wiggled into a bikini, then tossed the dress I had worn to tea aside, permanently ruling it out of my wardrobe. The ugliness at Château Printemps was more difficult to discard, but I was counting on a dip in the ocean to undo the kinks in my nerves.

"I already looked there." Sam sat back on her heels, bottom lip trembling and lashes fast spiking with moisture. "I left the screen in my window open just in case she wanted to go outside while we were gone. Maybe she ran away."

"She wouldn't leave you. Finish changing your clothes and we'll have an all-points cat hunt before we go swimming," I promised. Sam hadn't shed a single tear during the limo ride home, and suspecting that the effects of the confrontation with General Springfield were beginning to catch up with her, I added a reassuring "Don't worry, honey, we'll find her."

"That's what you said about Mommy."

I could have dealt with accusation or even flat-out anger, but I felt helpless in the face of her listless resignation.

"If somebody doesn't let me in soon, I'll have to start huffing and puffing." A pseudo-gruff warning came from the patio below.

Sam's malaise disappeared quicker than ice cream in August. "It's D.J.," she squealed, running to the open window.

Though her pace was faster, my legs were longer. We reached the sill at the same time. When I saw Jericho's ear-to-ear grin, the tatters in my afternoon began to mend.

"The sliding door is unlocked," I called.

"Hurry on down. I have five surprises for you."

Sam pelted out of the room, and after a mirror check showed me way too much skin, I slipped on a cover-up and followed.

He stood in the living room holding a silver-wrapped package. "Here's number one. It's actually a present for your mom, but I want you to play with it until she gets here," he told his niece, setting it on the coffee table.

When Samantha lifted the lid, exposing the miniature tea set inside, all of her excitement and most of the color in her face drained away. "You'd better keep it," she mumbled, quickly shutting the box.

From the quaver in her voice, it was apparent that the lone tear sneaking past her lashes was the vanguard of a deluge. Before the flood could develop, Jericho scooped her in his arms, his frown a combination of confusion and concern. "I guess I'm not very good at picking out girl-type toys."

"You did fine. This is just a bad day for china," I interceded, tacking on a brief account of the tea party.

Sam scowled. "I wouldn't have dropped that man's dumb old dish if he hadn't yelled at me."

"Don't you give Clayton Springfield another thought, doodlebug. He's not worth the energy," I said.

Jericho tousled her curls then restored her to her feet with the instruction, "Go fetch Maggie—I don't want her to miss the rest of the surprises."

Sam was all giggles as she bounced out of the room. Her uncle moved to stand beside me, expelling a long breath. "That's one terrific little kid. I didn't realize how empty my life was until she came along."

"That makes two of us," I agreed, studying him curiously. "Has an epidemic of good health broken out in Magnolia Grove, or are you just popping in between appointments?"

"Neither. One of the physicians who works at the Goose Creek clinic with me agreed to cover my caseload so I can hang out with three beautiful women. Are you, Maggie and Sam available?"

"We might be able to pencil you into the schedule." I worked to dampen a rising elation. "How long do we have to put up with you?"

He turned me to face him, the humor in his expression losing ground to a shadowed warmth. "Until now, our partnership has been ninety-ten, with you on the heavy end of the stick. I figure it's time for me to start pulling my share of the weight, so you're stuck with me for the duration."

"I'll be glad for the company," I said, reaching to touch the line of his jaw.

A giggle froze my fingers mid-air; I craned my neck to catch my housemates standing at the archway behind me.

"Is D.J. going to kiss Cricket, Maggie?" Samantha asked.

"I expect he might," Maggie said mischievously. Beaming, she made shooing motions with both hands. "Don't mind us, boy, get on about your business."

Jericho bent to plant a noisy smooch on my cheek, then marched over to give Maggie and Sam similar salutes. "Now that I've had my sugar for today, we're going to the cabana to check out surprises two, three, four and five."

He led us to the striped tent at the far edge of the patio at a leisurely pace, obviously enjoying the suspense he was creating.

"Hurry up, slowpoke," Sam demanded, tugging at his hand.

"Be very quiet and don't make any sudden moves." Carefully easing aside the canvas flap that covered the entrance to the cabana, he murmured, "Ladies, I'd like for you to meet DDT, Black Flag, Fly Paper and Raid."

Citronella, looking extraordinarily pleased with herself, lay inside nursing four newborn kittens.

"Oh, bo—" Samantha clapped a hand over her mouth, cutting off the end of the exclamation. The wonder that blossomed in her eyes reminded me of the first crocus of spring peeking through the snow. "How'd you know she had her kittens here, D.J.?"

"When I drove up, she stuck out her head and meowed the good news," he explained. "You can't play with the babies right away, but mama cat's going to need a lot of care for the next few days. I'm counting on you to bring her food."

Her small shoulders squared as though to accommodate the responsibility and her face assumed a solemn maturity. "Tuna crunchies are her favorite. I'll go get a bowl right now," she said, dashing back into the house.

"Change into your bathing suit while you're at it. D.J.'s going swimming with us," I called after her. I turned back to Maggie. "Are you up to a dip in the ocean?"

"Saltwater's bad for my arthritis. Besides, I called Charleston and talked to my friends, the Bristols, when we got back from tea. Their son Marcus is now a special investigator for the South Carolina state patrol, and they're having a cookout to celebrate the promotion. Plus, Bertie and Frank are leaving for Jamaica day after tomorrow, so this is the only time I'll have to see them." She pursed her lips. "I'm going to mosey over and reminisce a bit. Five cats and one inquisitive little girl should be enough to keep the two of you busy," she added innocently.

I blushed to the roots of my hair, an annoying habit I'd only lately acquired. "We'll drive you to Charleston."

"No such thing. If I have my own wheels, I can come and go as I please."

"Special investigator, huh?" Jericho massaged his jaw, his forehead creased in thought. "Marcus Bristol must have good connections with the Georgia authorities. Do you think he'd be willing to get some information about the Fairfax case for us?"

"I can ask. What do you want to know?" Maggie queried.

"I'd like to see copies of the autopsy reports if possible. It would also be interesting to find out why the Savannah PD is being so hush-mouthed. Sheriff Tillman's no legal eagle, but he's not a total incompetent, either, and the suicide did occur in his jurisdiction."

"It would help if we had some background on Ocean Manor, too," I chimed in. "The police must have interviewed the doctors and nurses who took care of Marietta Fairfax."

"It's as good as done." In full Kojak mode, Maggie marched off to the paper chase. "Don't wait up," she advised.

Jericho favored me with a lazy grin. "So, what's the agenda for the afternoon, lady?"

Suddenly at a loss for something to do with my hands, I niggled at a loop on the front of my terry-cloth cover-up. "I'm functionally illiterate when it comes to cooking, but if you're hungry I could throw together some cold-cut sandwiches. On second thought, maybe we should call out for pizza. I couldn't possibly screw that up," I rambled, avoiding his steady gaze. "I developed the film last night, but I haven't made prints yet. I could do it now, though, since you're here to entertain Sam. Or maybe I should go down to the newspaper office and start developing dossiers on CANTER's five senior vice presidents...."

His fingers closed over mine and the rest of my nervous chatter died in my throat.

"Our agreement sets aside Tuesday afternoon for R and R. You round up a blanket, beach towels and suntan lotion while I slip into something more comfortable," he directed, emphasizing the order with a playful swat to my backside.

"That definitely isn't in the contract."

"I just added a clause to the fine print."

When I returned to the patio five minutes later with the requisite equipment, uncle and niece had already hit the beach.

The good doctor wearing clothes was impressive, but in brief, snug trunks that accentuated the powerful configuration of his thighs, he made my toes curl under. His torso was well-defined without being unduly bulky and his skin was a satiny gold usually sported by surfers. Besides all that, the curly crop of dark hair that extended in a vee from his upper chest down the tight planes of his abdomen fairly begged to be toyed with. As I dropped the towels and began to spread out the blanket, I kept my focus firmly on the ground. In my experience, the safest way to handle temptation was to avoid it. That I managed to pull it off was an exercise of grace under extreme pressure.

"You can't go swimming in your robe, Cricket," Sam complained, tugging at my cover-up.

"I was just about to mention that," Jericho seconded.

"All right." Conscious of the extra pound or two Maggie's cooking had added to my hipline, I unzipped the terry-cloth garment and jettisoned it on the sand.

"Have mercy." Jericho's eyes popped open and he swallowed a couple of times. "You sure know how to jump-start a person's pulse," he said huskily.

Sam frowned her puzzlement. "What's that supposed to mean?"

"That it's time to hit the ocean, doodlebug. The heat on this beach is a real killer."

Jericho played every bit as hard as he worked, and for the rest of the afternoon he led Sam and me through every game he could devise. Since her best stroke was the dog paddle, she spent a lot of the time perched on his shoulders, laughing her delight as foamy waves eddied around his chest. Finally tiring of the water, we constructed lopsided sand castles, hunted for shells and investigated every sand crab hole within a hundred-yard radius of the blanket, and when the light began to fade, we gathered driftwood and started a fire. All things considered, I was happier than I'd ever been in my entire life.

"If I eat another bite, I'll bust my bikini," I sighed, licking the stickiness of a toasted marshmallow off my fingers.

Jericho arranged his features into an exaggerated leer. "In that case, you're more than welcome to the last hot dog."

"Why do you want her to tear her suit?" Sam mumbled. Her lashes dipped down to brush her cheeks for a long moment, but she resolutely lifted them, as though determined to banish the sandman once and for all. Jericho bundled her in his fleecy sweatshirt, then settled down by the fire with her on his lap. "Wanna hear the story about the munchkin who asked too many questions?" he queried, hugging her.

"Uh-uh. Sing the 'Get Around' song again."

He obligingly launched into an off-key rendition of a Beach Boys classic, softening and slowing the chorus as her head nodded to rest against his chest.

To my mind, the juxtaposition of his protectiveness and her trusting fragility was far more appealing than any of Raphael's Madonna compositions. Promising myself a future photo essay on the man-child connection, I sighed and stretched out on the blanket. The only thing missing was Alison.

The stars overhead resembled pearls scattered across a background of lush, peacock velvet, and the sea-scented breeze was underscored with the subtle breath of oleander. Although twilight was cooling the air, the sand still held the heat of the sun; I trailed my fingers through its comfort, soothed by Jericho's unorthodox lullaby and the swish of the incoming tide.

MY EYELIDS FELT AS THOUGH they had been glued together. When I finally forced them to open a crack, I was in the half-world between sleeping and waking, a curious limbo where a residue of dream images blunted the edges of reality. The atmosphere of my nightmare clung to me. The air seemed stripped of oxygen, stagnant with the overpowering odor of roses, and just beyond the dying embers of the fire, gossamer streaks of scarlet, emerald and amethyst intertwined, swirling together in a macabre dance that was paced by the ragged dissonance of my own heartbeat.

"I'm the one you want—let them go," I moaned.

The gentle hand that brushed the hair back from my forehead was solid, alive, the only warmth left in my universe.

"Nothing's going to hurt you, Rachel. You're only having a bad dream."

"Jericho?"

"Right here, love."

I clung to his fingers until the trio of rainbow shadows retreated into nothingness, then hastily hoisted myself to a sitting position. "Where's Sam?" A tear dribbled down the side of my face, but I was shaking too hard to do much about it.

He lightly whisked it away with the ball of his thumb. "I put her to bed about an hour ago. Before she went to sleep, she made me sing another verse of the 'Get Around' song to scare off any hobgoblins that might be lurking in the closet." He pulled me closer. "But in your case, I'd prescribe a hug."

Desperately needing the sanctuary he offered, I clasped my arms around his shoulders, resting my head against his chest. The thatch of curls that tickled my cheek were every bit as luxurious to the touch as I'd imagined them to be. "Not long ago, Sam was too afraid to sleep alone," I murmured.

He massaged my back, gently kneading the tension from my muscles. "You kept calling Vernon Avant in your sleep. Would you like to tell me about him?" he queried when my trembling started to subside.

Pulling away, I clasped my fingers tightly together and dropped them into my lap. Though I couldn't pin the name on anyone, it stood to reason it belonged to one of the actors in my childhood creep show. I'd never told another living soul the content of my recurring nightmare, but all at once, the details of the scene I'd seen a thousand times in my head came pouring out. It was only when I was nearing the end that the uniqueness of the latest version became clear to me.

"This time the child climbed up on the throne and went to sleep, and she was Sam, not me—I was floating somewhere near the ceiling. The ghosts started toward her and I tried to scream so she would wake up and run, but I couldn't make a sound, couldn't even move. There was blood...so much blood...and hundreds of crimson roses on the floor. When I looked down at the prisoner they had abandoned, it wasn't a man, at all, it was Alison."

"It wasn't real," Jericho interrupted, cradling my face between his hands. "When did you start having these nightmares?"

"I can't remember. It seems like they've always been there." The mere act of naming my fears weakened their hold on me, and his steadiness restored my precarious balance. "They came much less frequently after Mama and I moved to Tucson. I guess coming home made them kick in again."

He lightly stroked my forehead and the line of my cheek. "I can only imagine what all this is costing you, and I hope to hell the worst is over. If it's not, though, I'll be right beside you. Not that I think you can't handle it alone, but because I may have to borrow a little of your courage and grace to help me through."

The realization that I loved this man came to me clear and true. It had no beginning, middle or end, and I would travel its circle for all the days of my life. He lowered his mouth to mine, his lips and tongue demanding nothing more than entry but relinquishing all of their sweetness.

In spite of the perfection of the moment, or perhaps because of it, I couldn't let myself respond. I was centered in the very small eye of a very large hurricane, and I was afraid that the slightest movement would send me spiraling out of control.

Apparently mistaking my immobility for apathy, Jericho discontinued the kiss. Without apology, he laid my cover-up around my shoulders, then slipped on his sweatshirt. "Run on inside, so you won't catch cold," was his soft directive.

I rose to my feet, wishing I had enough guts to tell him how I felt. "Aren't you coming with me?"

His mouth twisted in a wry grin. "I'll be along as soon as the fire's out."

As I turned to trudge toward the villa, the headlights of the compact cut a bright swath across my path. The car peeled in at an imprudent speed, missing the rear end of Jericho's car by inches as it screeched to a rubber-burning halt in the driveway. It was an irresponsible performance even for Maggie.

"Something's wrong," I called over my shoulder, taking off at a dead run.

He caught up in a couple of strides. Just as we reached the Nissan, Maggie climbed out, clutching her purse to her bosom. Her glasses were askew and her stance was wobbly.

"Are you okay?" I slipped my arm around her waist.

"Fine—no thanks to that man who tried to run me off the road," she snapped, leaning heavily on me as we walked across the patio.

Jericho got his medical bag from his car, then followed us into the living room.

I settled Maggie on the couch. "Okay, tell us what happened," I said firmly.

"There wasn't much to it. I was about a mile from here when I noticed that a white panel truck was following me. The driver honked his horn and I thought he was signaling to pass, but then he speeded up and rear-ended me." She gingerly rubbed her neck. As Jericho approached with his stethoscope, she waved him off with an irritable "Put that thing back in your satchel. If I need your services, I'll ask for them. Aside from being spitting mad, there's nothing wrong with me."

"I'm calling the police." I reached for the phone on the end table.

"I didn't get a look at the driver and the license plate was covered with mud. Besides, we've got better things to stew over than the nut who hit me. The Savannah PD faxed Marcus all the information they had on Wallace and Marietta." She plucked her purse from the floor and triumphantly withdrew a manila folder. "I'll go make some sandwiches. We've got a long night ahead." As she rose from the sofa, she clutched her neck again, her mouth twisting in a pained grimace.

"The only place you're going is to bed," Jericho said firmly. "Aspirin should relieve your discomfort, but I'll leave you a light sedative for backup."

She must have been feeling worse than she let on because she headed off to her room without arguing.

"I suspect it's just a mild whiplash," Jericho said, handing me a plastic vial of pills. "Make her comfortable and see that she doesn't move around a lot. I'll be over first thing tomorrow, but if there are any problems tonight, call me."

"Aren't we going to read the Fairfax file?"

"It'll be more efficient to split the work. If you feel up to it, you can finish the prints, and I'll take the autopsy reports back to my place."

It was more a fait accompli than a suggestion. "Sounds logical," I said, matching my tone to his impersonal briskness.

He picked up his satchel and walked halfway to the sliding door before he turned back. "Rachel, I . . ."

Say you want to stay, I coached silently, translating the plea into a hopeful "Yes?"

His mouth thinned to a purposeful line. "I'll see you around nine in the morning."

By the time I checked on Sam and brewed herbal tea, Maggie had already drifted off to sleep, so I took the pot and the cordless phone into my makeshift darkroom and got down to business. The frames I'd shot at the house on Avalon Terrace went to the end of the queue—the last thing I wanted to see at the moment was Wallace Fairfax's body— and I ran the negatives from the "newly exposed" film I'd found in his home studio through the enlarger. That there were only twelve exposures out of the thirty-six that were possible was the first oddity that piqued my interest. One of my mentor's pet peeves had been squandering film. His penchant for conservation had dictated that each shot be carefully planned and executed, which was why, I mused, his pictures lacked spontaneity.

The dozen photographs that comprised his last work—a sequence that had been taken inside his place of business—were so blurred and haphazardly composed that they could've passed for the work of a neophyte Shutterbug. Technical flaws notwithstanding, they held an intense urgency that compelled my attention.

After hanging the prints to dry on a line I'd stretched the length of my work space, I stood back to study them. It took fifteen minutes and two cups of tea for me to notice a curious anomaly. The last three were crisp shots of the wall beside Wallace's desk, a step-wise succession homing in on the portrait of his wife. Armed with the suspicion that I was onto something, I went back to number one and worked forward again. The progression of photos mimicked the path I'd taken the day I'd visited Icons Unlimited.

"So what?" I asked myself aloud. The conclusion that Wallace had meant to lead me to Marietta was a non sequitur. There was no possible way he could have known or even guessed that I would develop that roll of film. Still, much of what had happened to me since I'd returned to Magnolia Grove was equally improbable—finding the purple bicycle, for example, and literally running into Alison's long-lost brother in the shopping center parking lot.

My immediate intention was to report the discovery to Jericho. The cordless phone I'd stationed on the vanity began to ring even as I reached for it.

"You do have the family ESP. I was just thinking about you," I answered.

"Somehow that doesn't surprise me, Mrs. McKinnon."

The man on the other end of the line was definitely not the Jericho Quaid I knew and loved. "Sorry, I was expecting another call. How may I help you?"

"By packing up that brat and going back where you came from." His voice was a nasty rasp, as grating as the scrape of fingernails across a chalkboard.

I swallowed hard. "Who is this?"

A pause, then a wheezy chuckle. "Just think of me as your worst nightmare. The love tap your car got tonight was just a warning, and I promise that you'll be very, very sorry if you don't take it."

There was a sharp click and the line went dead.

Chapter Nine

In addition to threatening phone calls and spending half the night with photographs of a corpse, my "least favorite" list included physicians who didn't show up on time and the six pounds of naked poultry with which I was now working.

As I dragged a soggy package of livers and gizzards from the latter item's innards, Samantha's response was an apprehensive, "What're you gonna do with that icky stuff?"

"I think I'm supposed to put it in the gravy," I answered, glancing at the clock on the oven panel. It was three-thirty, only half an hour before Caleb Soames was due to arrive, and with Maggie barely able to move her head, my Mission Impossible was to put together a presentable dinner.

"Oooo-yuck—I'm not gonna eat it."

"Neither am I," I muttered, dropping the giblets into the disposal. A quick peek in the oven showed me a pineapple cake whose top hadn't browned despite two hours of baking. After switching the thermostat to broil, I found a butcher knife and began sawing the bird into microwavable hunks.

"What's for dinner, chicken à la Lizzie Borden?" Jericho teased from the doorway. This time he'd come equipped with a gold florist's box and a drugstore shopping bag.

"If I'd wanted a food critique, I would have invited Phyllis Richmond," I grumped, giving the unoffending carcass another whack. "You're six-and-a-half hours late."

The complaint didn't appear to faze him in the least. "I just got back from a meeting with the administrator of the Willow View nursing home in Florence. Where's Maggie?"

"She lying down so her neck will feel better by dinner-time," Sam answered, bounding across the kitchen to plaster herself around his kneecaps. "Are those more presents, D.J.?"

He relinquished the bag with a flourish. "Go give Maggie the Barbie doll and you take the neck brace and the mystery novel. Of course, I expect she might switch with you if you beg hard enough."

"You're so silly," she giggled, pelting off with the loot.

"Wash up while you're upstairs. Mr. Soames will be here soon," I called after her.

Jericho sauntered over to relieve me of the butcher knife before he handed me the florist box. It contained a dozen long-stemmed red roses.

I couldn't decide whether the man hadn't been listening when I'd told him about the flowers on the floor in my nightmares or if he had a perverted sense of humor. In either case, what I perceived as blatant insensitivity prompted my sarcastic, "You really shouldn't have bothered."

"I didn't. The delivery man pulled up out front at the same time I did, so I thought I'd save him a few steps." His expression was troubled. "Who are they from?"

Feeling like an absolute fool for making the hasty assumption, I snatched the envelope from the box and ripped it open.

The enclosed card read

Gather ye Rosebuds while ye may,
Old Time is still a-flying.
And this same flower that smiles today,
Tomorrow will be dying

My knees wobbled, and as I leaned on the counter to steady myself, my hand hit the box of flowers and sent it spinning to the floor. Strewn across the white ceramic tile, the roses resembled splatters of fresh blood.

Jericho touched my arm, his eyes bright with concern. "What is it, Rachel? Who sent them?"

"General Springfield. He's sorry for the way he behaved," I quickly improvised, crumpling the note into a ball and shoving it in my pocket.

The lion's share of my rationale for the lie was that I didn't want to worry him, but submerged beneath it was a reluctance to depend on anyone's support but my own. Scooping up the flowers, I unceremoniously dumped them in the trash can. As much as I hated touching the things, the uncomplicated activity did give me a chance to regain my composure.

He raised a quizzical eyebrow. "I take it you aren't accepting Clayton's apology."

"Not today," I said grimly, reaching for my knife.

"Before you start torturing that poor bird again, I want to give you your present." Reaching into his shirt pocket, he retrieved a dented half-dollar suspended from a chain. He fastened the makeshift medallion around my neck. "It's a multipurpose magic charm, absolutely guaranteed to chase away things that go bump in the night. It also removes evil spells, changes bill collectors into frogs and deflects switchblades. I can personally vouch for that last one because when I was sixteen, it saved my life during a turf rumble in the Bronx."

My jaw sagged. "You belonged to a New York street gang?"

"Among other things. One day when we have nothing better to do, I'll tell you all the sordid details."

I felt protected with the weight of the coin against my chest, but for me, its magic came from the fact that it was a gift from Jericho. "Where did you get it?"

"Alison gave it to me as a keepsake the day the people from the adoption agency took her away." Eyes shadowed, he picked up the knife and began surgically dissecting the remainder of the chicken. "You don't mind if I add a few touches to your Lizzie Borden recipe, do you?"

"Mind? If you can produce an edible meal, I'll be your slave forever—or at least until next week," I sighed gratefully. I gathered from the sudden shift in subjects that he'd rather not relive the separation from Alison. Perching on the stool, I propped my elbows on the counter and moved on to neutral ground. "What did you find out in Florence?"

"That Mr. Soames was right on target when he said Marietta Fairfax was once a patient at Willow View. She stayed there for approximately six months...." He stopped to sniff the air suspiciously. "What's burning?"

"My pineapple cake," I squawked.

The next minute was an out-take from a Laurel and Hardy movie. When I hopped off the stool, my toe caught on a rung and I belly flopped onto the floor. Meanwhile, Jericho yanked open the oven and the plume of inky smoke that billowed out set off the detector in the ceiling. Wheezing both from the fumes and my impact with the tile, I hauled myself to my feet and staggered across the kitchen, my one aim to get some fresh air circulating. He must have had a similar goal because we bumped into each other at the exit. Both of us were struggling for control of the knob, but I overpowered him and jerked open the door.

Caleb Soames stood just outside. "Did I come at a bad time?" he asked mildly, handing me a bottle of wine.

The cough that rose in my throat came out a choked snicker, and it found a companion in Jericho's snort. In two seconds flat, we were hanging on to each other, helpless with mirth. It must have been contagious, because Caleb quickly added his booming bass laugh to the general hilarity.

"What in the name of all that's holy is going on in here?" Maggie snapped, marching in from the hallway.

When I turned, the combination of her best dress, the neck brace and the lone pink roller still poised atop her head set me off again.

Spotting Caleb, she snatched off the curler and ran her fingers through her hair. "Can't turn my back for a single minute," she muttered, moving past Jericho and me to face our guest. "I'm Margaret Peace, Mr. Soames. You'll have to overlook these two. They tend to get into mischief when they're left to their own devices."

"That's Caleb, if you please, ma'am. Don't be too hard on them—children will be children." Instead of shaking the hand she offered, he raised it to his lips in a gallant salute.

As soon as the alarm was silenced and the smoldering remains of my cake disposed of, my partner-in-crime and I were summarily shooed away by a pair of golden oldies who had obviously taken a shine to each other.

"I knew they would hit it off," I told Jericho smugly when we were out of earshot of the kitchen.

"Your matchmaking instincts are impeccable. That's a lot more than I can say for your culinary skills," he teased.

As he wiped a smudge from my cheek, Samantha bounced down the stairs to join us. "I smell smoke. Did you ruin dinner, Cricket?" Before I could answer, she turned to her uncle. "She burns up stuff all the time."

"Don't complain. If she hadn't torched the dessert, we would've had to eat it."

I aimed a playful punch at his midsection and tweaked her nose. "I've got better things to do than listen to your insults, sawbones. While I'm freshening up, why don't you introduce the munchkin to Caleb?"

He hoisted Sam onto his shoulder, whistling her favorite "Get Around" song as he transported her along the hallway.

In less than thirty minutes, the kitchen collaborators produced a meal that wouldn't have shamed Julia Child, and as we took our places around the glass table in the dining alcove, it quickly became apparent that Caleb Soames had come prepared to entertain Samantha. While his Disney imitations sent her into giggles, the chief material in his act, the adventures of two little girls for whom he had built a treehouse, held her spellbound. Me, too, for that matter. I'd forgotten most of the mischief Alison and I had devised.

By the end of dinner he had thoroughly aired our checkered childhood careers, so he moved on to his grand finale, an adroit slight-of-hand exhibition. Intoning nonsense syllables as he passed presumably empty fingers through the space behind Sam's ear, he produced a smooth, brown, oval stone. "You're now the proud owner of a magic pigwidgeon rock."

Her mouth rounded into an enthralled O. "What does it do?"

"It turns bad things that happen to you into good things," I interjected, drawing on the spiel I'd heard when I was her age. "It doesn't always work right away—sometimes it takes years and years—but if you believe in the magic and do the best you can to help it along, your troubles are bound to disappear."

Caleb rewarded my presentation with an approving nod. "You've got a good memory, child. Is the one I gave you still on the job?"

"More or less, although its powers seems to require a lot more nudging these days," I said, thinking of my inability to find Alison.

"Be right back. I gotta put my pigwidgeon in the 'posit box where it'll be safe." As Samantha bounced out of her seat, the telephone rang. She veered toward the extension. "I'll answer it, Cricket."

"No!" My cry was far sharper than I'd intended. Pushing back my chair, I added a more moderate, "I'll take it in the kitchen. We all need more coffee and there's no sense in making two trips."

Conscious of an exchange of curious gazes around the table, I covered the distance to the communications console in the next room at an unhurried walk. My hand shook as I snatched the receiver from its cradle. "Hello."

"Rachel, it's Meredith Fisher." I sagged against the counter in relief, but the editor's next words snapped me right back to attention. "That call you warned me to expect finally came. A Mr. Winters from the bank in Magnolia Grove wanted verification of your employment with *Southern Style*. He also asked a lot of questions about the little girl. He claimed to be processing your application for a real estate loan."

I gritted my teeth against a rising disgust. "If the whole damned town were on sale for a dime, I wouldn't buy it. What did you tell him?"

"I fed him the line you gave me." There was a short pause. "Are you in trouble?"

"Nothing I can't handle. Thanks for the cover. It's good for dinner at the Watergate Terrace when I get back."

As I cradled the receiver, Jericho came through the archway with a load of dishes. "Was that something I should know about?" he asked casually.

"A call from the magazine. I'll fill you in later."

Retrieving a full carafe from the coffeemaker, I detoured to the refrigerator for a fresh supply of cream and was heading toward the door when the phone rang again.

Intent on not slopping hot decaf on the floor, I tossed Jericho an absent "Get that for me, will you?" The request barely passed my lips before I realized it was a mistake. Setting the coffee and cream on the counter, I hugged my arms across my chest and prayed for a wrong number.

"Jericho Quaid, here."

He had his back to me, and though I couldn't see his expression, I could tell by the rigid set of his shoulders and the way his left hand tightened into a fist that he was far from pleased with what he was hearing. After what seemed like ages, he slammed down the receiver so hard that a chunk of plastic flew off the earpiece.

"The guy on the other end of the line listed some very creative games he intended to play with you if I didn't convince you to leave town. He mentioned that he'd called last night and also wanted to know if you got the flowers he sent. Why did you lie to me?" His voice was flat, almost gentle, but his face was contorted with anger.

Although I couldn't be sure whether his wrath was directed at me or the anonymous caller, I gauged it to be fifty-fifty. Unable to bear the disappointment and hurt in his eyes, I dropped my eyes to the floor. "I don't want this to spoil Caleb's afternoon. Can we talk about it when he leaves?"

"In depth and at great length." Spinning on his heel, he strode back into the dining area.

While I couldn't really fault him for his anger, the prospect of having to deal with it added a few more pounds to the already weighty load I carried. But the anonymous caller was chief among my worries at the moment, and the thought of his lurking in the vicinity made me long for the security of my Georgetown row house. Not about to let the creep reach out and touch me again, I took the phone off the hook, then picked up the coffeepot.

When I returned to the table, Maggie and Jericho were discussing the relative merits of Ella Fitzgerald and Sarah Vaughan, while Caleb cautiously teased the lock on the 'posit box with the point of a penknife.

"I lost the key," Samantha explained to me, as the hasp popped open. "I've got lots of neat stuff, Mr. Caleb. Do you want to look at everything?"

Acknowledging her invitation with a smile, he raised the lid of the treasure trove. "This is a might fine collection. It puts me in mind of the one your mother used to have....." Soames stopped abruptly, his congenial expression freezing to austere. He fished the diamond-encrusted watch fob from the box. "How did you come by this, child?"

In the press of events, I'd completely forgotten Sam had the thing, but the severity of Caleb's tone brought back the uneasiness I'd experienced when I'd first seen it. His taut question also silenced the jazz conversation on the other side of the table.

Eyes startled, Sam took a step backward. "I didn't steal it."

Caleb's face gentled. "I wasn't accusing you, honey. Where did you find it?"

"In my bed."

"Here in this house?"

"She had it with her when she came to Washington." Maggie modified the explanation.

Jericho left his seat to stand beside his niece, the attitude of his body protective. "What's the big deal about that piece of junk jewelry, Mr. Soames?"

"For openers, it's worth about ten grand, give or take a few coins, and that only includes the cost of the gold and gems. In terms of historical value, though, it easily hits six figures. This fob and four more exactly like it were made by Charles Lewis Tiffany just before the Civil War. They were commissioned by the Society of the First Horseman."

"S'cuse me. It's almost time for the Ninja Turtles cartoon show," Sam mumbled, poised for a strategic retreat.

Jericho caught her on the fly and, kneeling, turned her to face him. "It's very important that you tell us everything you know. When did you find it?"

"When I was five." Obviously anxious, she twisted the front of her T-shirt between her fingers. "A man came to see Mommy after my birthday party. I was asleep, but he started talking real loud and woke me up."

"Do you remember what he said?" I prompted.

"Not exactly. It was something about my daddy. After he stopped yelling, he came in my room and stood beside my bed for a long time. I was scared, so I closed my eyes tight and pretended I was asleep. Can I go watch TV now?"

"You still haven't told us how you found the watch fob, sugarplum," Maggie reminded her gently.

Sam heaved a gusty sigh. "That mean man musta dropped it while he was watching me, because when I got up for breakfast, it fell out of my blanket. Mommy took it away from me and threw it in the trash, but I got it out again when she wasn't looking," she admitted. "Please don't say anything about it when she gets back, Uncle D.J. I don't want her to be mad at me."

"She won't be mad. She'll be proud of you for telling the truth." He reinforced the assurance with a hug. "Run along to your television program, doodlebug. The third degree is over."

She collected her 'posit box, glancing wistfully at the glittering ornament Caleb had laid on the table.

"I'm afraid you won't be able to keep it, Samantha," our guest informed her kindly, patting her shoulder.

"That's okay. I like my new rock better, anyway."

As Sam headed off to her Turtles, Maggie offered a thoughtful theory. "It's my guess that Alison's late-night visitor is the man who's been chasing her for the past six years. Since we've already established that he's one of CANTER's vice presidents, we can use that extravagant knickknack he dropped to pick him out of the crowd. Who are the members of that horse club, Caleb?"

"The society is disbanded now, but when it was in full swing, any man who laid legitimate claim to Hamilton, Ogletharpe, Rochambeau, Springfield or Endicott blood could participate. The officers could only be direct descendants of the original five founders of the society, though, and they were the holders of the watch fobs. Before I go any further, I'd be obliged if someone told me a bit more about what's going on. I might be more help to you if I knew all the facts," he observed, drawing a cigar from the inside pocket of his jacket.

Maggie frowned instant disapproval. "Do you plan to light that thing in here?"

From years back, I knew that Soames and his Corona weren't easily parted. Sensing a miniconfrontation in the offing, I rose from my seat. "The chairs on the patio are much more comfortable than these, so let's move this conversation outside."

"Good idea. Maggie, why don't you and Caleb go out and get settled. You can start his update, while Rachel and I break out the wine," Jericho chimed in, snagging my arm to force-march me into the kitchen. We'd scarcely gotten through the archway when he turned me around with a tight-lipped, "Why didn't you tell me about the watch fob?"

"Because I didn't think it was relevant. This is the first I've heard of the Society of the First Horseman, and there's no way I could have identified it, much less connected it to Alison's disappearance," I snapped, jerking from his grasp.

When I started toward the wine bottle on the counter, he sidestepped to block my path. "I'll give you that one, but besides the phone calls and the note that came with the roses, if there's anything else you've either misrepresented or conveniently forgotten to mention, you'd better tell me now. We're supposed to be a team."

"Really? Then why did you go shilly-shallying off to Florence without so much as a by-your-leave? This may not have occurred to you, but if I'd gone along I might've been able to ask the people at Willow View some reasonably pertinent questions. I knew Marietta Fairfax as a living, breathing human being, not a name on a medical chart."

"I didn't ask you to go with me because I figured Maggie wouldn't be in any shape to baby-sit Sam." Although he appeared apologetic, contrition didn't alter the stubborn set of his jaw. "You intentionally cut me out of the loop, though. If we're going to work together, you've got to trust me."

"I only met you a few days ago, and the fact that—" I caught the words "I love you" just in the nick of time "—you happen to be Alison's brother doesn't necessarily mean that you're dependable. You don't demand confidence, doctor, and a winning personality and gorgeous eyes can't buy it, either. If you want my trust, you'll have to earn it, and that means showing up when you're supposed to, or at least calling—"

He pressed his fingers to my lips, seriously hampering my grand finale. "You're right, you win, and I apologize," he conceded sheepishly. "You're really awesome when you're angry. You look—"

"Please spare me the macho clichés," I snapped, swatting his hand away.

"Like a cat whose tail is plugged into a light socket."

I've always been a sucker for a fast punch line, and the impish smile that lifted his mouth was contagious. "Well, at least you're creative," I grumbled, working hard to suppress a chuckle.

He stuck out his hand. "Friends?"

After one final glare, I abandoned my anger. "Friends."

I clasped his fingers, and a current flowed between us. Not the electric, prickly-heat variety usually touted in paperback novels, but an unbroken stream that could carry us past forever, if we let it.

On our way back to the patio, I retrieved the think tank's brochure and handed Caleb a glass of wine. "I'll crosscheck the CANTER organizational chart while you give us the names of the current watch fob owners."

He rubbed his chin thoughtfully. "Albert Hamilton, but we can rule him out right from the jump. I guarantee you he still has his, and he hasn't been out of the house in recent memory. Number two is Clayton Springfield. He was chairman of CANTER's board of directors four or five years ago, but after his term was over he severed most of his ties to the foundation, so it's unlikely that he'd be driving one of the HORSE cars. Winstead Ogletharpe has a fob and

so does Barrett Endicott. There are a bunch of Rochambeau children, but I don't rightly remember which one's first
in the line of succession."

"Ogletharpe and Endicott are vice presidents, and so is a
Kyle Rochambeau," I said, adding my two cents' worth.

Jericho's eyes glinted with elation. "Now we're getting
somewhere. From what you know about them, Caleb, which
one of the trio should be put at the top of our suspect list?"

"That's a hard call to make. Winstead Ogletharpe is a
good thirty years older than the others, and he's mean as a
scalded skunk, but not so smart by half—witness the fact
that he's only an honorary CANTER vice president and his
generational peers among the five families are all members
of the board of directors. Kyle Rochambeau would do in his
own mother for the gold in her teeth, but he's a lot more interested in hunting big game than women. And Barrett Endicott is as sneaky as he is peculiar. When Barrett was
growing up, one rumor circulating below stairs was that he
had a secret hideaway somewhere in his suite. But who
knows? Nasty things had a habit of happening to servants
who crossed B.E.-III."

"All things considered, my money's on the weirdo,"
Maggie said briskly. "Now that that's settled, this might be
a good time for you to give us the background on the society, Caleb."

"In the beginning it was a social club—more or less. The
five charter members were all married to well-bred southern belles who held rather circumscribed views on romance, so when the boys wanted—excuse me, ladies—some
extracurricular activity, they'd slip into their ceremonial
robes, hop on their stallions and round themselves up a few
comely partners. If the girls required forcible persuasion,
the Horsemen were only too happy to oblige," he said, fingering his still unlit cigar wistfully.

Maggie plucked it from his hand and banished it to the
end table on her side of the wicker loveseat. "If I remember Revelations correctly, the First Horseman of the Apoc-
alypse was Conquest. I assume that's how they decided on
the name of their little fraternity."

"I guess it was a natural, since HORSE is an acronym for their surnames," I interjected. "Between listening to my fifth-grade history teacher and the sewing circle members who used to meet at the parsonage, I had picked up a lot of juicy gossip about Magnolia Grove's rich folk, but I never heard so much as a whisper about the society."

Caleb shrugged. "As far as I know, there hasn't been an official meeting since way before I was born. During the early fifties, the college crowd tried to stage a revival, but it only amounted to a drunken drive through the shantytown. It ended in the accident that crippled Albert Hamilton. I guess they lost their taste for carousing after that."

"Well, one of them is still in the business of terrorizing women," Jericho said. Rising abruptly from his seat, he began to pace a restless path back and forth across the flagstones.

"Where does CANTER fit into the picture, Caleb?" Maggie interjected.

"Mostly as a heavy-duty tax shelter for the five families. Plus, many an election—local, state and national—has been influenced either by the consortium's financial contributions or a creative bit of CANTER arm-twisting in the right places. Those bad boys have an exceedingly long reach. Which is precisely why you and Rachel should take Samantha back to Washington on the next plane out," Caleb said. He got up and walked around the loveseat to reclaim his cigar, finishing, "From what I know now, I'd say you all never should have come down here in the first place."

Although I'd engaged in the same twenty-twenty hindsight less than half an hour before, I popped from my chair with the firm assertion, "I'm not leaving this place without Alison, but I do think Maggie and Sam should go home."

"If you're all through talking about me as though I'm too senile to make my own decisions, sit down and shut up until I have my say," the elder subject in question commanded, glaring at the three of us. When her conditions were met, she laid out her case. "We're all in agreement that we need to get our baby out of harm's way, and I'm the logical one to take care of her, but Rachel is as dear to me as my own daughter, and I'm not about to leave her to the tender mercies of some degenerate. Sam and I can go to Charleston. I'm sure Frank and Bertie won't mind us staying at their house while they're on vacation.''

Soames shook his head. ''Won't do for the two of you to be alone. As soon as you can pack your things, I'm taking you to a place where Samantha will have space to run and other young'uns to play with.''

''Where's that?'' I queried.

''The less you know, the better. I'll act as middleman to carry messages back and forth. It'll be safer for Maggie not to call here, because the phone may be bugged.''

As we were planning the details of the move, it dawned on me that although I'd long since lost my pigwidgeon rock, it had left its magic behind. Imminent danger had bonded me and three people I loved dearly into a family.

IT WAS WELL AFTER DARK when Caleb's '79 Buick carried Maggie, Samantha and the five cats away to parts unknown. A portion of the package deal we worked out was that Jericho would move into the cottage with me, a proviso with which I wasn't altogether comfortable. Small touches to emphasize a point of discussion and ingenuous kisses that conveyed his support came as natural to him as breathing. While I didn't plan to come unraveled each time he tucked a stray curl behind my ear or tweaked my nose, the cumulative effect was bound to put a strain on my hormones. And if anything, I found the metaphysical element more problematic than the physical—the prospect of twenty-four-hour proximity to a man who was wired into my emotions was to say the least, disconcerting.

While he stashed the few belongings he had retrieved from home in the downstairs bedroom that had been Maggie's, I wandered around the living room, aimlessly plumping sofa pillows and realigning lamps. When I stooped to pluck a broken crayon from the carpet, I was hit with a wave of depression. In two short weeks, I'd gone from not knowing what to do with Samantha to wondering what I would do without her.

"What you're feeling is called the 'empty nest' syndrome. One of its early symptoms is obsessive tidiness." Jericho's diagnosis straightened me up in a hurry. He moved to lay an arm across my shoulders. "Let's get to work before—God forbid—you're overpowered by an urge to bake chocolate-chip cookies," he teased.

"Not to worry. Maggie wouldn't leave until I'd sworn I'd stay out of the kitchen." I eased away from the contact under pretext of fetching the sheaf of photographs I'd placed on the credenza. "Your choice—we can start with these or you can tell me about the trip to Florence."

Jericho sagged down on the couch and propped his feet on the coffee table, his expression gloomy. "Perhaps we should let the Fairfaxes rest in peace. I know you don't think Wallace killed Marietta, but even if we could prove he was innocent, it wouldn't do either of them any good. And since Sam said the man who came to D.C. was yelling about her father, there's probably a larger payoff in going to Stanhope College to investigate Noah Girard's suicide than in fooling around with Wallace's."

"There's a possibility that Alison's husband didn't kill himself," I corrected him, struck by the eerie concurrence of self-destruction. "And I believe foul play could've been involved in Wallace's death, too. What if the Horseman murdered them both?"

Jericho's lips pursed in amusement. "That scenario has way too many holes. For example, why didn't he do Alison in when he found her in D.C.? And why would he have gone to the trouble of smothering Marietta?"

Without an answer for either question, I resorted to a stubborn "I still think there's a connection." To shore up the argument, I trotted out the twelve photos of Icons' interior along with my theory that Wallace had left them as a message for me. "Sheriff Tillman must have a key to the place. Can you persuade him to let us in?"

"I'd have to do too much explaining. Plus, I'm not sure we can trust him since his job depends on the goodwill of the HORSE crowd." His feet hit the floor and he hauled himself from the couch. He grinned. "Locks are no problem, though. I've never met one I couldn't pick. Go slip into something black and slinky. We're going to check out your hypothesis."

Our conversation was sparse during the drive into the business district, partially due to my preoccupation with my upcoming debut as a major felon, but mostly because we couldn't make ourselves heard over the assorted groans, rattles and whines coming from the beetle's engine. My eardrums were grateful when Jericho finally pulled into a space on a deserted back street that ran parallel to Plantation. The few buildings that hadn't been razed were abandoned. The lower-class district was obviously undergoing a transition to upscale commercial.

"Icons Unlimited is a block over. Why are we parking here?" I climbed out of the car with a purseload of assorted equipment we might need.

"Because we're being sneaky. We're cat burglars, remember?" He tucked his hand in the crook of my elbow, drawing me into an alley beside a boarded-up laundromat.

As we passed a broken window set low in the side of the building, I peered warily into the blackness behind it, clutching the shoulder strap of my purse and crowding closer to Jericho. "What do we do if someone comes while you're picking the lock?"

"Improvise." He gave my arm a tiny shake. "Loosen up. Part of the reason we're doing this is to clear Wallace's name, and if you're right about the photographs, he practically invited you to search Icons."

The rationale was thin, but it held enough truth to soothe my conscience. I tried to keep my mind off the possibility of a jail term by talking. "Besides the fact that Marietta was a patient at Willow View, did you pick up any tidbits in Florence that might help us?"

"A few. The Fairfaxs's medical insurance didn't cover long-term residential care, and when the bill was four months overdue, Arlo Buchman, the nursing home administrator, served notice that Marietta would have to be placed in a state institution. But just before the deadline, Wallace paid the bill in full and had her transported to Ocean Manor. And this is the kicker—Buchman said that the monthly fee at the home in Savannah is triple the cost of Willow View."

"I'm not up on medical ethics, but I thought patients' files were supposed to be confidential. How did you get him to give so much financial information?"

"I'm Magnolia Grove's official coroner, remember? Either the guys in Savannah don't know about Willow View or they haven't gotten around to checking it out, so when I told Buchman I was investigating a murder-suicide, I couldn't shut him up."

By now, we had reached the cross alley that ran behind Icons. To my relief, no people were in evidence and there was enough light coming from floodlights anchored on the corner of each building for us to see what we were doing. When we got to the back entrance of the studio, Jericho retrieved a credit card from his wallet and slipped it into the crack between the door and the jamb.

I kept an eye peeled for trouble. "Wallace probably sold his old house in order to get the money. I'm sure he wanted Marietta to have the best of care."

"If that were the case, he would have left her where she was. Willow View has a crackerjack rehab program for patients who've been comatose. On the flip side, Ocean Manor is little more than a luxurious warehousing facility." He jiggled the plastic card impatiently and with little discernible result.

"Why don't you use the long metal thingy we brought?" I queried impatiently.

"This should do the trick," he assured me. "According to the chart in the file Maggie brought us, Marietta was given daily doses of a tranquilizer. In spite of the medication, she was making some progress in the weeks before she died."

"Let me get this straight. Are you saying Wallace didn't want her to get well?"

"I'm afraid that's the way it looks. The Savannah police have listed her death as first-degree homicide, mainly because three months ago, her husband took out a hefty insurance policy on her life."

I had been very hard-pressed to accept the idea that Wallace might have killed Marietta to end her misery, but a cold-blooded murder for profit was totally unthinkable. I was about to express that opinion in no uncertain terms when a police patrol car turned the corner at the end of the alley. My mouth dropped open, but before I could get out a warning, the vehicle moved toward us with its red lights flashing.

Chapter Ten

In a lightning-quick move, Jericho dropped the credit card in my bag and spun me to face him. At the same instant his left arm squeezed my shoulders, his right traversed my rear, compacting my thighs against his. Just before his lips clamped down on mine, he whispered a hoarse "Pretend to enjoy this."

Our embrace in the treehouse had been poetry, a delicate counterpoint of comfort and discovery, and his caresses on the beach read like a lyrical thesis on equanimity. But this kiss was unadulterated purple-prose lust. Forcing my mouth open, his tongue drove deep, challenging mine to a duel in which quarter would neither be asked nor given. I was defending my position admirably when he launched a sneak attack, tugging my blouse free to slide his hand beneath. His fingers kneaded the small of my back, then insinuating themselves under my waistband.

The show had to go on, so in the best tradition of the theater, I dug my nails into his biceps and did my level best to fuse us into a single body. Along about then, it came to me that if this were just an act, he most certainly deserved an Academy award for special effects. A small fragment of my consciousness wondered if our steamy cover would fool the cop in the cruiser; the remainder was too busy enjoying the sensations to give a damn.

"Break it up, you two! I don't want to have to call out the fire department." Tillman's directive cut through the pyrotechnics. My eyes popped open to stare directly into the heart of a spotlight. Jericho reluctantly released his grip and stepped in front of me, partially shielding me from view.

"How's it goin', Sheriff? Nice weather we're havin'," he offered in a lazy drawl.

The officer cackled. "The humidity's not bad, but the temperature out here is a real killer. Y'all do show up together in the strangest places."

I tucked in my shirttail, then moved out of Jericho's shadow. "We went down to the pier to look at the view, and we thought we'd take a shortcut back to Plantation," I stammered.

"Evenin', Miz McKinnon." The disembodied voice filtering through the glare held a trace of surprise. "I've been wondering why I haven't heard from you. I guess you've been too busy to develop those photographs."

From the heat in my face, I could tell that my skin was as red as it could get without bleeding. "I'll deliver them to you tomorrow," I assured him with all the dignity I could scrape together, which was precious little.

"I'd appreciate it. If you're planning on going to the service, you can drop them off at the office afterward."

"What service?" Jericho queried.

"Ol' Wally's being funeralized at eleven tomorrow morning at Friendship Methodist. He didn't have any relatives, and considering the murder and all, I don't expect many of his friends will show up. Since you're the town coroner, it might be proper for you to put in an appearance." The lawman turned off his warning lights, and as he slowly rolled away, called back a knowing "Y'all have a nice night, hear?"

I sagged against the brick wall, every joint in my lower extremities as spongy as angel food. It was hard to tell whether the condition stemmed more from Tillman's appearance or Jericho's creative improvisation. "Do you realize that by this time tomorrow, it'll be all over town that we were making out in an alley?"

"Beats being busted for breaking and entering." A devilish grin wafted across his face and he held out his arms. "That was one helluva performance, wicked city woman. How 'bout an encore?"

"Quit fooling around and open the stupid lock," I scolded, peering over my shoulder in case the cruiser made another pass-by. This time Jericho used the metal pick and it worked like a charm. Switching on the small flashlight I had supplied in our stash of equipment, he shoved open the door, and we stepped inside.

"Suppose we set off a burglar alarm?" I whispered apprehensively.

"People in Magnolia Grove don't use security systems. There hasn't been a break-in since I moved here."

"That might not be a useful statistic to bring up at our trial," I muttered as I tailed him along a hallway that eventually led into the main gallery. Beyond the flashlight's narrow reach, the darkness seemed to coalesce into a crouching entity, and the dead silence in the room was nearly as unnerving.

As we moved into the alcove that served as Icons' office, Jericho panned the beam around the walls until it illuminated Marietta's portrait. Her gentle eyes seemed to welcome us. Handing me the light, Jericho lifted the picture from its hook and laid it facedown on the desk.

One corner of the brown paper lining had come loose from the frame, and when he ripped it all the way off, I saw an envelope taped to the foam board underneath.

"Remind me never to doubt one of your theories again." Flashing me a congratulatory smile, he freed the envelope and stuffed it in his pocket. "Let's go over to my place and open it," he said as he rehung the portrait.

The relief I felt when Icons Unlimited's door closed behind us bordered on euphoria, but it changed into apprehension during the short trip to the office. Now that we had the envelope, I wasn't really sure I wanted to know what was inside.

The minute we stepped into Jericho's kitchen, he handed it to me. "Get started without me—I've got to go check the messages on my answering machine. Letitia Ledbetter's twins are due any day now, and she's having a few complications."

"Isn't Dr. Dumont handling your patients?"

"Yes, but he's hard to get hold of after office hours. There's stuff to drink in the fridge—be back in a second."

His estimate missed the mark by at least ten minutes, and while I waited, I straightened the mess of books and newspapers on the table, grumbling to myself about his defection. When he finally reappeared, I was nursing a shot of lemonade and a load of irritation.

"Dumont can't cover my caseload anymore. He says he's sprained his ankle playing golf. I finally got Dr. Ravenel to sub for me, but he can't start until day after tomorrow." He pulled up a chair beside mine, and appropriating my glass, motioned to the sealed envelope on the table in front of me. "Why haven't you opened it?"

"Because we promised to share everything fifty-fifty." Apprehensive of what might be inside, I pushed it toward him. "I did my part by finding it."

"Yeah, but I had to pick the lock."

The sudden tightness that squared his jaw as he tore loose the flap told me he was anxious, too. Withdrawing a rectangle of buff-colored paper, he scanned it, then wordlessly handed it to me.

It was a cashier's check in the sum of $38,068.75, issued by a bank in Columbia, South Carolina, and made payable to Wallace and Marietta Fairfax. A typewritten notation on the memo line in the lower-left corner read "Alison Girard/loan principal plus $13,068.75 in interest." When I flipped it over, I made an equally startling discovery: written above the two endorsements on the back was the instruction "Pay to the order of Rachel Bodine McKinnon and Samantha Girard."

Laying the bank draft carefully on the table, I clasped my hands together so tightly that my fingers went numb. "I don't understand any of this. Supposedly, Alison wouldn't accept help from the Fairfaxes when she was in college, and after her husband's funeral, she left without a word to them. So when did she borrow the money? And why such a large amount?"

Jericho shrugged. "Being on the run with a small child couldn't have been easy. She probably needed a nest egg to tide her over between jobs."

"She always hated the idea of owing money. Only a dire emergency would've made her go into that much debt." I picked up the check and stared at it, hoping for answers but finding more questions, instead. "This is dated the day after Alison called me, and that means when she left Boston, she went directly to Columbia. It doesn't make sense. It would've been simpler for her to buy the check when she came to Magnolia Grove, or better still, stay in hiding and send it to Wallace by registered mail."

"The only reasonable explanation is that she didn't have access to the money until she got to Columbia. If it had been deposited in some type of account, she could have had it transferred to Maine, so it must have been in a safe deposit box," Jericho concluded. Leaning over to commandeer a pad and pencil from the other side of the table, he began scribbling figures. "The original amount of the loan was twenty-five grand. Do you know what the prime interest rate is these days?"

"I don't know what the prime interest rate is, period. Money management isn't my long suit, so you'll have to explain where you're going with this."

Instead of responding, he reached for the newspaper and thumbed through the financial section until he came to a savings and loan advertisement. Muttering "Ten and a quarter," he resumed his mathematic maneuvers, finally circling the last calculation with a force that snapped the lead in his pencil. "Okay, here's the deal: the formula for simple interest is principal multiplied by rate, times the number of years—"

I waved him to silence. "You might as well be speaking in Sanskrit. Just give me the bottom line."

His expression held a curious intensity, a mixture of realization and consternation. "She borrowed the $25,000 from the Fairfaxes five-and-a-half years ago."

Even without his emphasis on the amount and timing, I would have perceived the harrowing conjunction of events. "The mugger didn't steal the money Marietta withdrew from the bank in Charleston. She gave it to Alison," I said dully.

"Sent it," Jericho amended. "It would've been too risky for Alison to come back to South Carolina at that point in time. The way I see it, the assailant's motive for beating Mrs. Fairfax was to get information. He probably knew she was the one person in Magnolia Grove Alison would contact."

"Are you saying that the Horseman—" The sourness that crowded my tonsils prevented me from finishing, and in any case, I already knew the answer. Rising abruptly from my seat, I went to the sink to splash cold water on my face.

By the time the kitchen stopped revolving, Jericho was beside me with a paper towel, dabbing my cheeks. Even at the risk of causing him pain, I had to make one final point. "I can only think of one reason for Wallace to have signed the check over to me and Samantha. Alison must be dead."

"The Quaid EKG system says you're wrong. She's still in my heart, right next to you and Sam and Maggie." He lifted my hand, first kissing its palm, then placing it flat against his chest. "Trust me on this—she's holed up somewhere waiting for the cavalry to arrive."

As much as I wanted to believe him, my own instincts warned that time was running out. "We might be able to pick up a lead at the bank that issued the check."

"That's a good possibility. Day after tomorrow, we'll drive over to Columbia, and while we're there, we can also go to Stanhope and see what we can find out about Noah." He rummaged through a cabinet over the refrigerator, and securing a dusty bottle of champagne, returned to present it to me with a flourish. "Your reward for being the best detective and cat burglar in South Carolina. We'll pick up a triple pepperoni pizza with mushrooms—hold the onions—at Emilio's on our way back to the cottage, and after the bubbly's chilled—"

A summons from the wall phone put the rest of his plan on hold, and from the medicalese he used during the conversation, I could tell the interruption was apt to be permanent.

As he cradled the receiver, I set the champagne on the drain board and pasted on an ersatz smile. "Let me guess— Letitia Ledbetter's water just broke."

He nodded, his expression distracted. "There's no telling how long the delivery might take, and I think you'll be safer here than in the cottage. I'll be back as soon as I can."

"Don't sweat it, I'm used to being on my own." The observation sounded vaguely petulant, so I added a chipper "I still have your credit card, and if I run out of things to do, I can max it out with TV diamondoids."

Granted, the joke was weak, but he appeared too preoccupied to acknowledge even that much. As he strode from the kitchen, I retrieved the check from the table and tucked it into my purse.

"Life goes on, McKinnon," I reminded myself aloud. "With him or without him."

AS IT TURNED OUT, without him was the operative mode for the rest of the night, and hesitant to invade his private domain on the second floor, I spent the balance of the time on the couch in his inner office. Neither Jericho nor Carrie Barstow had shown up by nine in the morning, and since the phone was going berserk and two people were queued up at the front door, I manned the nurse's desk and coped as best I could.

The Ledbetter twins had apparently made quite a production of their debut. The good doctor dragged in a half hour later, stubble-faced and hardly in shape to deal with patients, much less go to Friendship Methodist with me. Before he started to work, I popped into his office to firm up the plans du jour.

"I don't like the thought of you going to the funeral. Besides, we only have one car, and I don't have time to take you back to the cottage to dress," he began without preamble.

"I've already called a taxi. This is something I have to do, Jericho, and no one's going to make a move on me in broad daylight with a church full of witnesses." I handed him the message slips I'd filled out. "Since you don't have office hours this afternoon, you should try to get some sleep when you're finished with the bunch in the waiting room. I'll stop for food on the way back from the funeral. Do you want pizza, deli or Chinese?"

"I'm booked for a luncheon meeting with Whitney Delafield, the city commissioner of health services, and I probably won't be back until after one. When you leave the church, I want you to go straight to the cottage and lock yourself in," he answered, yawning as he absorbed himself in a chart. "Before you go, tell Mr. Crabtree I'm ready for him."

The distracted dismissal didn't thrill me, but with the taxi honking and the funeral looming on the horizon, there wasn't time to brood over it. After the taxi dropped me off at the cottage, I programmed myself into fast forward, dressed, made the return trip to town and pulled into the last available space in the parking lot beside Friendship Methodist Church with sixteen minutes to spare.

Contrary to the prediction of a sparse turnout, a mob jammed the left side of the lawn. In its middle, Sheriff Tillman held sway for the benefit of a television news crew. Since I'd forgotten the pictures, I hastily skirted the crowd to head for the front entrance of the church. From the nervous titters and snippets of gossip I picked up in passing, it was clear that the predominant motivation for attendance was morbid curiosity.

Inside the sanctuary, a scant dozen people—true mourners, judging from their bowed heads and strained expressions—were scattered among the pews. Before I could slip into a seat in the back row, Sleepy Zwisler beckoned me to the center of the church. As I walked reluctantly down the aisle, I noted with no small relief that the bronze casket positioned in front of the chancel rail was closed. The only floral tribute in evidence was a simple spray of white carnations atop its lid.

"Rachel, this is my wife, Daryl Ann," Sleepy said in a stage whisper, stepping aside to admit me to a space next to a very pregnant blonde:

"Pleased to meet you, although I'm sorry it had to be under such sad circumstances," she murmured as I took the seat. Handing me one of the programs she was holding, she confided, "I think it's a real shame that Mr. and Mrs. Fairfax are going to be separated, don't you? My daddy's bookkeeper is about to have a fit, because they had pre-arranged for their plots and everything, and now she'll have to send a refund all the way to Louisiana.''

Not sure how to cope with the disjointed outpouring, I made do with a generic "That's too bad.''

"Daryl Ann's father is the funeral director,'' her husband translated. "You see, Marietta's cousin, Wilbert, claimed her body and took it back to Baton Rouge for burial. He's their only kin, so he'll get all the estate.''

"We hear he's planning to put the house up for sale,'' Daryl Ann joined in. "Since I've been around corpses all my life, it wouldn't really bother me that Wallace's was found in the garage. The property should go for a rock-bottom price, and with our second baby coming and little Zeb needing another operation, it's our chance to own a nice home in a good neighborhood.''

Only one word in the monologue caught my attention. "Operation?'' I repeated it aloud.

"Junior was born with spina bifida,'' Sleepy supplied in an undertone. "He wears leg braces now, but Dr. Quaid says that—''

The rest of the prognosis was lost in the opening chords of the organist's prelude, but as the tolling of the bell in the steeple above announced the imminent beginning of the service, another piece of the puzzle fell into place for me. Perhaps Alison had needed the twenty-five thousand dollars for the surgery that had repaired Samantha's congenital heart defect.

I couldn't begin to imagine the pain she must have felt when she learned of Marietta's injuries. And the guilt. The realization made me understand why she had kept her past and her problems a secret from me as best she could. She had been trying to shield me from the Horseman.

It also caused me to take a closer look at the Fairfaxes' role in this drama. If Marietta's assailant had considered her a threat, it would have been logical for him to have killed her way before now, unless he needed her as bait. Had he financed her move to the expensive nursing home and paid her husband to keep tabs on visitors and people who called to inquire about her? More specifically on Alison? That would certainly explain the dramatic improvement in Wallace's financial status. Even if Wallace had been an unwitting dupe, he certainly must have figured out the whole scheme when Alison presented him with the repayment of the loan. Had he betrayed her to the Horseman, then in a fit of remorse, tried to atone by signing over the check to me and Sam?

The question propelled me to my feet and out of the pew. Given my suspicions, there was no way I could sit through the funeral. Mumbling an innocuous excuse in the direction of the Zwislers, I headed for the rear of the church, a nearly impossible trek in view of the incoming crowd that clogged the aisle. I was attempting to circumnavigate the bulk of a polyester-draped matron when I bumped into Barrett Endicott. Before I could get out an "excuse me," he tucked a proprietary hand under my elbow and turned to usher me toward the door. Wealth still had the right of way in Magnolia Grove. The speed with which the mass of humanity made a path for us reminded me of Cecil B. deMille's Moses parting the Red Sea.

As we walked down the front steps and onto the lawn, the tail end of the crowd gave us a respectful berth. My mouth was cottony with fear as I thanked my self-appointed escort for his assistance. I tried to move away, but he maintained his grasp.

"You just rescued me from a very tedious duty. Since the dearly departed was once headmaster of Palmetto Prep, the alumni association felt obliged to send a representative to the service, and it was my bad luck to draw the short straw," he confided, massaging the soft spot in the crook of my elbow with his thumb. "The very least I can do in return is treat you to a mint julep brunch at the country club."

"It's nice of you to offer, but I have other plans for the rest of the morning," I responded, pulling away with a jerk intended to demonstrate that his touch was disagreeable.

If he noticed my irritation, he didn't react to it. "You're a very beautiful woman, Rachel, but that isn't the only reason I'd like to spend time with you. I had the utmost respect for Reverend Bodine, and I owe it to him to see that his daughter receives a proper welcome home,'' he insisted in a pompous tone.

Even if he hadn't been one of the three prime suspects, I still wouldn't have liked the renovated B.E.-III. Everything from his drop-dead gorgeous face and his Armani-clad biceps to his self-assured arrogance was overdone to the point of caricature. And although I could think of thousands of escorts with whom I'd rather share a meal—the Hunchback of Notre Dame was a notable example—the date would give me a chance to dig for information. Where better to get the scoop on the descendants of Magnolia Grove's founding fathers than straight from a HORSE's mouth?

Heedless of Jericho's earlier warning to go straight home, I accepted the invitation, but I firmly vetoed Endicott's suggestion that I ride with him. I already knew the man drove like a maniac, faint traces of liquor wafted my way every time he opened his mouth, and I needed the means to make a quick getaway if I determined that he was Alison's pursuer, so I wasn't about to strap myself into his blue-and-white car.

The details of the tandem trip to Plantation Harbor Country Club were best forgotten. Suffice it to say our cars fractured all the traffic regulations in the municipal code and made the quarter-hour trip in a little under five minutes.

Although I'd never actually been inside PHCC, in my childhood I'd imagined it to be grander than Buckingham Palace. The reality was closer to Disneyland. The main entrance opened onto a glass-domed rotunda. In its center, a larger-than-life grouping of Neptune and provocatively posed mermaids were sculpted from Carrara marble. The interior designer, doubtless the same one who'd done CANTER's lobby, had taken the nautical motif way past excess. Every surface in sight abounded with seashells.

Barrett and I were the only patrons in a private dining room set on the ocean-view side of the rotunda. The maître d' bowed and scraped us to a window table where a waitress and two frosted mint juleps stood at the ready. There were no menus in evidence, but my escort had barely lowered his impressive physique onto the semicircular banquette before he began to order.

"The lady will have a portion of strawberries with Devon cream, to begin. Then shrimp-and-artichoke quiche, cheddar-baked grits, beaten biscuits with an extra portion of apricot butter, and for the grand finale, a fresh fruit platter accompanied by café au lait," he rattled off, adding with scarcely a pause for breath, "And I'll have my usual."

The most cherished of my pet peeves was having a meal chosen without my advice and consent. "I couldn't possibly eat that much," I protested irritably.

Barrett waved the waitress on her way as though I hadn't spoken. "There isn't a southerner alive who can resist Chef Clarence's specialties," he assured me, shifting in his seat. The move decreased the already limited space between us and briefly pressed his calf against mine.

The contact could have been accidental, so I gave him the benefit of the doubt, but I immediately scooted to a less vulnerable position and initiated a diversion. "I'm writing an article on the founding fathers of Magnolia Grove and their direct descendants to go with my photo essay, and if you wouldn't mind, I'd like to begin my research with you."

"Nothing would please me more."

I ignored the overt lasciviousness in his tone. "I was very impressed by what I saw of CANTER, and I'm sure your job entails a great deal of responsibility. Exactly what do you do?"

The toe of his shoe stroked my ankle. "Do you really care?"

Endicott's expression resembled the look Citronella usually wore when she was watching for a sand crab to emerge from its hole. It also reminded me that I was now playing the game on his turf, so I raised my guard and switched to offense.

"Perhaps it was a trite question, but I was too busy thinking of a courteous way to mention my 'hands-off' policy to frame a more pertinent one," I countered sweetly. "I'm not interested in the nitty-gritty details of your position, but I realize it took a great deal of effort and ambition for you to make senior vice president at your age. You must have started working at the consortium right after college."

"The main qualifications for a key to the executive washroom are power and image, and when I graduated from Clemson, all I had was a four-point average." The amusement in Barrett's voice was heavily undercut with rancor. He straightened, absently rearranging his silverware as he continued, "I ate my way through New Orleans before I decided that grad school at the University of South Carolina was the answer to my problems. Michael Springfield and I shared an apartment in Columbia—we both were going through a 'poverty is the way to salvation' phase at the time. You remember Mike, don't you?"

I nodded. "Amelia told me about his accident."

"Michael was almost like a brother to me, and his death hit me pretty hard. Not too long after, I headed for Europe to pull my act together. A hundred-eighty pounds later, I discovered that jet-setting was a lot more fulfilling than corporate networking. I suppose I'd be living on the Riviera right now if my father hadn't died. The old man couldn't figure out a way to take his money to hell with him, so a year ago, I came back to Magnolia Grove to keep Mother Dearest away from the cooking sherry and spend as much cash as I could in the shortest time possible." He completed the saga with a mirthless chuckle. Half of his julep disappeared before he continued. "The minute I got home, I was offered a vice presidency at CANTER."

The arrival of our brunch temporarily halted the discussion, and during the hiatus, I compared his story with the one Jericho and I had pieced together. If Endicott's time sequence were accurate, he couldn't be the right Horseman. The conclusion allowed me to breathe a lot easier, and with my suspicions about my brunch companion allayed, I found myself feeling sorry for him. The slick veneer was too thin to disguise the troubled, embittered man he obviously was.

"Besides the fact that Elias Endicott's great-great-grandson is a born-again hedonist, it there anything else I can tell you?" The object of my pity broke into my musing.

I smiled at him. "I'd like to know more about the descendants of the other founding fathers. Shall we begin with Winstead Ogletharpe?"

"Fine, but pleasure before business. I'd count it a crime if you to let this magnificent feast get cold."

Suddenly famished, I focused my attention on the multitude of chafing dishes the waitress had laid out in front of me. By comparison, Barrett's section of the table was positively naked. The "usual" he'd requested was an oversized goblet filled with what looked like an anemic strawberry milkshake. As I ladled fresh melon balls onto my plate, he lavished a loving glance on my fruit platter.

"Wouldn't you like to share this with me?" I asked.

"Please don't tempt me—at least not with food. It's the one gratification I won't allow myself." Handing me my untouched julep, he picked up his goblet and tapped it against my glass. "To Michael Springfield and Gideon Bodine, the only two people in Magnolia Grove who never called me B.E.-III."

After the first obligatory sip of the toast, Barrett abandoned his diet shake in favor of the julep, polishing it off with alacrity. And as soon as he set down the empty glass, the waitress whisked it away and provided a refill.

"Don't neglect the biscuits, Rachel, they're at the peak of flavor when they're hot," he urged, continuing with a dissertation on how the bread had been prepared. As he spoke, he selected the flaky rounds in turn, slathered them with dollops of apricot butter, then gently laid them back on the platter.

While he segued into a lecture on the cheese-baked grits, I came to the weird realization that I hadn't been asked to brunch because Barrett Endicott lusted after my body. I was being used as a surrogate digestive system. The thought totally destroyed my appetite. For the next fifteen minutes, I toyed with my food and tried to nudge the conversation back to the HORSE brigade, but when it became apparent that all I would get from him was recipes, I checked my watch and decided to close down the operation.

"It's after twelve! Where on earth does time go?" I interrupted his monologue, rising from the table. "I have an appointment this afternoon, so I'd better get going. Thank you for brunch, Barrett, and I really appreciate all the information you've given me."

"I have to go out of town for the weekend, but I'll give you a call when I return. There's a marvelous French restaurant in Charleston that you mustn't miss."

"I'll certainly keep that in mind."

To my relief, he didn't offer to see me to my car, and as I walked away, the waitress brought his fourth julep.

The bulk of the PHCC brunch bunch now eddied around the rotunda—matrons kiss-kissing, yachtsmen already two sheets to the wind, pastel-clad tennis buffs whose headbands had never encountered a drop of sweat—a microcosm of the bored and the restless frittering away the days of their lives. When I spotted a nattily attired Jericho posted beside Neptune and company I did a double-take, once because I was surprised, and twice because I was so glad to see him.

I hurried to his side. "You look terrific. This is the first time I've seen you in real clothes."

"What are you doing here?" he demanded, his expression startled.

"I just had brunch with Barrett Endicott. We met at the funeral and I decided to see what information I could—"

"Have you lost your mind?" Jericho cut into my explanation incredulously. Drawing me closer, he lowered his voice to a fierce whisper. "That was not only a dumb move, Rachel, it was dangerous. Suppose he's our man?"

"I'm pretty sure he's not. I'm on my way now to try to verify some of the details of the story he just told me."

"The only place you're going is back to the cottage. Lock all the doors and windows, take the phone off the hook, and don't move a muscle until I get there. Have you got that straight?"

I didn't care for either the content or the tone of the message, and it seemed to me that if he were really concerned, he would cancel his dumb health planning meeting and leave with me. Before I could raise the point, the well-endowed redhead who kept popping up in Jericho's vicinity made her third appearance.

"So sorry to have kept you waiting, Jerry, but the Porsche is giving me trouble again," she reported in a sultry alto. For all the attention she paid me, I might have been part of the statue.

"Whitney Delafield—Rachel McKinnon," he said, handling the intro as briefly as possible. There wasn't so much as a smidgen of guilt in his expression.

So much for his highly touted honesty. If that twit were the commissioner of health services, the sick people in Magnolia Grove were in dire trouble. I was fuming inside, but I'd rather have had my molars extracted with red-hot pliers than to let him know it. I returned his date's disinterested nod with one of my own. "You'll have to excuse me. I have pressing business to attend," I said crisply.

I'd almost reached the exit when Jericho caught up with me. "I want you to promise that you'll go home."

The last thread of my temper snapped. "One of us has got to work, *Jerry*. While you're tiptoeing through the juleps with Whitney, I intend to do some more research." With a final glare that would've withered a redwood, I turned and stalked away.

ALL OF THE MAGNOLIA GROVE news from April 1, 1923, through the past month had been stored on microfiche in the office of the *Harbor Light,* and when the editor-in-chief, a man whose age surely must have antedated running water, discovered that I was a Bodine, he was only too willing to grant me access.

"You'll probably be interested in the issues we put out during the time your father was at Mount Tabor. We used to run synopses of sermons in the Monday edition, and his always headed the column," he said, and as he doddered away, added a mumbled "A finer speaker never stood in the pulpit."

Although I agreed with the sentiment, I had enough on my mind without dealing with Papa. Jericho's alleged luncheon meeting, for example.

To my chagrin, I determined in the first five minutes of reading that Whitney Delafield, nee Rochambeau, was not

only a city commissioner, but had a PhD in health care ad
ministration from Harvard. She was also the first in line to
inherit her family's considerable fortune, had been di
vorced four times, and of late, had been seen in the com
pany of one of M.G.'s most eligible bachelors—unnamed
of course. The last tidbit notwithstanding, I felt as though
I were five pounds lighter: Jericho hadn't lied to me, after
all.

Barrett Endicott was more problematic. The fanfare sur
rounding his return a year before definitely ruled him out as
the D.C. Horseman, but he hadn't been given much ink
during his fat years. Most of the references I found were
tucked into the myriad articles about Michael Springfield's
death.

I was getting a headache from reading the type on the
screen, so I began printing out miscellaneous HORSE news
from the past seven years. The stack of copying paper be
side the projector was half an inch thick when I decided to
call it a day, but before I turned off the machine, I felt duty-
bound to check out a few of the quotes from Papa's early
sermons.

By and large, it was a disappointing exercise. The one-
paragraph squibs couldn't begin to convey the eloquence
and passion with which my father had delivered his mes
sages. But I did run across an old headline that captured my
attention: Vernon Avant Found Dead in Atlanta. Since that
was the name Jericho said I'd been muttering in my sleep the
night of our beach party, I scanned the extensive coverage
the *Harbor Light* had given the event. The unfortunate
Vernon, who at the time was head foreman at Ogletharpe
Textiles, left his job, his wife and his five children to run off
with a Charleston waitress two weeks prior to being pulled
from the Chattahoochee River.

I wondered how he'd entered my dream library until I
found a sidebar mentioning his regular attendance at Mount
Tabor church. Mystery solved, I zapped poor Vern back into
history.

It was after three when I returned to the cottage. The
Buick and the beetle were already in the driveway, and their

respective drivers were standing between their cars deep in conversation.

As I walked over to join them, Jericho's expression was a mixture of relief and anger, the latter predominating. "Caleb and I arrived ten minutes ago, and when we saw that you weren't here we were worried to death," he snapped. Before I could respond, he handed me a ring.

"That's the one I found in your family's burying ground, Cricket. I got to thinking that it might be important, so brought it over to see what you all could make of it," Caleb supplied.

It was a Palmetto Prep class ring, at least size eleven, I gauged. The stone was missing and the band was slightly bent. The embossed initials on either side of the empty setting were in such ornate old English script that they were nearly indecipherable, but when I finally made them out, a shiver zipped the length of my spine. "It belongs to Barrett Endicott," I said, swallowing hard.

"Tell me about it," Jericho said shortly. "You should be more discriminating in your choice of brunch dates."

I stifled the urge to make a similar observation and turned to Caleb. "Have you talked to Maggie and Sam yet?"

"Yes, and as a matter of fact, I'm on my way to see them right now. Sam forgot to pack her Barbie doll and she asked me to bring it."

"I think it's in my room. I'll run and get it," I said.

The two followed me into the cottage, and as I left them to head up the stairs, the recollection of B.E.-III's toe grazing my ankle made me shudder with revulsion. But that was small change compared to the icy dread I felt when I stepped across the threshold of my room.

The words Last Warning had been smeared in lipstick across the dresser mirror, and Samantha's decapitated doll was lying in the center of my bed.

The blood rushed down to my feet then back up to my head, throwing my heart into overdrive during the round trip. The increased circulation lifted me from whimpering terror to a rarified distillation of rage, and my field of vision narrowed until all I could see was the message.

Without rational thought, I found myself moving toward it with the base of a brass lamp balanced in my hands like a baseball bat. A karate yell and the entire weight of my body went into my swing, its force patterning the slivered glass with spidery cracks that fanned out from the point of impact. I was dimly aware of the thud of feet running up the staircase, but I paid the noise scant heed.

Hitting the mirror again and again, I punctuated my strokes with all the epithets I'd ever heard and invented a few of my own. It wasn't until my vocabulary and wrath were finally spent that Jericho moved to my side. He gently extracted the lamp from my fingers and, letting it drop to the floor, enfolded me in his arms.

Chapter Eleven

There were no marks to indicate forced entry on either the doors or windows, so the intruder had to have let himself in with a key. Even after the signs of the havoc I'd wreaked had been cleared away and the other rooms searched to insure that he hadn't left any other nasty surprises, it still seemed that his presence contaminated the cottage. Although it may have been irrational, I decided to stay. In my view, moving our base of operations to Jericho's house or my going into hiding with Maggie and Samantha would have been tantamount to running away, which was exactly what the creep who'd left the message wanted me to do.

While I was adamantly opposed to retreat, I considered a temporary strategic withdrawal a fine idea, particularly since Caleb's boat, the *Kingdom Come,* was the location we picked to hold a council of war. Once we cast off from the private dock in back of Hamilton Hall, Albert's gloomy mansion, the sun, a clean wind and the swish of saltwater against the hull of the sloop-rigged motor sailer allowed me to get a grip on both my paranoia and the events of the day.

After I had given Jericho and Caleb the details of the brunch conversation and some of the information I'd gleaned from the pages of the *Harbor Light,* I took a wild stab at putting together our case against B.E.-III.

"The class ring and tire tracks place him at the cemetery, and we know by the things I found in the treehouse that Alison was in the general vicinity. It stands to reason he was chasing her. He also could have mugged Marietta because he left for Europe very shortly after the assault. The Springfields hosted a big bon voyage party at the club," I said, summing up the pro side. "On the other hand, he was in Paris two years ago, so he couldn't have lost his watch fob in D.C."

"Come to think of it, he hadn't even inherited it at that time," Caleb observed as he set a course through the buoys marking the mouth of Plantation Harbor.

"I don't believe he made the calls, either. I'm almost certain he doesn't know there's a connection between me and Alison, and if that's true, he'd have no reason for wanting me to leave Magnolia Grove." To firm up the conclusion, I added, "He even asked me to have dinner with him next week."

Disapproval tightened Jericho's jaw. Securing his sail line to a winch, he claimed a seat beside me on the starboard bench. "Endicott is the only one of our three suspects who could have been driving HORSE I in Boston. Ogletharpe hosted a yachting party that weekend and Barrett was supposed to have taken Whitney Delafield, but he canceled the date at the last minute. Kyle, her younger brother, escorted her instead."

I stared at him in disbelief. "You told her about Alison?"

"Of course not," he responded impatiently. "If I had, she would've provided Barrett with an alibi."

I should've left well enough alone, but I couldn't. "It must've been tough to fit a report on Whitney's social life into a discussion about Magnolia Grove's health services."

"I generally have more trouble working it the opposite way."

"It's plain to me that more than one Horseman is involved in this. I told you the gentry in this town take care of one another," Caleb said.

I greeted the conspiracy theory with a hefty sigh. Our plot already contained more characters than we could handle.

"You're probably right, but since B.E.-III seems to be the front man, let's stick with him for the moment," I said glumly. "If Alison were free, she would've contacted one of us by now, so he must've stashed her somewhere. We need to think of a way to get into his house and search for that secret room."

"He wouldn't be stupid enough to hide her in his own suite," Jericho objected.

"Arrogance tends to make people careless," Caleb said. "Starting Saturday, his mother is hosting a regional bridge tournament, and her butler called to see if I'd send over a couple of the Hamilton servants to help out. I'll just go myself."

"The timing couldn't be more perfect. Barrett's going out of town for the weekend." Knowing better than to mention Caleb's failing eyesight and lack of speed, I drummed up another excuse to prevent him from doing the job. "I'd better go, though. Even if Alison isn't there, he may have something incriminating in his hideaway. I can disguise myself as a maid and take pictures—"

"That's the dumbest plan I've heard lately," Jericho interrupted in an exasperated tone. "You'd be spotted in a New York minute."

"Make that a bet and I'll take it," I shot back.

Removing one hand from the wheel, Caleb absently rubbed his chin. "It might work. The rich folk here don't pay much attention to servants, particularly the ones that are on loan from another house. Just to save a dime or two and avoid hiring extras for special events, they swap us back and forth as though we were baseball trading cards."

Jericho frowned at him. "You sound as though you approve of Rachel's harebrained scheme."

"It doesn't matter whether I do or not. When she sets her mind to something, not much in this world can stop her," Caleb responded. "I'm going over to Endicott Manor tomorrow so I can scout the general layout in advance."

"Neither one of you is going because it's much too risky, particularly since the chance of finding anything useful is almost nonexistent," Jericho said stubbornly.

"You didn't believe there was anything in Fairfax's studio, either," I reminded him.

"No, but I didn't let you go there alone."

"Let me?" I squawked.

"Coming about," Caleb warned, steering into the breeze.

As the sloop heeled into the turn, its tilt slid me against Jericho. He braced himself against the coaming and wrapped his arms around me, steadying us both. When the tacking was completed, he maintained his hold and I didn't object. Our captain's adroit maneuver had simultaneously taken the wind from the sails and our argument.

After lowering the mainsail, Caleb dropped anchor and broke out two fishing rods, distributing them with the instruction, "Put these to good use. You can hash out the undercover operation on your way to Columbia tomorrow."

Although baiting our lines beat baiting each other by a wide margin, I detected a false note in the harmony we managed to put together. Jericho seemed to be working too hard at enjoying himself—teasing, joking, making a big production of a sardine-sized fish I reeled in—and after an hour had passed, what I'd come to think of as his "doctor face" appeared more and more frequently. When I caught him checking his watch two times in one minute, I decided to let him off the hook.

"Don't you have rounds at the hospital tonight?" I asked.

"Not until seven-thirty, but there are a few things I need to do at the office beforehand," he said, favoring me with a smile. This time, it was a genuine, toe-curling, happy one.

"I guess we'd better head back, Caleb."

"Haul up the anchor and secure the sails, then. The motor will get us in faster." As Jericho hurried to do his bidding, Caleb added the aside, "That boy's going to burn out before he hits forty. What he needs is someone to teach him how to play."

"Don't look at me. It's been so long since I really had fun, I think I've forgotten how."

"So Maggie says. We'll have to do something about that."

Under the engine's power, the sloop cut the time back in less than half, and after Jericho secured the bowline around a piling on the pier, Caleb handed him the keys to the old Buick. "Run along and see to your patients. I'll drive Cricket back in my other car and keep her company until you finish your rounds."

"I appreciate that, partner." Jericho clapped him on the back and bounded off. He was fifteen feet away before he turned and came back to plant a kiss on my cheek. "Be home as soon as I can. Take good care of our captain."

Caleb's glance followed him to the car parked on the cement apron that backed the dock, then cut back to me. "You think right much of him, don't you?"

"Yep."

"Are you concerned about him and Whitney Delafield?"

I did a quick gut check, surprised at the answer I found. "I want him to be happy for the rest of his life, no matter who he chooses to spend it with."

"Suppose he chooses you?"

"That would be a problem for both of us. I know he can't live without his career and I'm not sure I can live with it."

"Things like that have a way of adjusting themselves." He slipped his arm around my shoulders and guided me to the garage in back of Hamilton Hall. "You're a fine woman, Rachel Bodine McKinnon. I expect Gideon is resting right well now because you've exceeded all his hopes and then some."

I could have put together a better response than my mumbled "Thank you," if I'd known what Gideon's hopes had been. I felt suddenly skittish about the subject. "I've been meaning to ask, Caleb, do you remember a man named Vernon Avant?"

"Sure do. What brought that on?"

"I ran across an article about him when I was at the newspaper office. It said he attended Mount Tabor."

"That he did, but he wasn't one of your father's success stories. Avant was a rogue, particularly around the ladies. The gossip was that he even knew Winstead Ogletharpe's oldest daughter in the biblical sense," he said, chuckling as he raised the garage door and turned on the light.

Escorting me past Albert Hamilton's stretch limo, he opened the passenger door of a mint-condition convertible and handed me into my place. It was an older model that brought to mind homecoming parades and "beach blanket" movies.

"I really like this car," I said as he slid behind the steering wheel.

"I bought it as a birthday present for myself when I turned sixty, but I only run it around the estate. A convertible is really a couple car," he explained, his expression holding embarrassment and a trace of wistfulness. "You and Jericho are going to drive it to Columbia. It needs to be aired out on the highway every now and again to keep it in tune."

"It's nice of you to offer, but—"

"You were raised better than to dispute your elders," he interrupted with a smug grin. "If a three-hour trip in this baby doesn't loosen the two of you up, you're beyond mortal help."

JERICHO AND I WOULD HAVE left Magnolia Grove at seven if it hadn't been for a kidney stone. He had been in the middle of rounds when its owner was rushed to the hospital for surgery, and it was past midnight before she was out of recovery. Since he had spent two consecutive nights under stress and with very little rest, I tiptoed into his room before dawn and turned off his alarm clock.

At ten-thirty, while I was doing my best to wrest a jammed apricot Danish from the toaster's innards, he hurried into the kitchen dressed and grumbling, "Why didn't you wake me up? The bank will be closed by the time we get to Columbia."

"It's open until four on Friday. I phoned earlier. I also called the administration office at Stanhope. Dr. Genevieve Foster was a professor in the school of music when Noah Girard was dean, and she took over his post. We have an appointment with her at two-thirty," I said, delivering a mug of instant coffee. "Plus, I made reservations at a hotel near the campus just in case we need to stay over until tomorrow."

Jericho's eyebrows peaked. "Did you also have a chance to solve the Middle East crisis while I was asleep?"

"I was busy stowing my things in the trunk of the car so the creepo won't have anything to mess up if he comes back.

And since I had time left over, I decided to fix your breakfast.''

The fogginess on his face eased into sunshine, and he kissed the bridge of my nose.

I pushed him gently to arm's length. ''What was that for?''

''For being brilliant, efficient and beautiful, and because you just ruined Ogletharpe Properties' toaster,'' he responded, pulling the appliance's plug from the socket. ''As soon as I throw a few things in my duffel bag, we'll hit the road.''

Caleb's prediction about his sporty car's effect on us was fifty-percent accurate. Jericho abandoned his suit jacket before he started the engine, and by the time we reached the Interstate, the knot on his tie was loosened and the collar button beneath unfastened. I, on the other hand, got tighter by the minute.

While I didn't doubt that I loved him now—whatever that meant—I began to wonder whether the attraction that drew me to him would have been so intense had we met under saner circumstances. In the world I knew, romances based on sharing danger and solving murders only lasted until the credits faded from the screen. As I saw it, the sensible thing to do was to back off for a while. If what I felt was real, there would be time enough to let it grow after the search was over.

Fortunately for my ''wait and see'' strategy, the weather diffused some of the convertible's mystique. A mist that had been creeping steadily in from the ocean since sunrise settled into a steady drizzle as we left Magnolia Grove behind.

''If you get any closer to that door, you're going to be on the other side of it,'' Jericho observed wryly. ''Scoot over here and let me massage the back of your neck. You seem tense.''

''I'd be a lot tenser if you didn't have both hands on the wheel. Highways are tricky in the rain.'' To remove the edge from the response, I smiled, sliding closer but still out of reach. ''Since we've got time to kill, would you like to explain how a country boy got into a New York street gang?''

"I didn't get into the Rug Rats, I organized them, and we were more like a mutual protection society than a real gang." His smile held more pain than nostalgia as he continued. "When I took off from Sumpter, I hitched a ride in a semi headed for New York. My game plan was to make a lot of money so I'd be able to come back and take care of Alison. The truck driver dropped me in the Bronx, and since I only had twenty dollars, I holed up in an abandoned carpet factory with a dozen other runaways."

The nonchalant tone of his voice told me he wouldn't welcome sympathy. I tried not to offer it. "You couldn't have been more than fifteen. How did you get to be the leader?"

"I was oldest and largest. We hung together for about a year, then we got caught between two real gangs that were having a turf fight. Besides the blow that Alison's half-dollar deflected, I took a knife thrust in the thigh. Motor Mouth, my second in command, went down with me."

"Was he badly hurt?"

"*She* didn't make it out of surgery. Her real name was Crystal and she was my first girlfriend, although we didn't do very much about it. After she died, I told the welfare authorities where to look for the other Rug Rats. I figured the kids would be better off in foster care than with me. That was the end of my 'godfather' career, and since by then I could pass for eighteen, I joined the navy." Jericho momentarily shifted his attention from the road to me, the expression on his face unreadable. "I can't seem to get the hang of protecting people I love, but this time I'll get it right if it kills me. That's why I can't let you go to Barrett Endicott's mansion."

It was the only time he had ever mentioned me and love in the same paragraph, but loving and being in love were two different emotions in my book. Since he usually didn't beat around the bush, my safest move was to take his oblique declaration to mean the former.

"I can understand how you must feel, but I'm not a child and there won't be any weapons involved," I reassured him softly. "We can talk about it later, though, and if I can't convince you that I'll be okay, I promise to drop the plan."

He nodded agreement, and I gathered from the tight line of his mouth that this wasn't the right moment to go into the rest of his biography.

I'd always considered that I'd had a rough time as a kid, but in comparison to his, my teen years were a breeze. I'd always had Mama, and she never let me want for anything important. When I thought of all the things Jericho had missed—high school pep rallys, the senior prom, just knowing there was someone around to back him up, for Pete's sake—I wanted to cry. Sensing that my tears were the last thing he needed at the moment, though, I dug into the tote bag I had stuffed with the evidence we'd collected so far and retrieved the sheaf of articles I'd copied at the *Harbor Light* office.

"I put all this stuff in chronological order this morning while you were asleep, and I've already been over it once. The only thing I found interesting is that Endicott tried to save Michael Springfield's life, and that doesn't do much for our case," I said, arranging the papers in a stack on the space between us. "I'll give you a quick synopsis of the accident first, then I'll read you the parts about B.E.-III. Maybe you'll be able to pick up something I missed. Want to try it?"

"Why not?" he said, but he didn't sound enthusiastic.

"The two of them had been out celebrating Michael's birthday and his return from South America. Supposedly, Mike had been drinking heavily, but insisted on driving his brand new Ferrari. When he swerved to avoid a dog that ran into the road, Barrett—who wasn't wearing his seat belt—was thrown out of the car."

"Which goes to prove that passengers shouldn't sit too near their doors," Jericho commented dryly, peering through the windshield. "Looks like the sky's clearing up."

I avoided both observations and continued reading. "According to Endicott, the vehicle kept going for two hundred yards more before it went out of control and hit a tree. The high-octane fuel in the tank ignited on impact and the resulting explosion scattered debris over a wide area. Ironically, the only item that survived intact was a gift box that had contained an identification bracelet Mr. Springfield was given for his birthday." I shuddered as I tacked on a personal opinion. "Lord, what a horrible way to go."

"I can think of worse. There probably wasn't time for Springfield to feel pain or even fear," Jericho said. He switched off the air conditioner and rolled down the window. "Get to the part where Barrett stages his rescue attempt."

The rain-washed breeze coming in felt fresh and seductive against my skin, but I ignored it and flipped over to the next page. "William Pendergast, a motorist who arrived at the scene scant minutes after the crash, reported that Mr. Endicott, heedless of his own safety, was running toward the inferno. 'He was hell-bent on getting his friend out of that car. If I hadn't knocked him out, he would have died right along with Mr. Springfield,' said Pendergast."

"That doesn't sound particularly heroic. Anything else?"

"Not about Barrett. It says here that the Springfields offered a $10,000 reward to anyone who found the ID bracelet. I'll bet that was Amelia's doing. Clayton probably didn't care one way or the other," I mused aloud. "They've got one of the most screwed-up relationships I've seen lately. I wonder where it went wrong?"

"At the altar. As I understand it, the marriage was more of a merger. Clayton had a pedigree but not much money to back it up, and Amelia was the daughter of a nouveau riche pork processor from Spartanburg. They both got what they wanted at the time, but I guess neither of them was satisfied in the long haul."

With that bit of wisdom, Jericho took the upcoming exit to a highway rest stop and, pulling into an isolated parking space at the end of the lot, turned off the engine.

"Is something the matter with the car?" I asked, frowning.

"Yep. No self-respecting convertible can stand being driven with its top up when the sun's shining and a drop-dead gorgeous woman is riding in the passenger seat." He punched a switch on the dashboard, and, as the cloth roof folded itself back into the boot behind the rear seat, he plucked the sheaf of papers from my hand. "Let's trash the Horseman for the rest of the drive. It's turned out to be a lovely day, and I'd like for us to enjoy it together. We could even pretend we're on our way to a beach party. This car is the perfect prop for it.''

"Make-believe games can be dangerous, Jericho."

"Not if the players are straight with each other." Freeing my hair from the comb that held it twisted at the nape of my neck, he fluffed it around my shoulders. "Before we start, let's get Whitney Delafield out of the way."

I heaved a sigh. "I suppose I owe you an apology for thinking you lied about her, but you'll have to admit that she doesn't look much like a health commissioner. I assume you're the 'unnamed eligible bachelor' she hangs around with."

"We have an interesting arrangement. She and Barrett have an on-again-off-again affair going, and on the down cycles, she goes out with me to make him jealous. It never works because he's more interested in a dancer from Charleston."

"Whitney's using the wrong strategy. She'd do better to stock up on Twinkies." The devil made me continue. "What do you get out of the deal?"

"Hopefully, a health center for the people who live in the trailer parks. She's pledged a half million of her own money, and she's pumping the consortium for the rest. Aside from that, we're good friends and we split our date expenses straight down the middle." He locked his gaze onto mine, his eyes guileless and untroubled. "I'd go a long way to help someone I care about, but I could never make love to a woman I wouldn't want to share my life with."

It was hard to determine whether that was a reassurance, a warning, or a simple statement of principle. In any case, I was in no shape to analyze it. I had finally succumbed to the convertible's spell.

"I'll go to your beach party on one condition," I said, kicking off my high-heeled sandals before I slid close to him.

Grinning boyishly, he draped his arm around my shoulders. "Name it."

"You have to sing me the 'Get Around' song."

THE SMALL OFFICE that housed the dean of the Stanhope school of music was the stereotypical retreat of an absent-minded professor. Threadbare oriental carpeting was on the floor, floor-to-ceiling shelves were stacked haphazardly with thick tomes and a clutter of papers rested atop a filing cabinet. The spare, elegant woman behind the desk seemed as out of place as a ballerina at a square dance. Since Gene-vieve Foster was hardly the type to favor meerschaum pipes, it wasn't hard to deduce that the collection in the rack on the desk belonged to a former occupant.

By a prearranged agreement with Jericho, I took the lead in the interview and opened deferentially. "We appreciate your taking the time to see us, Dean Foster," I said after the introductions had been dealt with.

"It's my pleasure. My department doesn't get nearly the attention it deserves, and a mention in *Southern Style* will be ammunition for next year's budget debate," she responded warmly.

Oops. "When I told your secretary I worked for the magazine, it was only by way of introduction," I said, try-ing to correct the misunderstanding. "Dr. Quaid and I are here about a personal matter. We'd like to ask you a few questions about Alison and Noah Girard."

Her eyes narrowed to mere slits. "To what purpose?"

"I'm Alison's brother, and Ms. McKinnon and I are try-ing to locate her," Jericho interjected. "She was here in Columbia recently, and we thought perhaps she might've dropped by for a visit."

Dean Foster went from suspicion to full-blown animos-ity in two seconds flat. "To be perfectly candid with you, Dr. Quaid, if she had come here, she wouldn't have been welcomed. You'll have to excuse me—I have a meeting to attend."

When she rose from the cracked leather desk chair, Jeri-cho and I remained rooted in place.

"My sister is in trouble, Dean Foster, and we suspect that the reason she's disappeared may be linked to Noah's sui-cide. Anything you could tell us—"

"Suicide?" the woman cut him off, her brows knitting into an expression of pure hatred. "Alison Girard may not have pulled the trigger, but it was her betrayal of her marriage vows that put the gun in her husband's hand. She wanted her lover, but she wasn't about to divorce her meal ticket. Noah took his own life so she would be free.''

"Is that your own speculation or do you have proof of it?''

Although the tone of Jericho's question was gentle, I could see anger glinting in his eyes.

"I was the one who found Noah. Before the paramedics arrived, he asked me to tell Alison he loved her, then he said it was better to end it. Those were his exact words, and I assure you they were his last ones. He was unconscious when the ambulance came and he died the next day at Stanhope Hospital.'' Regarding us with a contemptuous smile, Foster resumed her seat. "If and when you find Noah's precious wife, you can deliver his final message. In all the excitement, it slipped my mind.''

That brought me to my feet in a hurry. "You're jealous of her, aren't you? I've never laid eyes on this office before, but I'll bet even money it's exactly the way Noah left it. My guess is that you loved him, and you—''

"Thank you for your time, Dr. Foster. We won't impose on you any longer.'' Jericho interrupted my tirade, grasped my arm and hustled me from the office.

"Why were you so polite to that witch?'' I sputtered when we reached the outside of the music building. I jerked away from him. "You believed what she said, didn't you?''

"I believe she was telling the truth about the message. Pretend that you're Noah and repeat it for me.''

"Tell Alison I love her and it's better to end it,'' I parroted irritably.

"You've got the tense of the last part wrong. Try it this way: 'Tell Alison I love her. It was Barrett Endicott.'''

I stared at him as the implications of the awful discovery hit me. "Oh, my God! That's why she was so sure Noah didn't commit suicide.''

"The message couldn't have made her suspicious because she never got it,'' Jericho reasoned, glancing at his watch. "It's nearly three and I think we'll get more done if we split up. You take the bank and I'll nose around the hospital. Let's meet in the lobby of the hotel at five, and after we register, we'll compare notes over dinner."

"Sounds good to me. What are you going to look for?"

"I won't know until I find it." He leaned down to brush my mouth with his lips, and as he hurried away, left the final instruction. "Keep your cool, tiger. I don't want to have to bail you out of jail for slugging an uncooperative bank teller."

The directions I'd gotten over the phone took me to Congaree Federal Savings and Loan without a hitch. My big problem was the length of the lines that stretched from every station. After what seemed an interminable wait, I reached the first teller's window and handed her the check. She returned it with only a cursory inspection.

"Marc Favors initialed it, and if there's a problem, you'll have to take it up with him," she informed me before I could state my purpose for standing in her line. Waving me toward the queue left of me, she beckoned the next customer.

When I finally got to Favors, he was a lot more courteous about his refusal to assist me.

"I remember Mrs. Girard, but information on the transactions she conducted is privileged," he said with a regretful smile.

I immediately hopped on the plural. "Can you at least tell what other business she took care of when she purchased the cashier's check?" I queried, giving him my most compelling Alison's-in-trouble story.

Although he listened sympathetically, his answer was still the standard statement of bank policy. I was turning away in defeat when he stopped me.

"I can't cash this check for you because it's made over to both you and Samantha Girard, and she hasn't endorsed it."

"I don't want to cash it. I just—"

"But since you're both the beneficiaries of the trustee account Mrs. Girard opened with us, I can add it to the balance if you'd like," he interrupted my protest.

I gave him the draft and a smile that contained all the gratitude I could pack into it. After a minute of rapid computer entries, he presented me with the current balance.

With the new deposit, it was nearly $200,000.

As soon as I recovered from the shock, I moved closer to the window and lowered my voice. "You've already been so kind, and I don't want you to get into any trouble, but I have to ask this. Did she open the account with either cash or a personal check?"

The side-to-side motion of his head was barely perceptible.

I felt as though we were playing charades. "An electronic transfer from another bank?" I guessed urgently.

After a surreptitious glance toward the manager's desk, he said with a sigh, "Oh, what the hell, it's only a job." Regarding me with melted chocolate eyes, he scribbled a few lines on a slip of paper and pushed it across the counter. "Good luck, Mrs. McKinnon. I hope she's okay."

JERICHO WAS TWO HOURS late when he hurried through the front entrance of the hotel, and the second I saw the taut weariness on his face, I knew his half of our upcoming show-and-tell session wouldn't be as encouraging as mine. I intercepted him halfway across the lobby.

"I'm sorry I kept you waiting so long. I got tied up at the hospital," he apologized, avoiding my gaze.

"No problem. I had some shopping to do after I left the bank," I said, handing him his key. "We're already registered. This hotel has a very nice restaurant, but if you like, we can order room service."

"I'd like to freshen up before we decide."

Those were the only words I got from him until we reached the third-floor adjoining rooms we had been assigned. Though I'd decided to let him tell me his news in his own sweet time, I couldn't hold back my own.

"The money Alison used to repay Fairfax was part of a $200,000 payment from Noah's life insurance. I called the company and asked about their rules. In a case of suicide, they still pay the face value of the policy, but the beneficiary can only claim the money after a two-year waiting period."

"That was terrific detective work. I guess I'd better fill you in on my part of it." Jericho's tone was as flat as week-old beer. He ushered me into his room, and drawing me to the couch, settled down with a sigh that originated in the soles of his shoes. "It took some doing, but I tapped into the hospital computer and found Noah's records. If the bullet hadn't killed him, he would have died of cancer in a few more months."

I straightened abruptly. "That's how Alison knew. Noah wouldn't have killed himself because of the two-year waiting period in his insurance policy. He would've wanted her to have the money as soon as possible."

"I think so, too, but there's more," he said, stopping to clear his throat noisily. "Alison delivered Sam at Stanhope so I was able to access their records, too. It was a difficult birth and Sam required a transfusion."

I sensed that his hesitance was the prelude to a bombshell. "Can you cut to the chase?" I asked warily.

"Alison's blood type is O-positive and Noah's was A. Since Sam's is B negative, there's no way possible that Noah could have fathered her. The laws of genetics dictate that she has to have the blood grouping of one or the other of her parents, and we know for sure that Alison is her birth mother."

I swallowed hard. "I know for certain that Alison would never have cheated on Noah. She had to have been pregnant before she married him, and I'll guarantee you that he knew it because she wouldn't have tricked him into thinking that Sam was his daughter," I said fiercely.

"Hold up, tiger—I'm on your side." He captured my clenched fists between his hands, hanging on to them tightly. "I'm not making a moral judgment. How Sam got here is completely irrelevant to the way I feel about her or her mother, but it does explain why they've been hunted all these years."

I sucked a huge breath of air, held it until my pulse rate returned to normal and then expelled it wheezy-whoosh. "Are you saying that Barrett is Sam's natural father?"

"That's the only thing that makes sense to me. It seems that you've been right all along about his obsession with

Alison, except that it also includes Sam. Maybe in his own twisted way, he wants the three of them to be a family.''

"If that's so, then he won't harm Alison. All we have to do now is keep Sam away from him until we rescue her," I said with more confidence than I felt.

"Piece of cake.'' A trace of a smile lifted the corners of his mouth then vanished in a yawn. "If you don't mind a late dinner, I'd like to hit the shower. And I have a whole load of thinking to catch up on."

"Me, too. I'll call you in an hour or so."

The hiatus fitted part one of my master plan for the evening—to a tee. Once in my own room, I scurried into the disguise I'd previously laid out: green cosmetic contacts, stage makeup to change the contours of my nose and chin, a too-large maid's uniform padded with tissue in strategic spots and flat-heeled loafers stained with baby oil to simulate wear and tear. The pièce de résistance was a Dolly Parton wig I coaxed with some difficulty into straggly bangs and a bun at the nape of my neck. The transformation took twenty minutes of hard work, but the payoff was worth it. As I surveyed the lumpy reflection in the mirror, I didn't recognize it as my own.

The alter ego I'd mentally christened "Laverne" grabbed an armload of towels from the bathroom, slipped the key in her pocket and went to knock on Jericho's door, calling a nasal, "Maid service."

It took a long minute for him to answer the summons. As he stepped aside to admit me, he wore a pleasant, but blank expression, and his gaze flickered over me briefly before it landed on the towels.

"Thanks, but I have all I need," he said, preparing to shut the door.

I stuck Laverne's shoe in the opening, drawling, "I came to turn back your bed."

He nodded, moving to the desk to immerse himself in some papers.

His inattention boosted my confidence to the point where I hummed a tune as I worked. Not stopping with the bed, I adjusted the blinds, polished the television screen, then clomped over to his side and flicked imaginary dust from the desktop.

"You need anything, you just call housekeeping," I told him. "We got extra toothbrushes, combs and such as that."

He didn't even bother to look up. "I'll keep that in mind."

"Y'all have a good one," I twanged, heading toward the door.

"Just a second—here's a little something for your trouble, miss," he said, coming up fast behind me.

His gratuity was a healthy pat to my rear end.

I jumped forward with a startled "Ooooch!" Before I could pull my act together, Jericho spun me around and planted a smooch on my "tango tangerine" lips.

"If you had vacuumed the rug, I might've upped the ante," he said, hugging me as he chortled his glee. "I wish you could see the look on your face, Miss Petunia."

"Laverne," I corrected him with a punch to his midsection. "You have to admit I had you fooled at first. What gave me away?"

His grin was the epitome of smugness. "Hotel maids seldom wear fifty-dollar-per-squirt perfume."

"Good point. I won't wear it to Endicott's mansion."

Some of the mirth fled from his eyes. "I won't try to stop you, but I'll be outside riding shotgun," he said firmly, giving me an additional tip. "On your way down the hall, Laverne, you can stop next door and tell Rachel I'll be ready to take her to dinner in fifteen minutes."

"Make that twenty, and you've got a deal," I said, beating a hasty retreat through the door that joined our rooms.

I could have—perhaps, should have—canceled part two of the plan, but I'd blown a bundle on the second outfit, and since I'd probably never wear it again, I was determined to get my money's worth. My hands were shaking as I dispatched the maid face and applied subtle makeup. It took a hunk of my twenty minutes just to get myself zipped into the teal-blue chiffon formal. The matching satin pumps nipped my toes, and I felt like an absolute fool when I set the pearl tiara atop my freshly fluffed hair. After another spritz of cologne, I picked up the carnation boutonniere I'd bought for Jericho and headed back to the game.

"All set," he said as soon as I knocked, but it took a couple of seconds for me to work up the courage to open the door. When I did, he was standing by the window holding two champagne glasses. Except for the lamp on the desk, the lights had been extinguished and there were at least two dozen candles placed around the room: apparently he had written his own script for the evening. He didn't move, didn't make a sound, as I walked toward him.

"I know this looks dumb, but I figured that since you went to the navy after you stopped being a Rug Rat, you missed your senior prom. And I've always wanted to be the queen of—" The rest of the silly speech died in my throat, silenced by the shining in his eyes.

In that instant, I had no further need for make-believe. What I felt far surpassed being the belle of the ball, a prima ballerina, the angel atop a Christmas tree, or any of the characters in the splendid, preposterous fantasies I'd had. There were a million things I needed to tell him, but only one seemed truly important.

Oddly enough, we said it at the exact same time.

"I love you."

Jericho set down the glasses and held out his arms. "May I have this dance?"

I tucked the boutonniere in his lapel. "We don't have any music."

"We'll make our own."

Only three turns into our silent waltz, he lifted me from my feet. My tiara tumbled off somewhere between the desk floor and the nest of pillows he tucked under my head, but it didn't matter because the rest of my prom ensemble soon followed.

We didn't make music, we were music, a complex improvisation of sweetness and need in which grace notes were tiny touches and small kisses that teased as much as demanded. He sensed what I wanted before I did, and he was lavish in the provision. His body was glorious in its power, and as he moved into me, pushed me to the limits of pleasure and then beyond, I knew him to be my first love and my last.

In an interval between surfeit and hunger, Jericho propped himself up on one elbow and brushed my tousled hair back from my forehead. "Thank you for the prom. It's the best gift I've ever been given."

I opened one eye and ogled him. "Wait till you see what I have planned for graduation."

"The physical part was marvelous, but you made love to my soul, too." His fingers moved gently along the curve of my neck, tracing a path toward my breasts. "All day long, I've been trying to think of some clever way to ask you to marry me, but I guess straight out is best. Will you?"

Cupping his face in my hands, I pulled him down to kiss him.

"Was that a yes?"

"It was an 'I love you.' And as much as I do, I've got a lot of things to work through before I can make a decision. Can we put it on hold for a little while?"

"For as long as you need." He laid back on the pillow and nibbled my ear. "Meanwhile, let's talk about my diploma."

Chapter Twelve

There were sixteen bridge tables set up in the ballroom-sized main salon of the Endicott's mansion, and the sixty-four players seated around them were as dedicated as if the fate of their fortunes rested on the next hand they were dealt. As the tournament progressed, the losing pairs gathered in small knots on the terrace outside to verbally replay their mistakes, backbite their respective partners and run down the winners of the preceding rounds. Although replenishing drinks and whisking away full ashtrays from the tables where play continued was a less-demanding job than circulating around the terrace loaded down with hors d'oeuvres, I volunteered for the latter in order to avoid Amelia Springfield. She and her partner were number one seeds in the region, and the first time I'd approached her foursome, her gaze had lingered on my face a shade too long to suit me. But her focus quickly returned to her cards, and as I finished serving her, I might have been invisible for all the attention she paid me.

Mrs. Endicott oversaw the outdoor festivities, and it was easy to see where her son had acquired his affinity for alcohol. Clarisse, a reedy woman whose sun-abused skin had the sheen and texture of her alligator pumps, knocked off flutes of champagne as if Prohibition was due to be reinstated in the next five minutes. The more she drank, the nastier her attitude toward the hired help became. When the empty glass she aimed in the general direction of my tray fell short of the mark, she banished me to the kitchen with a sotto voce curse that would have made a longshoreman wince.

"You clumsy twit," the harried major domo growled at me in the kitchen. "One more mishap and I'll send you back to Soames with a personal recommendation that he dismiss you."

It was just the opening I needed.

"I'm an upstairs maid, Mr. Jarvis, so I'm not use to serving," I whined. "I could do you more good if I was to tidy up the lavatories. You know how messy rich folk can be when they've had too many cocktails."

"Well, don't just stand there, go to it. The cleaning equipment is in the closet by the pantry," he snapped. "Do the ones down here first, and use the back steps when you're going to the second-floor powder room. I don't want any of the guests to see you."

"Neither do I, sir," I said, suppressing a chuckle as I beat a hasty retreat.

The plan was moving along better than I'd expected, but as I removed the camera from a pocket under my apron and stashed it in the bottom of a bucket I found in the designated closet, I cautioned myself not to get too cocky. The best that could happen if my cover were blown was that I'd be arrested for trespassing. After a quick check of the sketch Caleb had made for me, I snatched up my pail and headed up the rear staircase.

The entrance to Barrett's suite was near the end of the hallway, conveniently set across from one of the powder rooms I was supposed to be tending. After a precautionary knock, I turned the knob and pushed open the door. There must have been some sort of electric eye gadget in the jamb. When I stepped across the threshold, a bank of fluorescent tubes in the ceiling flickered to life, a fortuitous circumstance since there were no windows in the room.

The man definitely wasn't into creature comforts. The only furnishings were a narrow platform bed, a desk and a straight-backed chair. Every surface in sight was a blinding white, and there was no indication that a human being occupied the space. There were no pictures, no books, not so much as a throw rug to soften the ceramic tile floor. And the adjoining room was even less comfortable. With its multitude of exercise equipment, it resembled a medieval torture chamber. A utilitarian commode, sink and shower completed the bathroom ensemble, and six pairs of tinted contacts were aligned on a glass shelf beneath the medicine cabinet—the secret, no doubt, of Endicott's heavenly blue eyes.

Since there was nothing even remotely worth documenting, I didn't bother to break out my camera. I was fighting discouragement as I slid open the door to the walk-in closet. It was a twelve-foot-square haberdashery showroom carpeted in white shag. I gaped incredulously at the vast assortment of suits, sport jackets and slacks hung from the racks. But too much to search was as bad as too little. At best estimate, it would have taken me an entire day to go through the floor-to-ceiling drawers that lined the whole of one wall. Frustrated, and starting to get twitchy, I was about to throw in the towel when my attention was drawn to a small black object near the baseboard opposite the door. My heart was thumping overtime as I knelt to pick up my first real clue. The gold P.P. on the smooth face of the onyx square told me it was the stone that came from the setting of Barrett's class ring. It was then that I also noticed an odd pattern of wear on the carpet, extending the length of the closet and disappearing under the wall in front of me.

"There's got to be a door," I muttered, hit by the effects of a rush of adrenaline. It took me nearly five minutes to find the right spot to press, and when the panel finally gave way, my trusty bucket and I hurried through the opening.

The softly lit chamber beyond the closet was obviously where the real Barrett Endicott lived—amid the clutter of Twinkie wrappers and soda cans on the thick carpet, hunkered on the massive daybed piled high with cushions and comic books, plugged into a collection of heavy metal that included every weird group that ever cut an album. It was a teen hideaway, with one notable exception. While most juvenile males favored *Playboy,* the magazines I found stashed under his mattress were back issues of *Bon Appetit.* The discovery would have been hilarious if I'd had time to laugh.

As it was, I shoved them back in their hiding place and got on with the job.

The only neat area in the entire room was a yard-deep rectangular recess at the far side, a niche that resembled a built-in bookcase without shelves. When I went to investigate, I saw that its side walls were plastered with candid snapshots, either of Alison alone or posed with a pudgy Barrett. He wasn't as heavy as his high school persona, but he was a long way from the current debonair playboy. The two posed on the campus of Stanhope College. For the life of me, I couldn't see how she had fallen in love with him.

Barely controlling an impulse to rip them from their moorings, I nipped in my bottom lip and concentrated on the larger-than-life photograph of Michael Springfield that was atop a low table in the alcove. The portrait was flanked by votive candles and a flower arrangement, and in front lay a mahogany box made in the shape of an-old fashioned coffin.

It took quite a bit of internal urging to make me lift the lid, and when I finally did, a solid gold identification bracelet, not surprisingly, engraved M.S., glistened against the black velvet lining. As I pushed it aside to get at the sheaf of letters underneath, it flipped over and I read the inscription. "To my beloved Michael in his thirtieth year."

If this had been a movie, an organ would be playing a sinister Bach fugue in the background. The memory flashes that came to me in rapid succession—Amelia's disclosure that her son's birthday had been celebrated a few days before he died, the newspaper clipping that touted Barrett's unsuccessful effort to get back into the Ferrari, the documented explosion that turned the Springfield scion and all of his belongings into unrecognizable debris—all made me suspect that previous accounts of the accident might not have been accurate. It was possible that Barrett could have acquired the ID bracelet at some time before or during the fatal drive, but since the Springfields had wanted it returned badly enough to offer a huge reward, I couldn't imagine why he would have kept the morbid souvenir. My hasty decision to slip it in the pocket of my apron was based purely on desperation. Since I seriously doubted that Barrett would want Amelia to know he had the gold chain, whatever the truth of the matter, it could be used against him.

All too conscious of the passing time, I retrieved my camera and hastily recorded the details of the bizarre den. Although I didn't usually sanction blackmail, I wasn't above trading Barrett the negatives for Alison's safe return.

In less than twenty seconds, I stashed the camera under the rags in my bucket, slid the secret panel shut behind me and sprinted back to the entrance to the suite. I didn't see anyone when I eased open the door and peered cautiously into the hallway, but I hadn't taken account of the blind corner near the head of the stairs.

Barrett's tipsy mother and Amelia Springfield rounded it just as I stepped across the threshold. Backtracking would have made me appear even more guilty, so, gripping the handle of my bucket tightly, I walked toward them humming an off-key hymn under my breath.

"What have you been up to, girl?" Mrs. Endicott said sharply. "No servants are permitted in my son's suite."

I stopped dead in my tracks, but before I could answer, she accused, "You were stealing, weren't you?"

"Oh, no, ma'am. I came up to tidy the powder room, and since I ain't never been here before, I kinda got lost." I stammered in my best redneck twang. Her companion was giving me a thorough once-over, so I ducked my head. "See, I'm one of the maids you borrowed from Mr. Albert Hamilton, and I'm just helpin' out for the day."

"What's in that bucket?" Mrs. Endicott demanded, her eyes narrowing to mere slits.

"Nothin' but scouring powder and a bunch of rags. I like to earn my pay, so I thought I'd straighten the gentleman's bathroom while I was in there." I mentally gauged my chances of shoving her aside and making a successful run for it. They were slim to none.

"Don't make such a fuss, Clarisse. You know how rigorously Albert screens his employees. I'm sure she's telling the truth," Mrs. Springfield intervened. "You go back to the tournament now. This girl can help me get the spot out of my dress."

Barrett's mother walked away muttering about the unreliability of poor white trash and Amelia grasped my wrist firmly, pulling me into the powder room on the opposite side of the hall. After she had locked the door behind us, she snatched the bucket from my grip and dumped its contents on the floor.

"Just as I suspected." She pounced on my camera and flipping open the back, unreeled the exposed film from the roll. "I interceded because of my affection for your mother, Rachel, but we don't take kindly to this kind of reporting here in Magnolia Grove."

From her frigid tone, I knew the ruined pictures were the least of my problems.

"I swear to you on Mama's memory that's not the reason I'm here." My inquisitor's sternness relented the tiniest fraction, so I pressed the advantage. "It's a very complex situation, and I don't have time to explain it, but for Samantha's sake, please don't expose my cover."

"That's a lot for you to ask of me. Clarisse Endicott is a valued associate, and Barrett has been like a son to me since—" She closed her eyes briefly, and when she opened them again, her gaze was hard as a diamond. "You've got exactly one minute to tell me what you were doing in his room."

My available options narrowed down to one—the truth.

"I was trying to find evidence that Barrett is holding Alison Girard against her will."

"Who?"

"My best friend. Her maiden name was Compton, and she's Samantha's mother. Endicott's been tracking her for years." The deepening puzzlement on her face told me I was making a hash of the explanation, so I took another tack. "I don't think he's aware of the connection between me and Alison yet, but I must be making him nervous because he called *Southern Style* to check my credentials. And in the past few days, I've received anonymous phone calls and macabre warnings. Someone even broke into the cottage."

"Do you actually believe that Barrett Endicott III could be responsible for that?" she asked, clearly flabbergasted. "I don't wish to offend you, but what possible interest could a man of his station have in your belongings? And why on earth would he abduct this Alice person?"

"Alison," I corrected tightly. "Jericho and I suspect that Barrett is Samantha's natural father—"

"What has Dr. Quaid got to do with all of this?" she interrupted.

"He's Alison's brother."

"If your purpose in telling me this ridiculous story is to confuse me, you've succeeded admirably, but I'm not fool enough to believe a word of it." Amelia's expression went from incredulity to open scorn.

Since she was reaching for the doorknob, I had no choice but to play my last ace. "Maybe this will convince you that Barrett's not the sterling character you believe him to be." I retrieved the identification bracelet from my apron pocket and handed it to her.

For a long moment, she stared at it silently, her face so white it was nearly translucent. "Oh, my dear God, no," she finally whispered. "Did you find this in his suite?"

I nodded. "There's a secret room behind his closet." That I'd guessed right about the bracelet didn't allay my guilt for having used it as a weapon against Amelia. "For what it's worth, I think Barrett really loved your son. There's a shrine to Michael's memory in his hideaway."

She appeared not to have heard me.

"My boy was so bright and beautiful, and no matter how hard Barrett tries to change himself, he'll always be a stupid, bungling fool. Deep down in my soul, I knew he was jealous of Michael, but to strip my precious baby of the last gift I ever gave him..." Amelia trailed off, slumping against the vanity as though her agony were too heavy to support. For a moment, I thought she would burst into tears, but she recovered her composure. "Have you contacted the authorities?"

"We don't have enough evidence to go to the state troopers or the FBI and Sheriff Tillman wouldn't dare pursue the case. Besides that, we're afraid that a full-scale police investigation would tip our hand. If Barrett knew we were close to nailing him, he might harm Alison."

"He can be very vindictive. How do you know she isn't already dead?"

I shuddered at the blunt question. "The most we're hanging on to is hope. Jericho and I think he may be holding her until he gets Sam, too, although we haven't figured out why he would want both of them."

Amelia's expression and body language indicated that she was firmly entrenched in my camp now. "A daughter is literally worth millions to him, my dear. There's a stipulation in his father's will that disinherits Barrett if he hasn't produced a child by the time he's forty. Because of his obsession with body-building, he's been taking massive doses of steroids for years, and now he's irreversibly sterile."

Her revelation put a fresh edge to my desperation. "No matter what we have to do, he's not going to get to her."

"Clayton would never permit me to help you openly—he and the others always close ranks to protect their own—but I can give you money," she offered eagerly. "And I have a villa in the Blue Ridge Mountains that my husband doesn't know about. I can take Samantha there so she'll be out of harm's way until you find her mother."

"I appreciate your concern, but she and Maggie are already hidden in a safe place. Jericho and I aren't about to move them until Barrett's no longer a threat. All I really need from you is a promise of silence, Amelia."

"You have that." She put her arms around me, holding me close. "And also my prayers."

AT BEST, BARRETT HAD betrayed Amelia's trust. At worst, he might have held some responsibility for her son's death. And although I didn't believe she would deliberately break her pledge to me, given the depth of her grief, it was very possible that she might not be able to control herself when she saw him. Which could be as early as the next day, since that was when he was due to return from wherever he'd spent his weekend.

In most of the Agatha Christie novels I'd read, there had come a time when the protagonists, previously stymied by red herrings and plot twists, plucked an esoteric clue from thin air and brought the muddle to an ingenious resolution. Hercule Poirot and Miss Marple we were not, so Jericho and I decided to pull the case together and turn it over to Marcus Bristol, Maggie's friend on the state police force.

It was late afternoon when we first piled all our sundry reports and photographs on the table in the breakfast nook and sat down to arrange them in some sort of logical order. What we came up with after hours of painstaking labor was a flimsy patchwork of circumstantial evidence and suppositions that still left three crucial questions: who was the owner of the watch fob, where was Alison being held, and why had she risked coming back to Magnolia Grove in the first place. Absent even the flimsiest of answers to the latter two, persuading Bristol to do more than fill out a routine missing person's report would be difficult. And with what we had now, if we accused one of the richest men in South Carolina of multiple homicide, we'd be lucky if we weren't carted off to the funny farm. In all likelihood, Barrett Endicott would never pay for his crimes.

When the flow chart I was drawing to detail the major events in our investigation began to look like a tangle of spaghetti, I abandoned it and wandered over to the freezer to take out a couple of microwave dinners. "We'd be in better shape if Amelia hadn't ruined that roll of film," I said glumly, peeling the end from one of the boxes. "But at least we know why Barrett is after Sam. Do you have any idea how we can verify that the disinheritance clause is in his father's will?"

"No, but I don't think it matters one way or the other." Jericho got up to pour himself yet another cup of coffee, then dumped it in the sink untasted. "When Endicott rammed Alison's car in Boston, he had to know Sam was in it. If she's his meal ticket, it doesn't make sense for him to risk harming her."

"A lot of things don't make sense—least of all, how Alison could've fallen in love with him. And after she got her hands on that insurance money, she should've picked up Sam and taken the next plane to Timbuktu."

"Maybe she was just plain tired of running." Straightening his hunched shoulders, he favored me with a weary smile. "And now her brother is just plain tired of rubber chicken covered with low-cal glue. Let's order a triple pepperoni pizza."

"With anchovies and extra cheese." I put in my bid as he started for the phone.

It rang before he got to it.

"Damn," I muttered. There hadn't been any calls all evening, but this was prime time for my threatening caller. "Don't answer it, Jericho."

He already had, and his initial reaction was relief.

"How's it going, Caleb? We're about to take a pizza break, and...no, the TV's not on, we've been working...slow down, I'm not following you. Oh, my God! When did it happen?"

I covered the distance to the phone console in the space of a heartbeat, slapping the speaker button so that I could also hear and respond to Caleb.

"Endicott must've been hightailing it when he hit that curve, and he'd probably been drinking. Maggie and I were watching a movie on channel three when they broke in with a special report on the accident."

When I understood what must have happened and that Maggie and Sam weren't directly involved, my body temperature thawed, but only a few degrees. "Was Barrett alone?" I forced myself to ask. "No," Caleb said, after a very long pause.

Jericho dropped the receiver and strode to the small television on the counter.

The scene that flickered onto the tiny screen was a glimpse of a nightmare. The pile of metal I saw was so badly mangled it was scarcely recognizable as an automobile. The camera zoomed to a close-up of the still-intact HORSE I license plate, then cut away to a reporter.

"It is a chilling coincidence that Mr. Endicott's life should come to its end on this deserted stretch of highway. Almost seven years ago and a mile from where I now stand, he was thrown clear of a similar accident that killed his best friend, Michael Springfield, the scion of another of Magnolia Grove's prominent families. As fate would have it, this time Barrett Endicott's seat belt was securely fastened, but the air bag that might have reduced his trauma failed to inflate." He paused to beckon someone off camera, and a familiar uniformed bulk stepped into the picture. The reporter continued, "This is Oswald Tillman, who's been the elected sheriff of Magnolia Grove for the past ten years. Sheriff, can you give our viewers any information on the female passenger who was with Mr. Endicott?"

"One of my boys found a purse near the wreckage. Can't say positively that it came out of the car, but there aren't too many other possibilities. The driver's license that was inside belongs to an Alison Girard of Kennicot, Maine," Sheriff Tillman revealed, running a nervous finger around the collar of his shirt. "We tried to contact the Maine address, but the phone had been disconnected."

I squeezed my eyes shut tight and tried to find a prayer, but there was nothing but pain in my soul. Jericho's arms encircled me, and when I finally gathered enough strength to raise my head and look at him, his eyes were clear and steady.

"It's not Alison," he said softly.

As much as I ached to believe that, I couldn't get past the sight of the twisted wreckage. When he reached to switch off the set, I held back his hand, determined to hear it all, no matter how bad it was. By now, the remote segment was over and two anchors in the studio were discussing the grisly details.

"As I understand it, both bodies have been taken to the county hospital pending autopsy. Is that right, Peter?" a perky blonde chirped.

"That's correct, Pam," another anchorman confirmed. "Barrett Endicott has been positively identified by his longtime friend, Whitney Delafield, but due to the extremely poor condition of the body of the woman who has been tentatively listed as Alison Girard, a visual ID will be difficult. Since she's from out of state, we're asking any of you viewers who might have know—"

Jericho cut Peter and Pam off with a determined flick of his wrist. "It's not Alison," he repeated.

Maggie apparently commandeered the receiver at the other end of the still-open phone line, because her voice floated through the speaker. "Caleb's gone to wake Samantha, Rachel. Now that there's no longer any danger, we're coming home."

The most I could do was nod.

"Don't tell her about the accident," Jericho warned.

"We weren't going to. That's best left to you and Rachel. You all hang on, we'll be there in twenty minutes," Maggie said, finishing the conference call.

Jericho cradled the receiver on our end, then extended his arms to me. I went into them gratefully.

"I feel that she's still alive, Rachel. I wouldn't lie to you, not even to save you pain." He bent his head to kiss my forehead and my eyelids. As his lips grazed my mouth, he murmured, "I need you to help me hold on to that faith."

"It wasn't Alison who died in the crash." At first, I said it because he asked it of me, but as it became a mantra in my head, I began to believe it. "She'll be okay now that Barrett's gone. All we have to do is find her."

"I love you more than my own life," he said, pressing me against his chest. After a long moment, he pulled back from the embrace. "Will you be okay if I go out for a little while?"

I knew very well where he was going and what he had to do, but I steeled myself and smiled. "Bring the pizza back with you, and don't forget the anchovies and extra cheese."

The twenty minutes it took for Caleb to bring the rest of my family home were probably the longest and loneliest of my entire life. While Caleb carried our sleeping child back to the bedroom Jericho had been using, Maggie clasped me in a hug.

"Looks like you're holding up right well, daughter, but that's what I'd expect of you."

The designation touched me deeply. "Don't give me any credit—I'd be a complete mess if it weren't for Jericho," I admitted. "And anyway, there's no need to fall apart just yet. Alison is still alive."

Her eyes widened. "Was there another special bulletin?"

"Sort of." As Caleb came back into the living room, honesty made me continue. "Jericho has this internal link with her. It's a little like mental telepathy, only he can't read her thoughts." Said aloud, this seemed patently ridiculous, so it surprised me when the two of them exchanged a relieved glance.

"Sounds right to me," Caleb said, grinning. "I'll have to ask him the secret so I can add it to my pigwidgeon repertoire."

"When's the last time you had a decent meal?" Maggie asked.

"The last time you cooked. We haven't had time to do any shopping, so there's nothing in the refrigerator but a couple of TV dinners. Jericho's supposed to bring back pizza."

"No such thing," she objected. "The old man and I will run out to the all-night convenience store and pick up a few things," she added with a proprietary pat to Caleb's arm.

"Better than that. Albert Hamilton's got enough food in his pantry to feed all of China. That's where I'll take this youngster to do her shopping," he chimed in.

I noted the easy give-and-take between them with a secret smile. Apparently my love wasn't the only one in bloom.

Just before they left, Caleb presented me with a hardback composition book.

"It's one of Papa's journals," I said when I'd examined the front label. My father, the habitual scribbler, had undoubtedly filled scores of similar notebooks in his lifetime. Mama had kept most of them, but for some reason, I'd never gotten around to reading one.

"I found it when Maggie and I were going through boxes of things I've collected over the years." The expression on his face was shadowed solemnly. "I was going to give it to you when you were ready to leave, but it might be of more use to you now."

The words *thank you* wouldn't come, but Caleb seemed content with my silence. When the front door closed behind the pair, I laid the book on the end table and went back to check on Sam. More than anything, I needed her giggles, her chatter and maybe even a quick cup of imaginary tea, but she was sleeping so soundly I didn't have the heart to wake her.

I nearly paced a hole in the carpet near the end table, trying to avoid looking at the composition book, but I didn't have much success. To divert my attention, I plopped on the couch and flicked on the television with the remote control gadget.

Every channel was replete with crash stories, and not surprisingly, I couldn't work up the slightest twinge of regret that Barrett Endicott was on a fast freight to hell. But it did give me some satisfaction that even in death, he was being upstaged by Michael Springfield. Newscasters went on ad nauseam about the coincidental aspects of the two wrecks.

Although my ingrained skepticism raised the possibility that neither had been accidents, I was too tired to examine the idea closely. I needed to get my thoughts off Barrett for a while, but I didn't want to miss anything important. The compromise I finally worked out was to press the mute button and pick up the journal.

"Okay, Gideon," I sighed. "Let's see what you have to say for yourself."

The first half of the diary contained scraps of sermons and lists, even a joke or two. Whenever I found myself getting interested, I turned the page: I wasn't exactly on speaking terms with the Right Reverend Bodine at the moment. The recorded dates were during his last year, and toward the end of the volume the writing got progressively harder to read.

"Now isn't the time for you to dig into all of this, Mc-Kinnon," I warned, tensing against the onslaught of an old grief. But unable to stop myself, I flipped to the final entry.

My Rachel is fiercely independent, never walking when she can run, always first in line and last to leave a fight—and she usually wins. From the day she was born, I was afraid to tamper with that spirit. I convinced myself that she could fly higher on her own wings, and that the best gift I could give was my faith in her courage and in her ability to stand alone. But lately, I'm not so sure that was the right way. And now that there's not much time left for me to share with her, I wish I'd told her more often how much I love her, how proud I am of her accomplishments, how rare and beautiful a soul she has and that I've always needed her more than she needs me. I leave it to my daughter and to my God to forgive me if I've failed her for if I have, I'll never be able to forgive myself.

"It was the right way, Papa," I whispered.

"There's General Springfield," Samantha piped up from the doorway, pointing to the silent image on the television screen. She hugged BeeCee tightly to her chest. "I'll bet he's still mad at me," she offered gloomily.

I laid the journal on the couch beside me, quickly thumbing the remote to turn off the set. As soon as Clayton disappeared, Sam padded over and settled into my lap. Her small body was trembling.

I wrapped my arms around her, grateful for her sweetness and innocence. "He probably doesn't even remember that you broke his plate, honey."

"Wanna know why I was so scared when I did it?"

"You thought he was going to slap you."

"Uh-uh. Because he sounded just like the man who yelled at Mommy when I was little," she confided through a yawn. "I'm thirsty. Can I have a glass of Kool-Aid?"

Revelation came in a series of razor-sharp flashes that sliced through my consciousness. I could almost see the General standing over Samantha's bed, staring down at her with the same cold fury that had been in his eyes the afternoon of the tea party. He had to have recognized her when she dropped the dish of petits fours. And ironically, the story I'd told Jericho when the roses had arrived the next day was only partially a lie. Clayton Springfield had indeed sent them, but not as an apology. The inescapable conclusion was that he'd also checked out my *Southern Style* cover, run Maggie off the road and made the anonymous phone calls all because he wanted no part in the child who was, perhaps, his own granddaughter. It was equally clear that Barrett Endicott had been a pawn in the game, and given the vicious pursuit in Boston, his marching orders had apparently been to get rid of Sam and Alison once and for all.

"You're smooshing me, Cricket," Sam interrupted the dark vision. She wiggled restlessly, adding a plaintive, "Milk with chocolate syrup would be even better than Kool-Aid."

I loosened my grasp, forcing a semblance of normalcy to my tone. "Maggie and Caleb have gone to pick up all sorts of goodies, and they should be back any minute. Will ice water do until then?"

"I can wait," she said, sighing. "Where's D.J.? I want to tell him all the neat stuff I did while I was on the island."

"Island?" I echoed vaguely.

"That's where me and Maggie went. Mr. Soames has a big house, and he says all of us can come back there every year when school is out. Mommy's going to like it a whole lot 'cause there's a room with a piano that she can play. And you and me and D.J. can go swimming while she practices," she said, going on to detail a list of delights future summers might hold.

The more she prattled about her plans, the harder it became for me to hang on to the mantra. Even if Alison were alive, Clayton Springfield might still have her, and I sensed him to be a much more formidable foe than B.E.-III. I got up and went toward the patio door to recheck the lock.

I was halfway across the living room when the phone rang, and Sam pounced on it before I could object.

"Hello," she said eagerly. Her voice became shy. "Uh-huh...he's not here. Okay...oh boy!" She offered me the receiver. "It's Mrs. Springfield. She says I can have one of her boy's dinosaurs!"

I slumped on the sofa and touched Papa's diary, the feel of it steadying my fingers enough to take the phone. "Yes, Amelia?"

"I'm so very sorry for your loss, darling. I would've called before now, but I've been with Barrett's mother." There was a weighty hesitation. "Clarisse is in no shape to raise a grandchild. I realize it's presumptuous for me to advise you, but it might be better if you and Jericho didn't mention your suspicions about Barrett to the authorities," she confided.

"That would be the last thing we'd do," I assured her, shakily. The earnest tone with which her opinion had been delivered triggered a massive guilt attack. I was certain that if Amelia knew the real story, she'd be beside herself with happiness. For a split second, I toyed with the idea of enlisting her aid, but given her husband's dominance, I didn't dare risk it.

"I realize it's very difficult for you to talk right now. I'd like to send one of my people over with food, but I need to know what you prefer. Would you mind if I spoke with Margaret?"

"She isn't in just now. I'll have her call you in the morning," I said, ready to pledge anything to get off that line.

There was a long pause at the other end. "You and Samantha shouldn't be alone at a time like this, Rachel. Would you like for me to come over?"

"No," I said in a harsh, tight voice. "But thank you," I added more gently.

As I hung up the phone, Samantha patted my arm. "You look scared, Cricket. Is anything wrong?"

"I'm just hungry. I wish Caleb and Maggie would hurry back with the food," I fibbed, rising to pull aside a slat in the vertical blind on the front window.

Approaching headlights fanned cones of brightness on the street outside, and when the vehicle was a short block from the cottage, I could see that it was neither Caleb's car nor Jericho's. Since ours was the only occupied cottage on the cul de sac, it was obvious to me that Sam and I were about to have a visitor.

There might have been other people besides the General who would come calling at this hour of the night, but I certainly couldn't think of any. Absent a convenient automatic weapon, I knew that my chances for a successful defense were at best miniscule, so I snatched my car keys from the credenza and hustled Sam out through the patio door.

We were nearly to the Nissan when the other car began its turn at the driveway. Tugging Sam into the shelter of the oleander bushes, I cautioned silence, circling her with my arms as we crouched down to wait.

As I had feared, Clayton Springfield emerged from the driver's side of a sleek sedan that had purred in and blocked my car. Since his foot soldier had gone down in flames, the First Horseman had come to do his own bloody work.

Chapter Thirteen

The guardian angel in charge of fools and babies that night must have been working an extra shift because the General conveniently left the car's headlights on and the motor running. Apparently in a hurry to finish us off, he covered the distance to the front porch of the cottage in four bounding strides, pulled out a ring of keys—courtesy of his fellow Horseman, Ogletharpe, no doubt—and unlocked the door.

He had barely stepped across the threshold when Sam and I sneaked into his car through the passenger side. I settled behind the steering wheel and ventured a peek at the cottage. A light went on upstairs and Clayton was silhouetted in the window.

"Buckle up, Sam," I warned. Shoving the transmission in gear, I peeled out of the driveway and laid a block-long track of burnt rubber down Pelican Cay Lane, jamming the horn to warn off a vehicle that was at the next cross street.

"We tricked ol' mean Clayton," she giggled. "And he can't come after us 'cause you have the keys to our car."

I knew very well that his transportation shortage would only be a temporary inconvenience. One phone call from him would bring new wheels in a hurry and probably a squad of goons in the bargain.

"We did good work, little buddy," I said, trying to keep my voice steady, "but we're not playing a game this time. It's very important that you do everything I tell you. Okay?"

Her head bobbed and she scrunched down in the seat. "Where are we going, Cricket?"

I hadn't thought that far ahead, but the answer was obvious. "To find D.J."

Since I'd never driven such an upscale car, the high-tech control panel was as confusing as the cockpit of a 747, and the horsepower at my command took some getting used to. Clayton was over a foot taller than I, and the seat was set so low I could barely see above the wheel. I couldn't locate the adjustment mechanism, so when I stopped for the merge at the exit from Pelican Cay, I swiveled around to see if there was anything I could use as a pillow.

The pile of material lying on the rear seat turned out to be a bulky satin robe, its white front embroidered with the horseshoe crest. A triangular hood with eye holes and a pair of gloves that were heavily encrusted with gold beading completed the ensemble.

The thought of Clayton—or any other grown man, for that matter—prancing around in the ridiculous getup would have been hilarious if the significance of the find hadn't hit me. He wouldn't normally drive around town with his Halloween costume at the ready, so it stood to reason that he must have been on his way to a HORSE conclave. In my view, the fact that the General had made a detour to the cottage beforehand signified that Sam and I were on the agenda.

I hurriedly refolded the robe around its accessories, and propping myself on the makeshift pillow, took off again. As I guided the sedan along Camellia, my tongue was so dry it was sticking to the roof of my mouth. From what I'd observed, I was fairly certain that Sheriff Tillman, et al, were in the HORSE's pocket, or at least wouldn't be willing to lay their jobs on the line to help me. To avoid attracting the attention of any stray cruiser that might be lurking in the area, I nudged the gas pedal until we were moving at a rate just below the posted limit. Not that my speed really mattered. At this time of night, with little or no traffic on the streets, it was impossible to be inconspicuous in a top-of-the-line car that every cop in Magnolia Grove would recognize as Clayton Springfield's.

The first thing to interrupt our flight to Jericho was that the route I thought would take us to the country hospital was blocked off for repairs, and my memory of the immediate area was hazy at best. There was a car phone on the dash, but I had no idea how to use it, and I didn't have the time to stop and experiment. The second, and by far the more compelling, was the distant sound of police sirens.

"Hold on," I cautioned urgently, hanging a right on a street I'd nearly passed. There was a lot to be said for expensive cars. The sedan cornered with all four wheels snugly against the pavement. The road ahead was a deserted straightaway, so I fed the engine more fuel.

If Samantha hadn't been with me, I might have tried to make it to Charleston, but in the likely event that Clayton's forces got on the trail, I didn't dare risk a high-speed chase in an unfamiliar car. My best shot seemed to be running for cover.

"Are you driving fast because the police are after us?" Sam asked, the tone of the question apprehensive.

Considering the circumstances, I thought it was best to level with her. "They might be," I admitted. "Remember the treehouse I told you about? We're going to stay there for a little while, just until we figure out how to contact D.J. and Maggie."

Her response was enthusiastic. "That's neat!"

"Look in the glove compartment and see if you can find a flashlight," I instructed, slowing the car as she unhooked her seat belt to comply.

After a little rummaging, she produced the item with an eager, "I got it. There's a funny-looking gun in here, too."

"Don't even touch it," I said sharply, a cold sweat beading my forehead as I leaned over to slam the compartment shut.

The luck that gave us the flashlight continued to hold. The sound of the sirens faded, and the only vehicle I encountered on the way through town was a red Porsche headed in the opposite direction. By the time we were nearing the outskirts of Magnolia Grove, Sam had dozed off.

My gaze flickered constantly between the road and the rearview mirror, and in one of my checks, I noticed the gleam of lights some distance behind. Camelot Court was coming up on my left, and I swung into the turn, cruising a few blocks of the subdivision at random. When I circled back to the main road, there was no traffic in either direction. I made it to the parsonage in five minutes flat.

As I parked the car in the shelter of Mama's camellia bush, the knowledge that I was scratching Clayton's paint job gave me grim satisfaction. I cut the motor and gently shook my small charge to wakefulness.

Since there was a damp chill in the night air, I took Clayton's folded outfit to use as cover, a move I was to regret further along in our trek to the treehouse. The slithery satin was hard to imagine. On the way through a patch of underbrush a few yards from our haven, a bramble snagged the fabric and the bundle slipped from under my arm.

"Are we almost there?" Sam asked as I stopped to retrieve the sundry parts of the Horseman getup.

I directed the beam of the flashlight at the base of the oak. "There's the ladder we have to climb. Do you think you can make it?"

She nodded assent, then took off. "Race you there."

I caught up with her just as she tagged the trunk. "This is serious business, and from now on, I don't want you to make a move unless I tell you to," I said firmly, handing her the flashlight. "You watch me while I take this robe up and dump it on the platform so you can see how to handle the ladder. But don't you dare try it until I come back down."

Sam was obviously a quick study. When her turn came, she scampered up in nothing flat. She was enchanted with our hideaway, exploring the corners as I refolded the satin costume into a pallet.

"You can take a nap while I try to figure out how to contact D.J. and Maggie," I suggested, sagging gratefully to the floor. I'd been running on empty all day, and the stress of the past few hours had sapped most of my reserve energy.

Plopping down beside me, she picked up the ornate gauntlet that I'd tossed aside while I was making her bed. "I'm not sleepy, now. Is it okay if I play with ol' Clayton's gloves?"

"Knock yourself out," I said absently, wishing I'd had time to grab some food before we left the cottage.

Sam rummaged through the pallet awhile before she asked, "Where's the other one?"

"Sh—" I cautioned, jerking to attention.

Sound traveled well through the still night air. One of the games Alison and I had played here as children was classifying vehicles that traveled the road past the parsonage by the noise their engines made. From the rising drone I heard coming from outside, I guessed that either a pickup or van was approaching.

She nudged me with her elbow. "Scoot over, Cricket. I want to see if you're sitting on the other glove."

I wasn't, and my frantic search failed to turn up the missing gauntlet either inside the playhouse or on the platform. Although I didn't dare shine the flashlight down on the path we'd taken to the oak, the three-quarter moon provided enough illumination for me to catch a glimpse of white caught in the underbrush where I'd dropped the bundle of satin. As I left the platform to scramble back inside I heard the distinct slam of a car door.

I didn't have the slightest doubt that Clayton or one of his minions would shortly put in an appearance, and although the playhouse itself was difficult to spot from below, a diligent searcher might wonder about the crosspieces nailed to the trunk of the tree—particularly if he had a clue to point the way. I had to retrieve the glove, but my rapid mental calculations told me I'd be cutting it very thin if I tried to climb back up the ladder afterward.

"Are you brave enough to stay by yourself for a little while?" I asked Sam, holding her tightly. Her heart was beating a mile a minute.

"I'll pretend Mommy's telling me a story—that way, I won't be scared." Swallowing hard, she added shakily, "I wish I'd brought BeeCee, though."

Snatching one of the stones on the shelf, I pressed her fingers around it and kissed her hand. "That's Mommy's pigwidgeon rock. Hold tight to it and everything will be okay. I'll be back for you as soon as I can."

She refused my offer to leave the flashlight with her, giving me her solemn promise not to move from her haven until one of our family came to collect her. Just before I left, she hugged my neck, then snuggled down in the robe I'd wrapped around her. "D.J. and I need you, Cricket. Please don't get lost."

I couldn't have loved her more if I'd given birth to her, and as I scurried to the ground, my father's message echoed in my ears. Praying that there would be no need for either Samantha or God to forgive me, I sprinted down the path to snatch the gauntlet from the briars that ensnared it.

It was scarcely in my grasp when I noticed a beam of light to my left, sweeping from side to side as its source approached me. Heedless of everything but the need to lead the hunter away from his prey, I spun to my right and took off through the bushes. With no conscious plan handy, I let instinct take me back to the time when I'd known every square inch of those woods. There was more growth now, to be sure, but the old paths were still there.

Although my cardiovascular system was strained at first— more, I suspected, from fear than exertion—I got into the run. I paced my breathing and began to rely more on diversionary tactics than speed, zigzagging so frequently that I almost got lost myself. On one double-back, my pursuer came so close to the tree I was hiding behind that I could hear the guttural rasp of his panting.

From the curses he muttered between gasps, I deduced that he was not a happy camper; I realized all too well that if he ever caught up with me, I was a goner, so I decided it was time to put some distance between us. Dashing off the beaten path into the underbrush, I flicked my flashlight on and off in rapid succession, side-arming it as far as I could before I slipped back to the well-remembered trail that would take me to Mount Tabor. He fell for the ploy, and I managed to get a sizable lead on him.

In the good old days, I could have made it from where I was to the church in two minutes flat and without raising a sweat. I had no idea how long it took me that night, but when I passed my family's resting place, I was staggering with exhaustion. Looking for a hiding place inside the sanctuary was not an option: for starters, it was probably the first place he would look. But the main thing that propelled me across the grove was the recollection of my Sunday morning brush with evil. I was as close to total collapse as I'd ever been by the time I reached Cotton Mill Run, and the only thing that kept me going was the determination not to fail. I'd dragged myself a country block when the headlights of a car behind me went from high beam to low and back again.

The cycle was repeated, and the sound time, accompanied by a woman's voice calling, "Wait, Mrs. McKinnon."

If the man who was chasing me had a female accomplice, she had nabbed me. I was too tired to take one more step.

The car rolled slowly to a stop beside me and Whitney Delafield stuck her head through the open window. In the backwash from the high beams, I could see that her face was puffy and mottled, as though she'd been crying. Recalling that she'd had the grisly task of identifying what was left of Barrett, I would like to have offered her sympathy, not for the loss so much as for her grief.

"Thank God you're safe. When I ran into Jericho at County Hospital, he said he hadn't been able to reach you and he was afraid you were in trouble. He would've come looking for you himself, but one of his patients required emergency surgery," she said before I could greet her. "Where's the little girl?"

Something in her tone set me on edge. I really couldn't tell whether it was paranoia or the stress of the chase, but at that point in time, I wasn't willing to trust anyone who had more than $2.98 in the bank. And though the story was superficially plausible, it had one flaw. How had she known to come looking for me along this deserted stretch of nowhere? Jericho had no way of knowing I'd be driving Clayton's car, so Delafield had to have seen Sam and me after we left the cottage. And I'd kept to the speed limit all the way through town, so she would have had ample opportunity to intercept us and deliver her message. Why had she waited?

"I have friends who live in Camelot Court, and I left Samantha with them." The lie came as easily to me as gasping. If I was wrong about Whitney I could apologize after her alibi checked out. Leaning heavily against the side of her Porsche, I tried desperately to pull myself together.

Retrieving her cellular phone, she punched one button and, after a short wait, spoke into the handset. "Surgical suite? Whitney Delafield here. Please tell Dr. Quaid I found Rachel, and that we're on our way to Camelot Court to pick up his niece...of course I'll wait." She turned a strained smile toward me. "Jericho left instructions for the nurse to let him know the minute I called. While I'm on hold, you can give me your friend's address and tell me how to get there. I'm not familiar with the subdivision."

The net had so many holes that it wouldn't have caught Moby Dick. If our positions had been reversed, I wouldn't have had County Hospital's number conveniently programmed into my phone, and I surely would have invited her into my car before I asked for directions. Drawing on the last drop of my energy, I wheeled and sprinted toward the woods.

At first I thought the explosion was her Porsche backfiring, but that wouldn't have explained the whine that zipped past my ear.

"The next shot won't miss," she called after me.

I might have taken my chances if I hadn't seen a beam bobbing through the trees directly in front of me. By the time I raised my hands and turned around, Whitney and I were practically nose to nose. I heard footfalls thudding up from the rear, and as the stalker's rough hand grabbed my shoulder, his beam illuminated her features. They were twisted with an ugly purpose.

"We can do this hard or easy. What's the address?" she queried, aiming the gun at my midsection.

She might do me some damage, but I figured she had orders not to kill me. At least, not until I revealed Samantha's hiding place. "Gee whiz, Miss Scarlett, I just can't remember. Why don't you wake up all the nice people in Camelot Court and ask them if they're baby-sitting the little girl B.E.-III tried to murder?"

I wasn't prepared for the heavy blow that came down on the back of my head, but in a weird sort of way, I welcomed the darkness it brought. I'd be able to catch a few minute's rest before the beginning of the final round.

CONSCIOUSNESS RETURNED in slow, painful waves and with it came the suffocating scent of roses and the muffled knell of a church bell. The grandmother of all headaches was wreaking havoc on my brain, but I finally managed to force my eyelids open. I panned my gaze around a cramped cell that resembled the set of a low-budget horror movie. There was a gaslight by the door, festoons of cobwebs on the ceiling, the requisite skitter of motion in one of the corners—all that was missing was a skeleton in chains. Since my arms were now bound tightly behind my back, there was a fair possibility that I'd be auditioning for the role.

My restricted mobility, the metal bars that protected the rectangular peephole on the door and the stone walls that were probably a foot thick, made the likelihood of escape less than zero. I struggled to my feet. I'd only taken one step toward the wooden door when it creaked open and the crimson ghost materialized just beyond.

I almost laughed. Was the hassle I'd just gone through part of another dream? I clamped my teeth down hard on the tip of my tongue, my usual way of waking myself up in these situations. I must have sheared off a year's growth of taste buds, but the red-swathed figure refused to disappear. It was only then that I noticed the emblem emblazoned on the front of the costume. It was the crest that signified membership in the Society of the First Horseman.

The specters who'd haunted me all of my life were real. All things considered, the realization gave me very little comfort when the hooded Horseman strode into the cell and grasped my upper arm. He hustled me over the threshold and force-marched me along the length of a corridor into a large room, finally shoving me into a high-backed chair.

"Your first move will be your last," he said, taking up a rigid stance beside me and blocking the view to my right.

The words were unnecessary in light of the lavishly embellished gun tucked in the sash around his waist. No doubt, the gun was standard equipment for the well-dressed

Horseman. But even without the threat I wouldn't have left my seat. As I ventured a glance at my surroundings, past fantasy and present reality quickly began to mesh. The Society's secret meeting place, a high-vaulted, Gothic chamber brightly illuminated by hundreds of flickering candles, was inside the chapel on the grounds of the Springfield estate. At some time during my early childhood, probably on one of the occasions when my mother was sewing for Amelia, I must have wandered through the rose garden and into their stronghold.

In light of the brutality I had witnessed, I couldn't deal with the thought of my immediate future, so I concentrated instead on a black-draped table in the center of the room. The makeshift catafalque was surrounded by floral arrangements, and its somber covering was the backdrop for a garish purple Horseman costume, the ceremonial gloves of which were positioned atop the pectoral insignia like the crossed arms of a mummy.

As I came to the simple conclusion that the owner was the late B.E.-III, a small emerald-clad figure drifted into my line of vision and, shoulders shaken by audible sobs, rustled over to pay tribute to the fallen hero. Evidently, mourning with a hood on posed major problems, because Whitney Rochambeau-Delafield had to remove hers to blow her nose.

I now had all the information I needed to identify the family affiliations of the masked crusaders: Endicott wore purple, Rochambeaus wore green, Springfields wore white. Albert Hamilton, Caleb's employer, was confined to a wheelchair, so by default, the crimson Horseman who guarded me had to be an Ogletharpe. Just as I broke the color code, he moved over to comfort Whitney, and my view now included the white-clad Horseman seated in an ornate chair on a dais at the front of the chamber. The last time I'd seen that robe it had been in the treehouse, tucked snugly around Samantha.

After a minute or so of pure panic, common sense kicked in. If Clayton had already found his granddaughter, I was of no earthly use to him and I'd surely be dead by now. Ergo, the costume he now wore had to be a duplicate of the one I'd found in his car. Sam was still safe in her hideaway.

When a rapping at the entrance reverberated through the meeting hall, Springfield cracked a riding crop that was clutched in his gloved fist against the arm of the throne. My guard resumed his position beside me and Whitney hurried to the main portal.

She pulled open the massive wooden door with some difficulty. "Enter, venerable Knight Pegasus."

Albert Hamilton, I presume, I mused, choking back a hysterical urge to laugh at Delafield's ridiculous performance.

As predicted, a stoop-shouldered man, swaddled from head to toe in royal blue satin, maneuvered an electric wheelchair around the catafalque and steered an erratic course toward the corner nearest me.

By my count, the circle was now complete, and I didn't understand why everyone's attention was still riveted on the entrance. I didn't have long to wait for the answer. Jericho stumbled in, his face badly bruised and his hands tied. General Springfield, sans the uniform of the night, was directly behind, the muzzle of his pistol prodding Jericho's ribs.

I felt as though my bones were strung together with overcooked noodles, but I tried to get up, anyway. Capturing my gaze, Jericho shook his head in the briefest of warnings. His crooked smile sent the silent message that he loved me and that Alison was still going strong.

"I told you your girlfriend was safe, Quaid. Your cooperation will insure that she stays that way," his captor warned with a sneer.

What was wrong with this picture?

I stared at the man incredulously, then swiveled my neck to gawk. If Clayton weren't the grand poobah of the bunch, who was the white-robed Springfield on the dais?

Amelia bared her head, readjusting her coiffure as she rose to her feet. "I don't understand why you're surprised, Rachel. Women's liberation is de rigueur these days, even in Magnolia Grove." Her laughter was silvery, gentle, and as chilling as the hiss of a cobra.

My mouth flapped open and shut, but nothing came out.

She descended majestically from the platform, pausing beside Hamilton's wheelchair. "I'm glad you could join us tonight, Pegasus. We have a bit of business to handle before we start the memorial service, so you might be more comfortable if you remove your headpiece until then. Would you like for me to assist you?"

Although now didn't seem like a particularly good time to attempt an escape, Jericho must have thought so. He suddenly rammed his shoulder into Clayton's arm, knocking the gun from his hand. It went spinning across the table. The General retaliated with a right cross. Jericho went crashing to the floor. His captor followed up with a swift kick to the ribs, but Jericho must have been unconscious because he didn't even grunt.

A moan echoed in my head, but I couldn't let it out, couldn't even move.

"See that Quaid doesn't create more problems, but don't do anything rash," Amelia ordered. She signaled for Whitney to take her place beside me.

Leaving Jericho to Ogletharpe's tender mercies, Clayton strode over to scowl at his spouse. "Poor Albert has nothing to do with this. Why did you have to involve him, Amelia?"

"He's been away from the fold much too long. The original Society members always shared both their entertainment and the responsibility for it, and that pact kept them from turning on one another. Besides, the old fool will probably sleep through the rest of the proceedings." Her expression was a mixture of disdain and anger. "You're nearly as useless as he is. I gave explicit instructions for you to bring Margaret Peace. I'm sure she can give us the address we need."

"You're not as clever as you think, my darling. Camelot Court was only a rendezvous point. While Rachel had Whitney and Ogletharpe stumbling over each other's feet, the old woman took your granddaughter back to the place where they've been hiding all along." Grinning wolfishly, the General delivered the coup de grace. "It took a bit of persuasion, but Jericho finally gave me directions. Our people are on the way to Sumpter even as we speak."

"Oh, my God, no," I wailed, doing my best to validate the red herring. The longer we kept the Horsemen galloping around in circles, the better our chances of living through the night.

The tears that now ran rivulets down my cheeks needed little prompting. They had been close to the surface for a very long time. If the bruises on Jericho's face were the cost of the cover he'd given Maggie and Caleb, I shuddered to think of the price he would pay if he tried to save me. Dropping my chin to my chest, I stole a sidewise glance at the inert form sprawled at Oglethorpe's feet. I hoped with all my heart that my love would stay unconscious until the Society's business with me was finished. That wouldn't be very long unless I cut an ally out of the herd. The most convenient target was the emerald-clad Whitney standing beside me.

"If you love Barrett, you've got to help me, Whitney," I sobbed. "He murdered people for Amelia, and when she didn't need him anymore, she arranged the crash that killed him."

"He murdered Michael in cold blood. Our exalted leader couldn't let her son's death go unavenged—I understood that and agreed with her. And anyway, Barrett's better off dead than with the trashy bleached blonde who was taking him away from me." The muffled response came through the green hood. "When I begged him to break up with her, he laughed. I had no other choice than to run them off the road."

The confession was a major setback, but the astonishment that sagged Clayton's jaw told me he'd been cut out of that part of the conspiracy.

Amelia came to stand in front of me, reaching to lift the point of my chin with her gloved finger. "I'm sorry for your pain, my dear, really I am, and I'm grateful to you for taking such good care of my baby," she said softly. "I have no quarrel with you and Jericho. If the information he provided brings Samantha safely home to me, I swear to you on my precious child's grave that you won't be harmed. In fact, I'll see to it that neither of you ever wants for anything."

I truly believed she meant it, but I could also envision my love and I spending the remainder of our days locked away in a posh institution. If we were lucky, we'd be allowed to sip an occasional Valium cocktail together. My hatred for the woman gave me a weird kind of courage, and since I was two inches taller than she, I rose to my feet to press the advantage.

"If you had taken the trouble to have my phone tapped, you'd know that I've been feeding a story to the editor of one of the supermarket newspapers you so detest. Not the one about Alison, because unfortunately, we hadn't yet put all the pieces together. But in addition to searching for her, I came back to Magnolia Grove to gather evidence of a crime that was committed twenty-seven years ago."

I took in a deep breath to collect the rest of my outrageous bluff before I continued. "When I was a child, I saw Ogletharpe, Whitney's father and Barrett Endicott II beat Vernon Avant to death in this very room. Neither you nor your husband were present, but since the homicide happened on your property, and probably with your full consent, the case can be made that you were accomplices to murder."

After the stunned gasp that circled the chamber, there was dead silence until Jericho let out a loud groan. Ogletharpe jerked him to his feet, pressing his temple with the muzzle of the ceremonial pistol.

I fought back the scream that rose in my throat, hardly recognizing the steady voice that came out instead. "The story's due for release next week, Mr. Ogletharpe, and if you kill us, we won't be able to retract it."

After a heartbeat hesitation, his aim moved down to Jericho's chest, not a huge improvement in my opinion.

"Nicely done, Rachel." Amelia tapped her riding crop against her open palm in mock applause, her expression surprised, but not particularly concerned. "You couldn't have found proof to support that accusation, because we made very certain that none exists. You were only four at the time, and even tabloids require stronger evidence than hazy childhood recollections."

I was stymied until my glance slid from her face to the crest on her robe. "That's precisely why I sent the editor the watch fob the General lost beside Samantha's bed when he went to Washington two years ago. Only I said that it belonged to—"

"Shut up, you idiot," Clayton cut in.

He raised his hand as though to slap me, but before he could launch the blow, Amelia's crop laid open a deep gash along the side of his jaw. As her husband lunged for her, she sidestepped, dropping the whip and snatching her own pistol from her sash.

"You found Alison two years ago and let her escape?" she questioned incredulously. "Why, Clayton? You've always agreed that our granddaughter deserves the best we can possibly give her."

"Quite right—and the best we have to offer the child now is her mother. Your interference and my harshness ruined Michael's life," he countered, his tone flat and hopeless. "If he were here, I believe with all my soul that he would ask us to let Alison and Samantha go their own way."

I'd made a lot of mistakes in my time, but never one of such monumental proportions. My grandstanding had just added three names to Amelia's long list of victims: Rachel McKinnon, Jericho Quaid and Clayton Springfield.

The Society of the First Horseman immediately rallied around its leader. Even Albert Hamilton woke up in time to wheel himself in for the kill. Ogletharpe shoved Jericho to join me and Clayton in the center of the square formed by the four hooded stalwarts.

"I won't beg for our lives, but I am asking that you take us to Alison," Jericho managed now. "Rachel and I don't want her to die alone."

I'd already said more than enough, and as I moved to rest my head against his chest, I noticed that he had loosened the rope that bound his hands together. Not that it mattered much. Four guns could easily take out myself and the two unarmed men. Jericho inclined his head to kiss me one last time, but instead of the "I love you" I expected, he murmured, "Hit the deck when I say go."

I sneaked a glance to see if the others had heard the instruction. Those damned hoods made it hard to gauge, but the Horsepeople seemed to be more interested in the Springfields than us.

"Where is Alison, Amelia?" her husband asked gently. "You've won, and you can well afford to be generous in victory. Samantha will surely want to know what happened to the three people she loves most in the world, and you can tell her with a clear conscience that they're all happy together."

The triumphant glitter in Amelia Springfield's eyes retreated, then came back as bitterness. "She's in Michael's bedroom, a place in our home you never bothered to frequent."

"Go!"

I hit the deck, then all hell broke loose.

Jericho slammed Ogletharpe with a flying tackle just as Clayton stepped forward to grab his wife's wrists. I couldn't do much damage with my arms tied, but I figured a head butt to the stomach might give Whitney pause. I had gotten to the rising-to-my-knees part of the plan when her first bullet kicked up stone shards on the floor beside my thigh.

The second shot I heard didn't come anywhere near me. It spun the pistol from Delafield's fingers without even nicking her manicure.

"Hi-ho, Silver!" Maggie's yell came through the folds of the blue satin hood. She stripped it from her head and rose from the wheelchair, her weapon trained steadily on a spot between Whitney's eyes.

I had hoped for at least a regiment of state troopers to come crashing through the door of the chapel. What I got was Sheriff Tillman and two deputies. A crew, as it turned out, that was more than adequate to handle the "book-em's" for Delafield and Ogletharpe.

"Leave Amelia to me," Clayton insisted, still grasping his wife's wrists. They stood at the foot of Barrett's memorial, as motionless as figures in a wax museum, their eyes locked in mortal combat.

"Are you all right, honey?" Caleb shouted from the doorway.

Before I could get out an affirmative he dashed past me to plant an X-rated smooch on Maggie, an embrace that gave me renewed faith in the longevity of human hormones.

Afterward, it got kind of complicated with the two of them trying to untie my arms while Jericho was kissing me, and somewhere along the way my release turned into a group hug.

"Oh God, we've got to get to Sam," I insisted from the middle of the huddle.

"She's having a tea party with the real Albert Hamilton," Maggie reassured me with a chuckle. "The old boy will probably never be the same."

"As soon as Tillman found Clayton's car, I knew where you had hidden her," Jericho chimed in between nibbling my neck and tweaking my nose. "I'm sorry we had to put you through that business, but Clayton didn't have any idea where Amelia had hidden Alison and we had to string her along until we found out."

"Considering your touching request to be reunited with your sister, Dr. Quaid, it's surprising to me that your pathetic little group would take the time for revelations." Amelia's voice cut through our shared happiness. "Particularly when there's so little of it left."

Jericho stiffened, his face ashen. "What have you done to her?"

"I've taken excellent care of her. After all, she is my guest. But since she hasn't been resting well lately, I had a physician in Charleston prescribe a strong sedative for her. She was sleeping when I looked in on her before the meeting, and I didn't want to trouble her. I did notice, however, that the bottle was empty."

I'd never heard a sound like the one that came from Jericho's throat. It was a moan born of anguish, rage and an agony that was past human tolerance. He spun away, hitting top speed on his second stride.

"Go!" Maggie exclaimed. She pushed my back, propelling me after him.

"Through the foyer—second door to the right at the top of the stairs," Clayton shouted.

The only reason I caught up to Jericho was that he paused to yank his medical bag from the Volkswagen. Later, I didn't recall our desperate dash to Alison's prison, but the utter terror that accompanied each step would be with me for the rest of my life.

The door to Michael's bedroom was locked, but Jericho took it out with one lunging blow of his shoulder. As he headed through the splintered frame, he stopped as though he'd run into an invisible wall. "Dear God," he muttered hoarsely.

Amelia had indeed taken excellent care of her guest. Dressed in a white silk gown and peignoir, Alison was lying on the satin coverlet of a four-poster bed. Her hair, free of its temporary dye, was a golden cloud on the pillow, and her hands were folded across her chest, a pale pink rose that matched the polish on her nails carefully tucked under her fingers. In contrast to the bright spots of rouge that had been applied to her cheeks, her skin looked as though it had been carved from alabaster. As far as I could tell, she wasn't breathing.

Jericho's initial shock seemed to evaporate instantaneously. When he hurried to the bedside, he was the consummate physician, not the worried brother. He began a resuscitation attempt, pausing between breaths. "Get cold water and cloths!"

A Rachel I didn't know found what he needed, took over mouth-to-mouth while he retrieved equipment and medication from his bag, chafed Alison's hands to transfer warmth to them and tried to hold on to the thin thread of her life by the force of will.

While I shared the ordeal with Jericho, I quickly realized that medicine wasn't his work, it was a part of his soul. If the person on the bed had been a vagrant, that patient would have received no less of his care, compassion and skill than his own sister. It was then that I began to understand the wonder and privilege of loving a dedicated man, and the prospect of his late night calls and the dinners I'd eat alone didn't loom large anymore. With forever for us to spend together, it seemed downright stupid to quibble over a few hours missing here and there.

"She's coming around," Jericho said at the same time I felt Alison's fingers curl in my hand.

Tears began to sneak past her closed lashes.

"Don't worry about Sam. She's fine," I reassured her. "And I got her the purple bicycle."

The teeniest of nods acknowledged the report, and the flood of tears increased.

"Are you in pain, little one?" Jericho queried.

Her head moved from side to side. As her lashes fluttered open, her unfocused gaze touched his face then wandered over to mine. The true reason for her distress came out halting and fuzzy.

"I was afraid I would miss the wedding."

Epilogue

It was hard to tell exactly when the long night was over because sunrise hid behind a sodden cloak of fog, but of all the mornings behind me and those still to come, this was the one I would remember with the greatest clarity—principally, I guess, because I never thought I'd live to see it. Since I didn't want to waste a single second of it, at quarter past five I eased up from my pallet on the floor beside the bed at the cottage and slipped into jeans and a sweatshirt. My hyper-anxious scrutiny assured me that Alison was alive and well. Her rest was motionless, her breathing deep and even. She was cradling her sleeping daughter. I watched them for a long moment, and when force of habit made me pull the sheet across Samantha's outstretched leg, the incredible joy I felt took on a bittersweet edge. My godchild didn't need me anymore.

"I love you, Cricket." Her eyelids opened in the merest slits then squeezed tightly shut again. "If you learned to cook, you'd be as good a mom as Mommy," she said groggily.

I was too choked up to frame a coherent "thank you," so I acknowledged the provisional vote of confidence with a peck on her cheek and tiptoed from the bedroom.

Downstairs, as I slid back the glass door, all the muscles in my recently abused body yelled "foul" at the idea of a run along the beach, but somewhere between the patio and the cabana, I managed to marshal my legs into a shambling semblance of a trot.

"You're limping," Jericho announced as he jogged out of the mist to keep pace with me. I half expected him to whip out his stethoscope and order me back to bed.

Instead, he slipped his arm around my shoulder and slowed me to a walk. "After all the things we said last night, would I be redundant if I told you that you are a magnificent, courageous, gorgeous woman who I'll love until the last day I draw breath?"

"Yeah, but do it anyway. And don't forget to add grandstanding blabbermouth to your list," I answered, molding myself into the warmth of him. "You were so busy telling me how wonderful I was that you never did get to the story of how you and the General hooked up."

"When I got to the hospital morgue, I glanced through the preliminary paperwork that had been done pending Endicott's autopsy—dental charts, previous medical records, that sort of thing. Something struck me as odd, but by then, I was beginning to doubt my instincts about Alison and couldn't concentrate on the problem."

"Barrett had the wrong blood type," I supplied smugly.

"Quit hogging the spotlight, will you?" He rewarded my brilliance with a playful swat to my rear end. "After I started home, I was ninety-percent certain Alison was dead, so I drove around for a while, trying to work up the guts to come back and tell you that I'd been wrong. Clayton was standing on the front porch when I drove up, and all of a sudden, everything clicked into place. The two of us went a couple of hard rounds before he got a chance to tell me he was on our side."

"Don't be so quick to let him off the hook. If he was so concerned about Alison and Sam, he shouldn't have let his wife hound them all this time," I objected.

"He didn't have much to say about it because she was the abuser in the relationship. It just suited her purposes to pretend it was the other way around. She knew from the jump that it was her money he wanted, so from day one of their marriage, she collected blackmail material on him and all the other Horsemen. When she finally took control of the Society and set up CANTER to exploit her own agenda, she had enough to hang them all." Jericho stopped to settle himself onto the sand, pulling me down into his lap. "Clayton did the best he could, though. Amelia had Marietta Fairfax moved to Savannah so she could keep tabs on her phone calls and mail, but every time her spies got a solid lead, he managed to throw them off. At first he didn't really care about Sam. He just didn't want Amelia to have her."

"But when he went to Washington he changed his mind. He couldn't help but love Sam," I concluded. "All that still doesn't explain why Alison would voluntarily come back to Magnolia Grove."

"I was just getting to that. Amelia had begun to suspect that Clayton knew where Alison and Sam were hiding, but she wasn't sure and she was too smart to confront him directly. She convinced him that she had terminal cancer—even produced phony medical reports to prove it—and told him she wanted to see her grandchild and make amends for the trouble she'd caused before she died. So he called Alison in Maine and asked her to bring Samantha home. The rest is history."

"Not quite." I allowed myself a long sigh, staring out at the slate-colored ocean to gather the rest of my questions. "How did Barrett get tangled up in it?"

"Actually, he was a victim, too. He hung around Château Printemps a lot when he was a kid, and according to Clayton, Amelia suffered his presence gladly because she could use him to keep tabs on her son's activities. Barrett mistook her attention for love and did everything in his power to please her, including breaking up Michael's supposedly secret engagement to Alison."

The assorted story lines were beginning to run together in my head like a bad soap opera with too many plot twists, but I couldn't let it go just yet. "Mike comes off as a world-class wimp—or worse. Even if he didn't love Alison, he shouldn't have bopped off to South America with her pregnant."

"He didn't know. As a matter of fact, neither did she at the time. The day after Mike left, Barrett gave her a letter—forged, of course, as per Amelia's instructions—claiming that Mike was having second thoughts about the relationship. There was also a check for fifty grand, which

Alison promptly tore up. A couple of months later, she married Noah Girard." Jericho leaned down to nibble at the nape of my neck. "As soon as my goofy little sister wakes up, I've got to have a long talk with her about the cavalier way she deals with large sums of money," he said, sighing.

I pulled away, determined not to let him distract me. "Okay, Columbo, explain to me why Noah was murdered."

"That was the biggest blunder of all, the classic case of B.E.-III trying to please everyone he loved. As the time for Springfield to return from South America got close, Barrett started feeling guilty about his part in trashing the romance. He must have figured that with Noah out of the way, Michael would have a clear field with Alison and everything would be hunky-dory again. Clayton believes that Mike somehow discovered the crime and was going to the police. Barrett had to kill Michael by tampering with his car to save himself. He kept the ID bracelet, thinking it may have been further proof of Michael and Alison's affair. And he ran back toward the car, to make it seem as if he were trying to save Michael."

"No more—please! I've had enough intrigue to last the rest of my life," I interrupted him with a shudder.

"Me, too. Let's get to the part where the hero and heroine are so overcome with passion that they fall on the beach and start ripping off each other's clothes," Jericho teased, tugging at the tail of my sweatshirt.

I was more than ready to go along with the new script when the sound of a motor interrupted. I turned my head to stare back at the driveway and spotted the convertible. It had no sooner pulled to a stop than Caleb got out, dashing around to the passenger side to open the door for Maggie. After a kiss that would have been banned in Boston, they made a guilty beeline toward the kitchen door, for all the world like teenagers trying to make a curfew.

"What on earth could they have gone out for at this hour of the morning?" I mused aloud.

"They didn't go out, they're just getting in. After you went to sleep last night, Caleb took Maggie for a moonlight drive."

My jaw dropped. "You mean—"

"Yep, and more power to 'em. The family ESP tells me there's more than one wedding in our immediate future." Jericho grinned. "Speaking of which, when I last looked in on Alison, she woke up long enough to predict that two years and three months from now, you and I will have our first baby, a little girl."

Which only proved to me that the vaunted Quaid second sight wasn't all it was cracked up to be: my own instincts told me the child I was now carrying was a boy.

I would name him Gideon.

HARLEQUIN PRESENTS®

is

- ✓ exotic
- ✓ dramatic
- ✓ sensual
- ✓ exciting
- ✓ contemporary
- ✓ a fast, involving read
- ✓ terrific!!

Harlequin Presents—
passionate romances
around the world!

HARLEQUIN ROMANCE®

is

 contemporary
and up-to-date

 heartwarming

 romantic

 exciting

 involving

 fresh and
delightful

 a short, satisfying
read

 wonderful!!

*Today's Harlequin
Romance—the traditional
choice!*